More
to
Life

More
to
Life

ReShonda Tate Billingsley

KENSINGTON PUBLISHING CORP.

www.kensingtonbooks.com

DAFINA BOOKS are published by

Kensington Publishing Corp.
119 West 40th Street
New York, NY 10018

All Kensington titles, imprints, and distributed lines are available at special quantity discounts for bulk purchases for sales promotion, premiums, fund-raising, and educational or institutional use.

Special book excerpts or customized printings can also be created to fit specific needs. For details, write or phone the office of the Kensington Sales Manager: Kensington Publishing Corp., 119 West 40th Street, New York, NY 10018. Attn. Sales Department. Phone: 1-800-221-2647.

Dafina and the Dafina logo Reg. U.S. Pat. & TM Off.

ISBN-13: 978-1-4967-2412-0
ISBN-10: 1-4967-2412-7
First Kensington Trade Paperback Printing: September 2019

ISBN-13: 978-1-4967-2413-7 (ebook)
ISBN-10: 1-4967-2413-5 (ebook)
First Kensington Electronic Edition: September 2019

10 9 8 7 6 5 4 3 2 1

Printed in the United States of America

To those searching for their joy . . .

More
to
Life

Chapter 1

Living my best life!

That thought made me wiggle, shimmy, and shake. That was what I was about to finally do. No more back burner livin' for me. After years of putting my dreams on hold, I was about to step out.

"And I'm gonna do more than just step out," I said to my reflection as I spread the Fenty gloss over my lips, then smacked them together. I stepped back, gave a girlfriend snap, and added, "I'm about to do me."

And it was going to begin with Oprah. While I'd made sure my family had a Christmas to remember, I had given myself the best gift ever—tickets to the exclusive "Living Your Best Life" one-day conference with Oprah as the opening speaker. The conference promised to help you "reconnect with your passion so you could walk in your purpose." This was going to be life-changing for me.

I hooked my earrings in place, fluffed out my natural curls, propped up my girls, then admired how the magenta Diane Von Furstenberg wrap dress brought out my golden overtone and gave me a glow.

I glanced at my watch: 7:57. I was making good time. "Today is going to be a good day," I sang as I grabbed my purse and headed out of the room.

I started humming as I headed down the stairs. "I'm doing me!" I said as I hit the bottom step, almost colliding with my son as he came around the corner.

"Really, Ma?" Eric moved his bowl of cereal to keep it from spilling.

I squeezed his chin. "Good morning, my handsome son." Eric was in his junior year at college and over the past year had become the spitting image of his father.

He pulled away and cocked his head. "Um, what's wrong with you?"

"I'm in a spectacular mood, that's all." I did another shimmy.

"Can you not?" He laughed as he headed into the kitchen.

I was about to ask him why he was walking around the house with a giant bowl of cereal, but before I could say anything, the front door opened and my daughter, Anika, came bouncing in. As the baby of the family, she commanded attention whenever she walked in the room, so trying to hold a conversation with Eric would've been moot anyway.

"Hey, Mom," she said.

"Hello, sweetheart," I replied. "You're out early."

"I had to go pick up Kelli from the airport, remember?" she said, motioning to one of her Spelman classmates who was walking in behind her. "I took your car because Dad said my car won't be out of the shop until tomorrow." She handed me my keys.

I extended my hand to the young Kerry Washington-look-alike who resembled my daughter so much it was eerie.

"Hello, Kelli," I said. "Anika has been so excited about your visit."

They giggled and hugged each other. "I'm excited, too," Kelli said. "My dad remarried and moved here and I did not want to spend the holidays with my stepmom. She's like only five years older than me. So thank you so much for letting me stay here a couple of days. I wish I could stay the whole break, but I have to go take part in the family drama." She released a disgusted chuckle.

Family drama. I knew all about that. Well, I used to when I was growing up. *No.* I shook off those thoughts. Memories were not about to mess up my day.

"Well, any friend of my daughter is a friend of mine," I said.

Kelli set her bag down and walked into our spacious entryway. Her mouth dropped open at the double winding staircase and large crystal chandelier that hung in the center. "Your home is beautiful," she said, taking in the surroundings. "And your Christmas tree. How tall is it?"

"Nine feet," I said. "And thank you so much for the compliment." I cut my eyes at Anika. "Maybe you can help my daughter take the tree and other Christmas decorations down this weekend."

"You know you like the stuff stored a certain way, so I wouldn't want to mess that up." She batted her eyes like she was doing me a favor.

Kelli continued surveying the house. I understood her awe, though. I'd worked hard to make our six-thousand-square-foot home a showcase. I'd imported tile from Tijuana, flown in drapes from Dubai, and bought furnishings from Finland. Our home had even been featured in a *Texas Monthly* "Best Homes" feature story.

"This place looks like it could be an art gallery," Kelli said.

That made my smile widen. My work . . . in an art gallery? That would be a dream come true. I wanted someone to be moved by my creations, to appreciate how I pour my soul onto the canvas. Shoot, at this point, I just wanted to create, do something that brought me personal joy. That's what I wanted to walk away from Oprah's conference with today—the inspiration to live my best life because I wasn't doing it right now.

Oh, I loved my family, but I wanted a life where my passion to paint could coexist. I hadn't found that yet. But now that both kids were in college, I definitely felt like it was my time.

"Oh my goodness. Is this a Jean-Michel Basquiat?" Kelli asked.

Anika burst out laughing. "That is hilarious. No, that's an Aja Clayton, my mom. It's her little hobby."

I grimaced at the dismissive way my daughter spoke of the thing that gave me my greatest joy outside of my family. But she'd come by it honestly. Her brother did it, her father did it. And when her grandmother, Judy—Charles's mother—had moved in several months ago, she'd fallen in line and started doing it, too. I guess the fact that I just did painting on the side made them see it as nothing more than a hobby. But it was my passion, even if it was buried underneath the weight of my world.

"I'm impressed that you know Basquiat," I said, deciding to do what I always did and ignore the condescending remark.

"Yes, he and LaTerus, the Modern Renaissance painter from Harlem, are my favorites. I'm an art history major," Kelli said.

That warmed my heart to see someone share my passion. I'd been painting since I was a little girl. It was my escape from the dysfunction that was my life. I'd wanted to major in art but my guidance counselor, who was helping me fill out my college paperwork, had come right out and said, "Be realistic, Aja. Major in something real."

I'd cried myself to sleep that night, then selected social work as my major.

Now watching Kelli take in my work confirmed that had been the worst choice I'd ever made.

"Wow, you could make a living off this," Kelli said, looking at another painting that hung over the entryway table.

"Yeah, right," Eric said, emerging from the dining room. "They're called starving artists for a reason, and all this," he said, pointing to his athletic body, "and starving doesn't go together." He laughed.

"Kelli, that's my bigheaded brother, Eric," Anika said.

Eric walked over, took Kelli's hand, and lifted it to his lips. "Hello, beautiful," he said with the same charisma that made me fall for his father.

"Don't even think about it," Anika said, pulling her friend's arm and pushing her brother away.

"What? I'm just trying to be hospitable to your guest." Eric chuckled.

"Can you two save this fight for another time?" I said. "Kelli, make yourself at home. I have to get out of here for my conference."

"Where are you going?" Anika and Eric asked simultaneously.

I inhaled. Exhaled. Reminded myself this was going to be a good day.

"So I guess neither of you noticed that I'm dressed up." I pointed to my outfit.

They both looked me up and down. "Oh," they said in unison.

"My conference is today," I said. "The one I've been talking about for the past two weeks."

"Oh, that's right. You have that entrepreneur thingy. I forgot about that," Anika said. "Good thing we didn't stop on the way back." She turned to Kelli. "Talk about a scam. My mom is going to this conference where they get people to shell out $1,500 for a ticket so they can tell you stuff you already know."

I wasn't about to get into a debate with my children. Another glance at my watch. 8:08. I wanted to be in place by 9:30 since the conference started at ten. "Whatever. I'm heading out because I can't be late. There's no late entry."

Eric shrugged his indifference as he continued into the kitchen. I followed so I could grab a quick cup of coffee and some fruit.

"Okay, Mom," Anika said, following behind me. "But can you make us some of your homemade pancakes before you go?"

Any other time, I would've jumped at the chance to cook for my daughter and her guest. But not today.

"What part of I have to go do you not get?" I asked.

"Mom . . ."

I ignored her as I opened the cabinet and pulled out my coffee pod, then dropped it in the machine.

Eric set his bowl in the sink, with the dishes from last night that Anika hadn't bothered to wash. "Mom, did you fill out my immunization papers? They're due at noon," he said.

"So we're really not getting pancakes?" Anika asked.

I cut my eyes at her and she huffed.

"Can you get us an Uber to go to IHOP, then?" she asked. "My Uber app isn't working." She looked at her brother. "Or Eric can take us."

"I'm going back to bed. Besides, I don't have any gas."

Anika's eyes widened. "Ooh, speaking of gas. You're probably going to need some," she told me. "The light is on in your car."

"You brought my car back on empty?" I said, exasperation creeping in.

Anika just gave me a blank look and a "Sorry." She paused. "So no Uber either, huh?"

I took a deep breath. Now I was going to have to stop for gas. Thankfully, the convention center was only thirty minutes away, so I was still good. "Anika, you are more than capable of making you guys some breakfast."

"Fine. Come on, Kelli. I guess we'll just have to starve." She took her friend's hand and led her out of the kitchen.

"Mom," Eric said, "my paperwork?"

I sighed. I had meant to print that yesterday, but I'd had to go to Office Depot and get a new cartridge, and when I'd come home, the dog had chewed up one of my favorite shoes so I'd gotten distracted.

"No, I didn't get a chance to do it," I said. "Can't you do it?"

"Mom . . ."

I pressed the Start button on the Keurig. "Get your dad to do it. It's his insurance information. I really need to go."

"You know Dad doesn't know how to do that," Eric replied.

"Your dad doesn't know how to do what?"

I managed a smile when the love of my life walked in and planted a kiss on my cheek. Even in his running gear and his face covered with a layer of sweat, he looked like he needed to be modeling Under Armour gear in a magazine.

"How was your run?" I asked.

"Good. And Dad doesn't know what?" he repeated.

"Eric needs his immunization paperwork filled out," I said.

"Coach said if I don't have it in today by noon, I won't be able to play in the first game when we get back to school."

"Oh," Charles said. "That's a mom problem." He laughed like he'd really said something funny. "Babe, have you seen my driver? I have to be at the golf club in thirty minutes. I'm playing with the new Texans owner, and since I'm trying to snag that exclusive interview, I can't be late."

It was now 8:20. I wanted to tell him I couldn't be late either. But I just said, "Did you put it back in your bag after your game last week?"

"I could've sworn I did. But it's not there. Can you help me find it?" His voice was suddenly filled with frustration like he'd expected to walk right in here and I was going to tell him exactly where the driver was.

I shook my head. "I can't. I have to get to my event. The Oprah workshop."

"Oh. Is that today?"

I bit my bottom lip as I felt my enthusiasm waning. While what everyone else did was important to me, nothing I did seemed important to my family.

"I really need to get dressed," Charles said. "Can you help me look?"

"No," I repeated, keeping my voice even. "I have to get going. The event starts in an hour and a half and I want to be there early."

He eased up behind me, wrapped his arm around my waist, and kissed me on my neck. "Please?"

"Can you guys get a room," Eric groaned. "Mom, can you at least hook up the printer and print out the paperwork since you're making me figure this out on my own? I have to get it in by noon and you won't be back by then."

"You're a college student. You should know technology." I gently kissed my husband on the lips as I pushed him away. His kiss normally had a way of relaxing me, but today it wasn't working.

"No, I go to the computer lab and the printers are already hooked up," Eric said. "I don't even know where the cartridges are."

"Fine," I said. "I'll at least get the paperwork printed, but you're going to have to fill it out."

I ignored his groans as I headed to the office. "Just relax," I mumbled to myself. "You're good on time."

I grabbed the Office Depot bag, pulled the cartridge out, opened it, and replaced the old one. I released silent curses as I waited for my email to pop open so that I could print the immunization paperwork Eric's coach had sent.

"Finally," I mumbled as the PDF opened and I pressed Print. I had just reached to remove the paperwork when I noticed Charles's silver golf club in the corner of the office.

I sighed as I called out for my husband. "Charles! I found your driver."

I heard footsteps as he came racing down the hall. "Where was it?"

"For some reason you dropped it off in here." I pointed to the corner.

He snapped his finger. "Oh, yeah. I stepped in here for a call the last time I came from golfing." Charles leaned in and kissed me. "I knew you'd find it."

"Did you even look?" My voice had way more irritation than normal.

"Why are you snapping?"

I took a deep breath. "I'm sorry. It's just that this conference is very important to me and I feel like no one cares."

"Okay, you're being a little dramatic," he said with a smile. "We all care. I'm so glad you're leaving for your vacation in two days. You seem like you really need it. And I'm making sure you have the best birthday girl's trip ever, so don't get stressed."

"Okay, you're right." I released a slow breath.

"Come here, let me massage you." Charles pulled the rolling chair toward him.

A moan escaped me as Charles began kneading my shoulders. "Charles, I don't have time. And I thought you had to go, too."

"Oh, his assistant texted me. He pushed back our start time thirty minutes." He glanced at his watch. "But it is five till nine, so let me get out of here."

Five till nine? I wanted to scream. How had the time gotten away?

"Dangit," I muttered, swiveling around in the chair to pull the paperwork off the printer.

"Well, have fun at your event, babe." Charles leaned in to kiss me again. But he bumped my cup of coffee before making contact, and hot coffee spilled all over my dress and the paperwork I'd just printed.

"Are you freakin' kidding me?" I screamed as I jumped up.

Charles grabbed a Kleenex and immediately began rubbing.

"Stop! You're making it worse," I said. Charles backed away at my outburst. "It's fine. I'm fine. Just let me reprint this paperwork and go find something else to wear."

Charles eased out of the room and I prayed that I could get the papers printed, change my clothes, and get downtown in the next hour.

———⸭———

It was 9:45 and my heart was pounding.

My dream was fifteen minutes away from being deferred. Again.

"Come on, come on, come on!" I screamed at the car in front of me. I pounded the steering wheel as I screamed at the little old lady who couldn't decide if she was going to go left or right.

I'd stopped for gas—rushing so I'd only put $5 in, which hadn't even turned my warning light off. But I just needed enough gas to get downtown.

If I miss this conference because of my family . . .

I pushed down the lump in my throat and the mist trying to cover my eyes as I glanced down at the GPS. I knew the way to the convention center but had turned on the GPS just to track my time. It had my arrival as 10:19, and I was praying that I'd be able to shave off some time.

My prayers hadn't been answered.

"Move!" I screamed at another car that had cut me off and slowed my speed race by twenty miles an hour.

"Breathe, Aja. Breathe," I mumbled. I'd been talking to myself the whole ride, trying my best to keep my nerves in check. "I know they stressed no late entries, but they'll have a grace period."

They have to have a grace period.

The GPS had been right on target because it was 10:19 when I pulled into the parking garage of the convention center. My hands were shaking in nervous anticipation. I drove around the second floor, and all the parking spots were taken, so I drove up to the third floor. After circling around and watching the clock on my dashboard turn to 10:26, I pulled into a handicapped space.

"Screw it," I said, deciding I'd just have to pay the ticket if I got one.

I parked and prayed for a miracle as I darted through the garage, across the skywalk, and into the auditorium.

The check-in desk was empty and my heart dropped.

"Excuse me," I said to a woman I saw standing at a table near the second entry. "I'm here for the 'Living Your Best Life' event. I'm registered." I fumbled for my phone to pull up my ticket.

The woman looked at her phone like she wanted to remind me of the time. I wanted to scream that I knew what time it was. "I am so sorry," she said. "There's no late entry. They've already started filming."

My chest began heaving. "Is . . . is there any way they can let me in?"

She flashed a sympathetic look. "I am so sorry," the woman repeated. "We even gave a fifteen-minute grace period. But that's why we have you submit the waiver, so we can make sure you are clear on the policy."

I wanted to explain to her my hectic morning, ask her if she was a mother and wife and understood how families could suck the breath out of you. Maybe if she could relate . . .

"I can submit a request to see if they'll give you a partial refund." She had the nerve to smile.

"I don't want a refund." My voice cracked. "I just want to go in."

The woman patted my hand. "I'm sorry. There's nothing I can do."

I nodded, unable to form a "Thank you anyway" as I scurried to the ladies' room. I dipped in a stall as my chest heaved. I'd never had a panic attack, but I imagined this was what one felt like.

Every time I tried to do something for me, something happened. Every time I took two steps forward, life pushed me three steps back. All my life, I'd given everything I had to my family. All I wanted was this . . . this day.

I'd obviously wanted too much.

I buried my face in my hands and sobbed.

Chapter 2

Whoever said forty-five was the new twenty-five didn't send that memo to my body.

"Drop it like it's hot!"

My friends-for-life had formed a semicircle around me on the crowded dance floor as I shimmied to a Spanish rap song. I couldn't understand the words, but I felt the pulsating beat that had the entire nightclub on its feet. Simone, Nichelle, and Roxie were all shouting like we were back in college at some frat party.

I wiggled, did a semi squat, and continued my shimmying.

"Girl, you're dropping it like it's lukewarm." Roxie laughed as she retreated to the sideline. Her comment caused everyone around her to crack up. She swooped a tequila shot and lime from the waitress who was passing by, gulped it, bit into the lime, grimaced, then managed to add, "Come on, birthday girl, shake your tail feather."

I wanted to tell her to stop barking orders at me and to bring her own tail feather to the dance floor.

But before I could say anything, a voice from behind me said, "Don't be shy, *Mami.* Let loose. Let's give your friends what they asked for. Shake your feathered tail."

I spun around and faced the hunky, handsome Marc Anthony look-alike who didn't back up. He was so close his chest was pressed against mine and his gyrating hips pushed against me. There were two things wrong with this picture: My behind was too tired for all of this, and I was married.

Well, three things were wrong. The third? This was only day two. I still had two more days to go on this four-day birthday celebration that had taken me and my girls from Houston to the Dominican Republic. Forty-eight hours to go and I was partied out.

I'd had to summon up every iota of strength just to come on this trip. After missing the Oprah event, I'd been in a daze. I could barely find the energy to pack.

And my family had barely noticed.

Charles haphazardly asked me how the event was, but before I could answer, he got a phone call, then never asked again.

"Go, Aja, it's your birthday, it's your birthday!" Simone, the mastermind behind this trip, sang, bringing me back to the celebration I didn't want. Simone was singing but I was dancing, putting in all the work. That's how all of this felt to me right now—like work. Because hanging out in the resort's beachside club had not been my idea of a good time. If I'd had my way, we'd be relaxing at the pool, still sipping big drinks with little umbrellas, or enjoying a quiet, sand-side dinner as the music of the ocean played in our ears. Or maybe even . . . a nighttime massage from some hunky Latino with fingers that could reach straight down to my soul. Wouldn't that have been wonderful, to be massaged straight into sleep?

But even though this was *my* forty-fifth birthday celebration, my girls had vetoed all of my—what they called boring—plans.

Simone was the one who'd told me before we'd boarded the plane, "There won't be anything boring or quiet about this trip." She'd pointed to my portfolio of painting supplies as I placed them in the overhead bin. "And I don't even know why you brought that stuff. You will not be doing any boring painting. We're about to party twenty-three hours a day, because I'm going to give you an hour to sleep. That's the way I planned it."

But no matter what plans my friends had, this was it for me.

"Okay, I'm going to have to rest," I panted and held up my hands to my Latin partner. *"No más!"*

He chuckled. "I was too much for you, yes?"

I nodded. "Way too much."

"Boooo," Simone belted from the edge of the dance floor. "I can't believe you . . ."

Before she finished, I grabbed her hand, then pushed her into my dance partner. "Here," I told her, "you dance with him 'cause it doesn't seem like he's tiring, and clearly neither are you."

"That's right, *señorita*. I don't tire easily." He winked and wiggled all up on Simone, not missing a single beat, not caring that his female partner had sent in a sub.

I staggered from the dance floor, my steps unsteady, a combination of the three shots we'd taken before I hit the dance floor and my lack of sleep. I believed in eight hours, but in the two days we'd been here, the late-night talks in the suite had netted me no more than five.

Plopping down into the corner booth that had held our purses and shawls all evening, I released a moan of pleasure when the weight left my feet. Not that I was a big girl. I wore my 153 pounds well, but if my feet could speak, they'd probably swear they'd been carrying 250 pounds right about now.

"Girl, you can't hang," Nichelle said, approaching the booth. She swooped her long, waist-length hair up in a bun on top of her head, obviously trying to get some relief from the humidity that filled the area.

I shook my head and laughed as Nichelle and Roxie piled into the booth with me.

"I have been hanging all night," I replied. "And none of you were on the dance floor. All you were doing was cheering me on from the sidelines."

"And taking shots," Nichelle said as she held up her hand for the waiter to come by again. "Don't forget the shots. And I want a few more."

I groaned, and then my bestie out of my best friends said what I'd been thinking. "That's enough for me," Roxie told Nichelle. "You can have my shot and I bet you can have Aja's, too."

I nodded my agreement, then leaned back, and for a moment, I drifted away on the beat of the music that mixed with the ocean's waves just feet away from the club.

Turning my head slightly to the open side of the club that led to the beach, I sighed as I took in the setting and savored the breeze that had swept in from nowhere. This really was beautiful—all of it. The song of the ocean, the blackness of the beach, the shimmer of the moonlight reflecting off the water's waves.

A splendid place, a wonderful trip that had been a surprise gift from Charles. When it came to spoiling me, he was the master, and this resort was proof of that. This gift had been the culmination of a month of gifts. Forty-five, one for each year of my blessed life, he told me: a gift card here, a negligee there. Each gift more expensive than the last. Some were thoughtful, like the table art book he'd purchased from the National Gallery of Art in DC that featured some of my favorite artists like Jacob Lawrence, Gordon Parks, and Kara Walker. Others were special, like the photo of my late mother he'd had restored and mounted in a crystal frame. A few were grandiose, like this trip that Simone had planned and he'd paid for.

Yes, forty-five gifts for forty-five years from a husband who'd loved me for twenty of those forty-five. Who loved me to infinity and beyond.

So why in the hell was my heart not happy?

"What is wrong with you, Aja?" Simone asked, sounding like she thought she was my mother as she danced back over to the booth.

I turned my attention back to my friends. "What?"

"We're down here in this beautiful place and we can't get you to party."

"What do you call what I've been doing?" I asked with my attitude coming out in the swivel of my neck.

"Yeah, but you were only out there for three or four songs."

"Uh, I'm forty-five years old," I reminded her.

"That means you should have danced for forty-five songs."

"Girl, bye!"

"Or at least forty-five minutes," Nichelle added as if she were serious.

I said, "Just because you think we're still back at TSU . . . my body knows that we're not."

"Whatever." Simone held up her palm in my face. "I'm going back out there." She pointed to the dance floor. "Anyone gonna join me?"

Nichelle raised her hand. "After I have another shot. Where in the world is the waiter?"

Simone grabbed her hand. "Girl, we don't have to wait. Let's go up to the bar."

I watched the two of them do some kind of rumba from the table and wondered if Nichelle had already had too many shots. But then, this was Nichelle—there was no such thing as too many shots.

"Don't worry about her," Roxie said.

I glanced at my friend and grinned. "You're still doing that thing, reading my mind."

"We've been friends for a long time. I know what you're thinking just by the expression on your face. So don't worry about Nichelle. You know she can drink us all under the table."

"True." With her petite frame and doe eyes, no one would ever guess that Nichelle had been dubbed the chug-a-lug queen our junior year at Texas Southern University.

"But what Simone said—I want to know, too," Roxie continued. "What's going on? What's wrong?"

My expression shifted. Now I frowned. "Why're you asking

me that?" Before she could answer, I kept on, "I'm fine. I was just tired. I haven't danced that much in a while. I don't hang in the streets like y'all do."

"Correction. Them." She pointed toward the dance floor where Nichelle and Simone had rejoined Marc Anthony's twin. He was sandwiched between the two of them, and there was no man on the floor who wore a bigger smile. "You know I don't party like our girls."

I nodded.

"But that doesn't mean that I can't see something is bothering you," Roxie continued. "You act like you don't want to be here. Which is crazy 'cause you usually like to celebrate your birthday as if it begins in June and lasts all summer and fall."

Roxie wasn't telling any lies. For my fortieth, I'd celebrated the moment Anika had stepped out of her last day of middle school and I hadn't stopped until the spring semester of her freshman year of high school. Seriously, every single day, I did something special. And back then, my plan had been to raise every single stake for my forty-fifth.

But that hadn't happened this year. June came and Anika had to get ready for college. Then Eric became a starter on the basketball team at the University of Texas. And even once I got them settled in school, cutbacks at my job led to more hours and Charles found more things for me to do. And when Christmas rolled around, what normally was my pre-birthday celebration had turned into daily disappointment.

Until I found out about the conference. That had put me back in the celebratory spirit.

"So," Roxie interrupted my thoughts, "you wanna tell me what's going on?"

I shrugged. I would've told her if I had anything to say. But the truth was, I didn't know. Something was wrong, though; Roxie wasn't imagining that. And it was deeper than just me missing the conference.

I knew it had nothing to do with aging. I looked damn good for forty-five. Even before I'd made that visit to Dr. Cash for my Mommy Makeover, I was passing for a woman in her thirties. And I'd kept Dr. Cash's plastic surgery work intact with my four-times-a-week Zumba classes. So I felt great—at least, that's what I thought.

But as I counted down the days to January 10, a wave of disconsolation had swept over me. My Christmas spirit was gone, and my birthday jubilation had followed it.

"Nothing's going on," I finally answered Roxie. "I don't know why you're all making such a big deal because I wanted to sit down. My feet hurt. That's all."

"Hmm . . . mmm." Her hum told me that she thought I was a liar.

"Come on, Roxie, don't do this. Don't be Simone."

She shrugged. "For once, I think Simone has a point. It's in your whole demeanor and it's been that way since we've been here. Girl, you used to always be the first who wanted to party, but these past two days, you've been more like Debbie . . . and I'm not talking about the one who did Dallas. I'm talking about her evil twin, Debbie Downer."

"Not true," I said, hoping that she wouldn't believe her lying eyes.

She studied me the way we studied rats under microscopes in biology back in college. But I didn't blink.

Finally, she shrugged. "Look, the whole reason we're here is for you to let your hair down. Leave behind the stress of your life, your family, your job, your mother-in-law moving in with you, and just let loose. You've got to do that. This trip is good for you. Forget about home. Forget about your family 'cause I'm sure that's what's on your mind."

My family. The picture that would pop up on the internet if you googled "Perfect Family": me, Charles, Anika, and Eric, who was named after my beloved brother, who committed suicide when he was twenty-five.

My kids and my husband had been the center of my world for so many years. I'd been supermom until Eric had left for UT three years ago and then Anika had left for Spelman the August before last. I was so proud of them, which is why I couldn't explain the hole in my heart. Before devoting all of my time to them, I'd given my all to caring for my siblings: my younger sister, Jada, and Eric, who was four years younger than me. So, in essence, I'd been pouring into others for the past thirty years.

I was ready to pour into me.

I shook away that thought. I was a mother and a wife. That was my priority. That had been my life. And it looked like it would be my life for eternity.

Maybe I really was suffering from empty nest syndrome—except our nest wasn't really empty, and it hadn't been for the last two years. Not since Charles's mother, Judy, had moved in with us.

The thought of her made me sigh. Not that I begrudged Judy living with us. Lord knows, I wish my own mother were alive so that I could take care of her the way we were able to be there for Judy after she had a hip replacement. She was doing so much better, walking on her own, even driving. She was completely capable of living on her own now, but since she had all the plush trappings of our home, I guess she decided that there was no reason to leave.

"So you know what we gotta do, right?" Roxie asked.

I had to blink myself back to the conversation. "What?"

"If you don't want to hear Simone and Nichelle's voices when we get back to our suite, you're gonna have to get up with me and join them on that dance floor."

"But my feet hurt," I whined.

She slid from the booth, then grabbed my hand. "Doesn't matter. Leave your shoes here and let's go. Just a couple of dances and then, we'll all head back."

I moaned, but as I stood, I knew she was right. If I didn't do this, I'd have a lot of explaining to do. And since I couldn't explain what was going on to myself, I wouldn't stand up under any interrogation from my three best friends.

So I hit the floor and rocked my hips and shimmied my shoulders and pasted a smile on my face.

"Let loose, girl," Nichelle exclaimed. "We're here to have fun. It's all about you."

And then, when Nichelle forced another shot into my hand, I laughed out loud, then downed the tequila. I decided that my friends were right—I'd lost my shot to do me with the conference. I needed to try to just let everything go and have a good time—at least for tonight.

Chapter 3

"Rise and shine. The early bird catches the worm." The sound of Simone's singsong voice interrupted my drunken dreams.

I groaned as Simone bounced from room to room, banging on the doors to wake everyone up. Without opening my eyes, I grabbed another pillow and pulled it over my head.

"Aja," Simone sang my name as she busted into my bedroom, "we did not come to the Dominican Republic for you to sleep the days away. Get up, sunshine." And then she did something that she hadn't done since we were at Texas Southern: She snatched the covers off me.

I wanted to scream. Tell her to go away. Let me have just a few more minutes. But she wouldn't have heard—or should I say she wouldn't have paid attention to—anything I said because Simone was one of those birds who were always early and looking for other soul-mate birds to hang with in the morning. When she couldn't find anyone else, she made all of us get up with her. We paid the price for the fact that she liked to rise with the sun.

"Come on, Aja," she said before she assaulted me with her next weapon—she drew the drapes, bringing the sun in as her partner. Even with the pillow over me, the sun won. I pushed the pillow to the side and I blinked until my eyes were all the way open. Thankfully, I'd taken a BC Powder last night before we began our shot spree, so I didn't have a pounding headache, but I did have a "need more sleep" ache, and Simone was messing all of that up.

It took a moment for me to focus on Simone, standing over me with her arms folded. "The tour guide leaves in an hour," she announced. "We need to get up and get moving. I've already cooked breakfast . . ."

I may have still been half asleep, but I was awake enough to know that was a lie.

"Or shall I say Miguel cooked breakfast," she added with a cheesy grin.

With a lot of effort, I pushed myself up and rubbed my eyes, just as Nichelle staggered through my bedroom door. But even though she had done the most drinking, she looked hella better than me. I mean, at least she was standing on two legs. I could hardly feel my own legs.

"I still cannot believe you hired a chef for us," Nichelle said, yawning as she stretched.

"And I told you before, I didn't hire a chef." Simone pointed at me. "Her man did all this." She faced me. "And speaking of your man . . ." She darted through the door, and the way she'd just said that, I wondered if somehow Charles had made his way down here. But before Nichelle had a chance to stretch again, Simone was back. "These just came for you," she sang, sounding like she was about to break out into a love song as she handed me the giant bouquet of white roses.

"Wow," Roxie said, strolling into my bedroom through the adjoining bathroom.

I was mesmerized by the flowers. White roses were my favorite, but they weren't in season. "Where did these come from?"

"Where else?" Simone said, setting the bouquet on the nightstand. "Your boo thang."

"Charles sent those?" I leaned over and sniffed.

"How many boo thangs do you have?" She laughed. "Of course he did, along with this." Simone held up her wrist.

This time when I squinted, it wasn't because I was still feeling last night's shots. I was trying to figure out what was sparkling from her wrist. "What is that?"

She exhaled a long sigh. "Only the most gorgeous diamond tennis bracelet I've ever seen." She modeled the jewelry like she was on *The Price Is Right.*

My legs suddenly worked; I jumped out of the bed. "And you have on my gorgeous bracelet?"

"You were asleep."

"And so that means wear my gift?" I said, trying to grab her wrist and my bracelet. "And I wasn't asleep because you woke me up."

She hid her arm behind her back. "Well, you were still in the bed with your eyes still kinda closed when I first peeked in here. So . . ."

"If the box had my name on it, why did you even open it?" I held my hand out for her to return the bracelet.

Simone shrugged as she released the clasp and took the bracelet off. "Because I wanted to see what it was." She dropped the string of diamonds into my hand.

"Awwww," Nichelle said, bouncing onto my bed. "When I grow up, I want a man who showers me with gifts the way Charles does you."

I hooked on the bracelet, then held it up in the light of the sun. Every shade of the rainbow bounced off the bracelet's multicolored diamonds.

"Twenty years and y'all are still going strong," Roxie said.

"Yeah, talk about being lucky," Nichelle said. "My man just got a raise at UPS, so we might be able to go to Galveston for the weekend."

"Don't front. You got a good man and you know it." I laughed.

Nichelle sat up and grinned. "I do, don't I?"

"Well, I'm glad y'all got good men 'cause Lord knows Ben is enough of a dog for us all."

All of our eyes turned to Simone, who was in the middle of a divorce that was so bad, she and her ex had taken restraining orders out on each other. I felt horrible about all she'd been going through and was glad that even though we called this my birthday trip, it was an important getaway for her, too.

"Wait." Simone clapped her hands. "We did not come all the way down here to talk about this. You have forty-five minutes and counting," she said, sounding like some kind of teacher trying to corral her class. "Let's get up and get going."

Roxie and Nichelle dragged themselves out of my bedroom behind her and I stretched before I took a quick sniff of my roses once again.

Lowering myself to the edge of the bed, I grabbed my cell phone, hit the FaceTime icon, and pressed my husband's photo.

It took a moment for the video call to connect, but then there was Charles's glowing face. The face of a popular sports anchor that had filled TV screens in Houston for two and a half decades. Everyone swooned over Charles Clayton—and I'd snagged him.

"Hello, my love," he said with his smile taking up more than half the whole screen.

"Thank you for the flowers and the bracelet," I said with my own smile.

"Just a little something to continue celebrating the blessing of your birthday."

"It's beautiful, babe, and I've really enjoyed everything that you've given to me, but no more gifts, okay? You've passed the forty-five mark already."

"So? Why can't I buy you as many gifts as I want? We work hard, we have the money, so what's our money for if not to enjoy it?" He chuckled. "And how many parents with two children in college can say that? Thank God for the academic brilliance that blessed our children through your DNA."

While he laughed, I sighed. He was right; we had more money than most since Eric's college was covered by his athletic prowess and Anika had received a full academic scholarship. But that wasn't what I was talking about. Charles loved to give me gifts, and that was wonderful—except that wasn't my love language. I wasn't into material things. I mean, yeah, who wouldn't love white roses that accompanied a tennis bracelet? It was just that the gifts didn't touch my soul. They never had.

I'd even bought that book *The 5 Love Languages* and given it to Charles, but he'd never read it and he'd never asked me why I'd bought it for him. It wasn't all on Charles, though. I'd never told him either. I just never wanted to seem ungrateful.

"Really, Charles, no more gifts, okay?"

"Please, who doesn't love gifts?" He didn't give me a chance to answer that question before he asked another. "So, are enjoying yourself?"

I fought back a groan. Charles always did this—talked over my concerns or tossed them aside completely. I was sure that he no longer even heard me.

"Aja?"

Now there was concern in his voice because if he wasn't buying me something, he was worried about me. I said, "It's nice. We're about to go out sightseeing now."

"Great. That's what I want to hear. Well, enjoy yourself. But hey, real quick. What's the Wi-Fi code?"

I sighed. "Honey, I told you before, it's on the side of the router."

"I know, but uh . . . I kinda forgot . . . Where's the router?"

I bit my lip. Charles had a master's from Notre Dame, yet he acted like a helpless child sometimes. No, I take that back—most of the time. At least when he was home. I knew so much of his behavior could be traced right back to me. From the beginning of our marriage, I'd taken over all thinking for him, as if he were my child. There were times when I felt more like his mother than his wife.

I said, "It's in the dining room over the fireplace," without adding that I'd told him this before. "Turn it to the side," I droned on, "and the Wi-Fi password will be right there. The last line." I figured I'd give him very specific instructions so he didn't call all the way back to the Dominican Republic to ask which line was the code.

"So, I gotta go all the way down there?"

I frowned. What was he talking about? All the way down where? From the video call, I could see that he was in our bedroom. All he had to do was go downstairs, take less than one hundred steps from where he was to the dining room.

He continued, "You don't know the password off hand?"

Because heaven forbid you should have to do some actual work. "No, sweetheart, I don't know. Just go look, okay?" My tone didn't sound that much different from when I talked to Eric or Anika— when they were ten years old!

"Fine," he said. "Enjoy yourself. I love you." He ended the call before I could tell him that I loved him back. It was obvious words weren't his love language. I guess he didn't need to hear what he already knew.

Tossing my phone onto the bed, I sighed, feeling a bit down. It was hard to be mad at Charles, though. He spent most of his life doing two things: loving me and loving our children. It was just that I was tired of his CEO position. Especially since he was more than capable of doing anything. It was just easier to tell me to do it. I needed my husband to grow up.

"But they're the monsters you created."

Roxie's voice was so loud in my mind that I had to look up to make sure she hadn't walked into my bedroom. But she hadn't. Her words were just there because that's what she always told me whenever I complained about Charles or the kids.

"You'd tie their shoes if you had enough time. You're always saving them when they don't even need to be saved."

Those words that Roxie had spoken were true. But I wasn't going to sit there and beat myself up about what I'd done in the past. I wanted to live for today, in this beautiful paradise. I'd made up my mind that though I didn't know what was eating at me, I was going to enjoy the rest of the time here.

And if I didn't start getting ready now, Simone would be back banging on my door.

I stood and dragged myself into the bathroom. I just had about fifteen minutes to get myself together.

⟶•⟨⟶

"Let's roll," Simone said, right as I stepped out of my bedroom.

"But I'm hungry," I whined.

"Me too," Nichelle and Roxie said in unison.

"Too bad," Simone said. Then she grinned and pointed to a platter on the dining room table. "Just kidding. I have bagels since you all are too late for breakfast."

We grabbed the bagels and headed out to the SUV where the driver that Charles had hired to drive us around during our stay waited.

"Where to, ladies?" he asked.

"We're going to the excursion. The one that's scheduled for 11:15," Simone replied.

"Ah yeah. You'll enjoy that one," he said.

While my girls chatted, my eyes were on the window, taking in the scene of the blue waves crashing against each other. My eyes were on the scenery, but my thoughts were on my conversation with my husband. That five-minute call was the epitome of our marriage. If anyone had listened in, that call would have told them all they needed to know about Charles and me.

It didn't even take us ten minutes before we were pulling into a lot that was framed by vendors on the perimeter.

"We have about an hour before we have to get on the boat/bus, so he said we can stop here and do a little shopping."

"Are you kidding me?" Roxie said. "We could've spent this time back in the suite enjoying breakfast."

"Or sleeping," Nichelle added with a yawn.

"I wanted to make sure we were on time," Simone said. "Remember, I'm the Virgo of this group. The rest of y'all . . . we would have missed this altogether. Plus, who doesn't want to do a little shopping?"

When the driver slid open the SUV door for us, the shouts of the men and women selling their wares from the tables greeted us. He helped us all climb down from the back seats and then told us that he'd be just a block away waiting for us.

"Okay, well, since we're here, let's go shopping," Roxie said.

"I wonder if any of these folks are selling shots."

"Really?" Roxie, Simone, and I said at the same time to Nichelle.

She shrugged. "It's happy hour somewhere in the world." Then she laughed as if she'd been kidding, but I wasn't so sure that she was.

I stretched as I took in the scene. A foghorn blared from the ocean as sea hawks clacked along the coast. Boats of all shapes and sizes lined the harbor—from small dinghies to luxury jet boats. There had to be at least forty vendors lined along the street and another twenty on the beach.

We began to stroll past the vendor tables; I was on the lookout for handmade souvenirs for my family. I didn't have to look hard or far. At the first table, I found a woven bracelet for Eric and then earrings made from spoons for Anika. The next table, I picked up a couple of bottles of oils that the woman convinced me would get rid of evil spirits. I chuckled as I made that purchase for my mother-in-law.

As I approached the third booth, a woman smiled before we even stopped. Her hair was braided into two long plaits and she wore a bright yellow skirt and red, white, and blue shirt that looked like the Dominican flag.

"Greetings. Can I interest you in some energy rocks?"

"Rocks?" Nichelle said.

"Talk about a scam." Simone laughed.

"Um, yeah. We can pick those up on the beach," Nichelle added.

"Stop being rude," I whispered over my shoulder as I picked up one of the rocks. I set it in my hand and twirled it around in my palm.

"Wonder powers activate!" Simone said.

"Ignore my friends," I told the lady. "Tell me about the rocks."

"The one you're holding emits positive energy. I have some for healing and emotional growth." The woman beamed as she spoke, sending out her own positive energy, it seemed.

"Girl, my seven-year-old hit her brother in the head with one just like this," Nichelle said, picking up a yellow rock.

I was about to once again chastise my friend's rudeness when a beautiful painting behind the woman caught my eye. The painting was incomplete, but an assortment of oil paints sat on a table next to the canvas. I smiled as I looked from the painting out onto the harbor.

"That's here, huh?"

The woman beamed at her work. "Yep, painting brings me peace. I love to tell stories on the canvas."

"Me too." I was mesmerized by her attention to detail, down to the seagulls perched on the buoy. "I love the serenity of creating and how—"

"Come on, Aja," Nichelle said, cutting me off.

"You guys go on. I'll catch up with you." I waved my friends forward because I wanted to talk to the woman. While my girls supported everything I did, they, too, gave no regard to my desire to paint. Because it didn't fit into the "safe" career box, most people didn't get it.

"Okay," Simone and Roxie laughed as they moved on to the next booth. Nichelle followed, though her steps were slower as she was texting.

When we were alone, I turned back to the lady. "You'll have to excuse my friends," I said. "They're not always so rude."

"It's okay," she replied. "Not everyone is a believer." Her smile was still bright.

"So, there are really rocks that do the things you say?" She nodded as I noticed more paintings on the ground, leaning against her table.

"Is that some more of your work?" I moved closer, then thought to ask, "Do you mind if I see?" When I noticed her apprehension, I added, "I'm a painter myself."

That made her relax. "I just do this for me, really," she said. She pulled out a painting of a weathered old man with a gap-toothed smile. Every crease in his face was noticeable. His eyes were hollow, like he wanted you to peer into his soul. "This is one of my favorites." She proceeded to pull out another painting. "This one, too. I call this one *Life*. It's a woman who is trying to find her purpose in life."

"Wow," I replied, marveling at the sad woman walking on the beach, staring aimlessly out to sea. "These are amazing. You really should sell these."

"I should." She chuckled. "And for the right price, I might consider it. It's just that my paintings are so personal." She looked at the painting that she'd just pulled out, then looked at me before handing it to me. "This one reminds me of you."

I didn't reply as I took the painting and instantly connected with it. I stared at it, mentally processing every detail.

"Are you okay?" the woman asked.

I shook myself out of the trance that picture seemed to be luring me into. "Of course. Why would you ask me that?" I replied. Before she could answer, I said, "I just got caught up in your painting. It's amazing."

She studied me, looking at the picture, then back at me, then she added, "The sadness in her eyes matches yours."

"Um, what are you talking about? She's definitely happy," Nichelle said over my shoulder.

I didn't even realize she'd come up behind me.

"This is her birthday," Nichelle continued as if she felt she had to take up for me. "We're here celebrating her forty-fifth. She has an amazing family. An amazing life. What does she not have to be happy about?"

After Nichelle's litany of my happiness, I returned my glance to the woman.

The lady said, "She may have all of those things." The woman spoke to Nichelle, but her eyes were still on me. "But she's like the lady in my painting, walking without a purpose."

"She has a purpose. To party her ass off." Nichelle took the painting from me and set it down on the table with a little more force than I would have liked. "It was nice to meet you, but we gotta go." She grasped my hand and pulled me away. We'd only taken a few steps when Nichelle said, "Oooo-wee, talk about a buzzkill."

As my friend dragged me away, I glanced back over my shoulder . . . and the woman's eyes were still on me. We were still close enough for me to see that the delight that had been on her face when we first appeared was gone. Now it was full of concern, which was crazy since she knew nothing about me.

"Come on." Nichelle yanked me as if she thought I needed protection. "She's probably one of those fake psychics who try to scare you into buying their stuff. She was probably trying to get you to pay her ten dollars for a rock she picked up out of her front yard. And she probably tells everybody that they look like her paintings."

We met up with Roxie and Simone, then made our way out of the marketplace. But my eyes kept returning to the woman. And each time I looked at her, I found her looking at me.

"Come back and see me," she called out.

"Yeah. We're good," Nichelle replied.

But my friend wasn't speaking for me. Something in my gut told me I needed to get back to see this woman before I left the island. Something told me that she held the key for whatever I was seeking.

Chapter 4

Of course I didn't believe in any energy-emitting rock, but the old lady's words had planted themselves inside my head and weighed on me all day. I'd thought about her words while we were out on the tour, as we returned to the resort and lay on the beach, and as we spent the night partying with our newly made island friends.

"Walking without a purpose."

Now, even as I lay in bed, I couldn't get rid of her words.

Nichelle had to be right. That was like when one of those psychics told you something that was going to happen anyway—like you were going to move soon. Eventually everyone moved. And lots of people were walking without purpose. What did that mean anyway? Nothing. And even if it meant something, that woman couldn't possibly read me like that. Not in the three seconds that I'd stood in front of her.

Could she?

I pulled myself out of bed and tiptoed around the bedroom, even though I was alone.

I wanted to be careful not to wake any of my friends, especially since it was—I glanced at the clock on the nightstand—a little after 5:30. There was no way I wanted to stay in the bed, not even for another hour, just thinking about that lady's words about my aimless purpose.

Inside the bathroom, I once again tried to move in silence. But when I turned on my electric toothbrush, the door that led to Roxie and Nichelle's bedroom opened.

Roxie stood there, wearing boy shorts and a tank top.

"What are you doing?" she mumbled.

"Just go back to sleep," I said, rinsing off my toothbrush.

"You're brushing your teeth? Where are you going? It's still dark outside."

"I can't sleep and I was thinking about checking out the sunrise yoga that was on the schedule." I paused. "You wanna come?"

"Girl, bye," Roxie said before she staggered back into her bedroom.

I rushed back to my bedroom and slipped into one of the cute exercise leggings and matching tops I'd brought with me. Never did I really believe I would spend any time exercising. But right now, yoga sounded so good. I needed to relax my mind.

When I was dressed, I slipped out of the suite, then stopped at the activities desk to pick up the yoga mat.

"You know where the sunrise class is?" the woman asked.

I nodded. "They told us when we got here."

She smiled, then turned her attention to the couple behind me. They were a perky older couple dressed in matching exercise gear and headbands. I was surprised at how awake the resort was, since the sun was just beginning its ascent. But I guess this was one of the attractions of the island—the rising of the sun.

Strolling down to the beach, I already felt better. It was the fragrance of the flowers mixed with the ocean air. I inhaled; this alone was almost enough.

As I approached, I was surprised to see so many women, and a handful of men, lined along the edge of the beach with their yoga mats already positioned in the white sand.

"Come. Come join us." The woman, who I assumed was the in-structor, waved at me. "Come, right up here."

She pointed to a spot right in the front, and when all eyes turned on me, I paused. Maybe this wasn't such a good idea. I'd done one Bikram hot yoga class about six months ago, and that had almost taken me out. I wasn't sure if it was the thick heat or the downward dog that had run me out of that place. My reaction had surprised me. When I'd decided to go to the class, I figured it would be nothing. I'd been a cheerleader in high school *and* college. But like my college days, my cheerleading days were long gone, and with them, my flexibility.

I wanted to run back to the suite, but with everyone watching me, I faked a smile, made my way to the front, and set my mat next to a plump woman with a smile that was too wide for six in the morning.

"Good glorious day," she sang in what sounded like a British accent.

"Hello," I replied.

"First time?"

I nodded.

"You'll enjoy it. Yona is fantastic. You'll feel relaxed and re-leased before you know it."

Well, if this woman could do it, I certainly could. And already it was better than Bikram because the early morning breeze was cooling and calming.

My yoga neighbor had been right. Yona hummed and woo-sahed until my entire body felt relaxed. The only problem I had was I couldn't completely clear my mind. At the end, when we lay back in what Yona called the restoration pose, I closed my eyes and forced my weight from my body into the sand, the way Yona instructed. But when it got to the part where she told us to free our minds, too, I just couldn't do it.

Not that I didn't want to. It just seemed that the rock woman's words were stronger than my own will. Maybe that was because now that she'd said it, it did feel like I didn't have a purpose. I mean, I was a mother and a wife, but outside of that, I had nothing. It did feel like there was something I was searching for. But what was it?

I kept asking myself that question even as we slowly raised up, then stood. I clapped along with the rest of the class, then thanked Yona and said goodbye to my yoga partner.

As I rolled up my yoga mat, my glance moved down the beach and I paused. No, I did more than that—I froze. At the sight in front of me.

Was that the lady from yesterday sitting at the edge of the resort's beach? What was she doing here? Though I was able to answer that question right away.

She sat in the sand, her legs crossed yoga style, her two long ponytails draping down her shoulders. Her easel was positioned in front of her. She was painting the sunset.

My heart fluttered at the sight of her. I pushed myself up straight, then with a deep breath—as if I needed courage—I eased toward her. I didn't get too close, though. I wanted to give her space because she had closed her eyes like she was trying to paint a mental picture.

But then she said, "You can come closer."

My mouth opened wide. She hadn't turned toward me, she hadn't even opened her eyes. For a moment, I wondered if she was speaking to someone else. But when I looked over both of my shoulders, I realized she was talking to me.

And then I was sure of it when she said, "Come."

I tiptoed toward her. "Hi. Uh, this is Aja," I said, feeling so weird that she was speaking to me without having any idea who I was. "I met you yesterday at the marketplace. I talked to you about your paintings."

She still didn't open her eyes, but she nodded. "Yes, the

painter." She took a deep breath and then exhaled so slowly it felt like it took a minute. Only then did she open her eyes. She was silent as she brushed wide strokes across the canvas. I watched her in awe as she painted blue ocean waves. She finished a wave then turned toward me. She studied me for a moment before she said, "Are you looking for your purpose?"

"How do you know that?" I asked. "Are you some kind of psychic or Dominican witch?"

The woman laughed as she resumed painting. "Psychics aren't real. Neither are witches. I'm just an old lady with a gift of discernment. So I know much. Like I know your friends, they're here for fun, but you're here in search of something more."

"What?" Now I knew she didn't know what she was talking about. "I'm here for fun, too. I'm here to celebrate my birthday."

She shrugged, unfazed by my tone. "So you can't be lost because it's your birthday?"

Her words made me pause. Now she was saying that I was lost? "I . . . I'm not . . . lost."

"Are you trying to convince me?"

"No, it's just that—"

The woman shrugged and cut me off. "All I can tell you is what I see. You're the lady in my painting. You should take that painting with you."

Okay, Nichelle was right. This woman was just running a con to get me to buy a painting.

"Fine, I'll buy the painting," I said.

She didn't miss a beat as she said, "It's not for sale. But you can come by later and I'll gift it to you." She picked up her bag from the sand, pulled another brush out and began contouring the wave. For a moment, I was afraid she was going to leave me standing on the edge of paradise.

Quickly, I asked, "What did you mean when you said I'm not walking in my purpose? You don't even know me."

"True. I don't." She dipped the brush in yellow paint. "I love yellow. It's the color of happiness. Are you happy? In your life . . . are you happy?"

"Am I happy?" I repeated her question to give myself a little time. "Why would I not be happy? I mean, of course I am. I have an amazing husband. He is a very successful sportscaster, we have two wonderful children who are coming into their own, money in the bank, I have a productive job . . . and oh, did I mention how fine my husband is?" I huffed. "So now you tell me . . . why wouldn't I be happy?"

"I don't know. You tell me."

"I'm happy," I repeated. "I'm happy. Very, very happy."

"Wow. You need to say it that many times to convince yourself?" She took a deep breath, then set her brush down on the easel tray. "Look, all I'm asking you to do is to look inside yourself. Life is for the living, not the existing."

"So, you're saying that I'm just existing?"

"Like you said, I don't know you, so I can't say," she said. "Are you?"

Now she was doing too much and I was reading too much into what was probably nothing more than a sales pitch to buy more of her wares.

"Okay," I said, tucking my yoga mat under my arm so that I could leave, "I was just . . . I was just asking, trying to find out what you were talking about yesterday."

"You shouldn't ask questions until you're prepared for the truthful answers." The woman smiled. "But it's okay. You don't have to listen now. Just know that at some point, you will hear me." She paused. "My name's Jewel. I'm in the marketplace almost every day. Come see me if you want to talk." She smiled. "Or paint." Then she turned and resumed her painting.

Since it was obvious she was done talking, I thanked her, then turned and walked away.

My mother used to have a saying—when you go digging, be prepared for what you unearth.

Those words hung over me as I trudged through the sand. I needed to decide if I wanted to dig any more to get to the root of what was wrong. As soon as the thought crossed my mind, I knew the answer to that was yes. Otherwise, I would forever be searching for answers as to what was wrong with me.

Chapter 5

Today had to be a first. The first time since I'd met my friends our freshman year in college that I'd awakened before any of them. Granted, it was because I couldn't sleep, but still I was surprised when I returned to the suite that not even Simone was awake.

So, I settled on the balcony, sitting in one of the oversized wicker chairs and watching the sun continue its ascent into a sky that was still lit with a panorama of colors. This place was absolutely beautiful. There were no signs that a hurricane had ravaged the area a couple of years ago. It was pure utopia and seemed like the perfect place to come and relax—sans party animal friends—and clear your head.

I probably should have been in my bedroom packing, since we had a flight home this afternoon. But I wanted to be still for a moment. Really, what I wanted to do was reflect on Jewel's words.

"You're here in search of something more . . . Are you happy?"

"Good morning."

I turned and faced Simone, who stood at the balcony door, yawning and stretching.

"What are you doing up?" Her eyes widened a bit as she studied me. "And dressed, too."

"I went to sunrise yoga. Wanted to do something on my last morning."

"Oh." She yawned. "You should have awakened me. Anyway, let me call Miguel to get our last breakfast, and while he's doing that, I'm gonna pack." She paused and looked over her shoulder at me. "You packed already?"

I lifted my chin, and that was enough for Simone. She stepped back inside the suite and banged on Roxie and Nichelle's door.

I didn't move, not even when I heard Roxie and Nichelle moving around the suite. I just stayed in place, staring at the sun and wondering about Jewel's words.

"You're not walking in your purpose."

I couldn't shake Jewel's words, I couldn't shake what felt like a cloud that she'd left with me.

"What's wrong with you?" Roxie asked, joining me on the balcony. "You're not acting like a woman on a birthday celebration."

I shrugged as I feigned a smile, and in my mind, I debated if I should tell Roxie what I was thinking, what I was feeling. But how would I put my emotions into words?

So, all I said was, "I'm good. Just sitting out here, enjoying the view of our final morning."

"Well you've gotta be tired, as early as you got up," she said.

"And you must be hungry, too," Simone peeked her head outside. "Breakfast will be ready in about thirty minutes, I think. Are both of you packed?" Simone asked as if she was some kind of tour guide boss.

Roxie said, "Yeah," and again, that was good enough for Simone.

"Let me go make sure Nichelle is up, because if Simone goes in there all Susie Sunshine, she's liable to get cussed out."

I laughed and said, "I'll be in in a minute." I stared at the beautiful blue water for a few more minutes.

Finally, I stood and followed Roxie inside. I headed into the kitchen and the aroma of the crepes and bacon enveloped me, pushing all my thoughts and troubles aside.

"Okay." Simone clapped her hands. "We can enjoy our breakfast, but remember, the car service will be here at eleven."

We chatted over breakfast, reminiscing about our days on the island, remembering the drinking and the dancing, the drinking and the touring, the drinking and the shopping.

"And speaking of shopping, I forgot to tell you guys about that crazy lady yesterday," Nichelle said with a shudder.

"What crazy lady?" Roxie asked.

"Remember the one with the rocks?" As Nichelle went on to explain about our conversation with Jewel after Roxie and Simone had walked off, I drank my orange juice slowly, so slowly, the glass was still at my lips when Nichelle finished.

"Yeah, she does sound like she was running games," Roxie said. "I don't know how I missed all of that."

"Well," Nichelle began, "I say we get dressed now, then go down to the bar and have final shots."

"At ten in the morning?" Simone said.

"Girl, it is happy hour somewhere." Nichelle stood and waved her hands in the air. She danced her way over to the console where she'd hooked up her iPhone to the speakers. She hit her music app and Salt-N-Pepa sang out:

"Oooh baby, baby . . ."

That was our signal. Simone and Roxie jumped up from the table and rushed into the living room, swiveling their hips as if they were in the "Push It" video, performing a routine we'd done back in our college days. I couldn't believe they still remembered it.

My three friends danced in the middle of the living room, competing with each other the way we used to back in the day when we'd have dance-offs. It took a few minutes for anyone to see that I hadn't joined them.

Roxie motioned for me to get up. "Girl, what are you still doing over there? You better get your butt up."

"She just knows that she can't win this," Nichelle said, doing a dip that was impressive. "And I say whoever loses this, pays for our shots."

"Ah, push it," Simone sang.

I watched my girls, and though I didn't join them, they did make me smile. They danced that whole song, argued about who won, played it again, danced-off again, and then dragged themselves to their rooms. Didn't these chicks remember how old we were now? Didn't they know that there were probably more days behind us than in front of us?

"We only have about twenty minutes," Simone sang out from her room. "I asked the bellman to come up at ten forty-five."

I waited until my friends were all in their rooms and then, with a sigh, I pushed myself up and cleared off the table. Of course, I didn't have to do that, but I needed something to do with my hands, and these thoughts kept playing in my mind.

"You're here in search of something more."

I poured a fresh glass of orange juice, then returned to where I'd been sitting. I went back to just sitting, just thinking, just wondering, just deciding.

When the doorbell to the suite rang, I was still sitting in the same spot.

"I got it," Roxie shouted and she rushed from her bedroom, dragging her suitcase behind her. She set it against the wall before she opened the door. As the bellman wheeled the cart into the suite, she said, "All good things must come to an end. Come on in."

"Hello, ladies. I'm here for your luggage," he said.

Roxie pointed to her black Gucci baggage, then Simone came out of her room, followed last by Nichelle.

After he placed all the bags onto the rack, the bellman turned to me. "Ma'am, do you have your luggage?"

That was when all three of my friends turned to me. Their expressions told me that they had just noticed—I was still in the same place, wearing the same thing, no luggage in sight.

"Aja, what are you doing?" Roxie asked. "Why are you still sitting there?"

"I'm enjoying this glass of orange juice," I said.

Simone glanced at her watch. "Um, can you either get that juice to go or finish up before we miss the plane?"

It took me a few moments to find my words. I was searching for something. Then it dawned on me. I wouldn't find it if I got on that plane. "I'm not going," I said as the realization swept over me.

"I have a million and one things to do when I get back," Simone continued, as if she hadn't heard me. "So the last thing I want to do is miss our flight. I also don't want to be running through the airport."

But while she jabbered on, Roxie and Nichelle had heard me clearly. I knew they had—it was all in their stares.

"What did you just say?" Nichelle asked.

Before I could answer her, Roxie jumped in with, "Girl, you need to stop playin'."

I spoke up and repeated my words. "I said, I'm not going."

A silence fell over the room.

"I'm sorry." Roxie blinked a couple of times as if that would help her understand my words better. "What do you mean you're not going?"

I set the glass on the table and sat up erect. "I'm not going back." My words were stronger this time and I actually smiled. "I'm going to stay in the DR."

The bellman turned his glance from me to the others as if he not only did not want to get in the middle of this but he had other guests to help, other tips to receive.

"Um, here you go." Roxie handed him a twenty. "Can you

make sure our bags get on the right SUV? Our driver is waiting in a black Tahoe under the name Aja Clayton." She glanced over at me. "We'll help our friend bring her bags down."

He put the money in his pocket, nodded, then exited the room.

Roxie turned back to me. "Okay, I have no idea what's going on, but you need to go in there and get your bag because it's time to go."

She spoke to me in her no-nonsense tone as if she were my mother. So I folded my arms and spoke back to her with conviction. "I don't know how many other ways to say this . . . I mean, if I could speak another language, I would repeat it several ways. But I'm. Not. Going."

"You're not going home?" Simone asked as if she were just now understanding my words.

"Right, I'm going to stay here." Just voicing that caused a sense of peace to sweep over me.

"We've been here four days," Nichelle said. "That's not enough for you? So how long are you going to stay? And don't you have to get back to work?"

I shrugged. "Yes, I have to get back to work, and maybe forever. Maybe I'll stay down here forever."

"Aja, don't be ridiculous," Roxie said.

"Yeah, I know we had a good time and all, but you can't just stay on the island throwing back shots. Our reservation is up today," Nichelle said.

"I'm going to call down now and extend it. And if they can't give me this suite, that's okay. I don't need all this room anyway. I'll move to another room."

"Okay," Roxie said, sliding in the seat across from me. "Tell me what's going on. Why are you trying to stay in the DR? You're not ready to go home?"

I sighed. "No, it's not that. It's just that . . . remember that old lady?"

Roxie frowned. "What old lady?"

"Oh no," Nichelle said before I could further explain. "She's talking about the lady I just told you about. The one with the rocks and the paintings."

"Yeah, well, she talked to me," I said.

"She's creepy and crazy," Nichelle said. "You let that old quack get in your head?"

"It's not that." I shook my head. "Look, even you, Roxie, kept asking me what was wrong on this trip."

Roxie frowned.

"Remember when we were at the club the other night?" I said. "You kept asking me what was wrong. I knew it was something, I just didn't know what. But I know it for sure now."

"You know it because of the old lady?" Simone asked.

I nodded. "She told me that I wasn't walking in my purpose. And that's it in a nutshell. I'm not doing what I was put on this earth to do."

"Oh, Lawd," Simone and Nichelle sang together, though Roxie just kept her eyes focused on me.

"She asked me if I was happy. And if I had answered her truthfully, I would've told her that I wasn't happy."

"What in the world does happiness have to do with adulting?" Nichelle asked.

"You're not happy about what?" Simone added.

"I'm not happy about anything. Because Charles made the choice not to have a lot of guy friends, outside of work it's like I'm his everything, and sometimes it's just too much."

"Wow, you're bothered because your man wants to be with you instead of running the streets?" Simone asked.

I exhaled my exasperation. "My life just doesn't feel like my own. I feel like I'm suffocating under the weight of all those I love."

"Shoot, aren't we all?" Simone said. "That's what happens when you grow up. But what are we supposed to do about that? Go back to when we ran the streets?"

"No. I'm too old for that," I said. "But there's got to be more to life than this. I mean, does the fact that we become wives and mothers mean that our dreams have to be put on the back burner? Or die altogether?"

"I don't understand. Charles supports your dreams," Roxie said. "Remember, he bought your first painting."

"In 1999," I replied. That had been one of the things that had made me fall in love with Charles. When we dated, he took such interest in my passion. He'd been the anonymous donor who had paid $500 for my very first painting. He'd won my heart—then put my painting in a closet, told me that all he wanted now was for me to be his wife and bear his kids. And that's exactly what I did.

I was ready to take my paintings out of the closet.

"I work. I take care of the kids. I work. I take care of a husband. Day in and day out. That's my life." I paused, looking at them as if I was pleading for their understanding. "I want to do something I love, something that gives me joy right here," I said, tapping my heart.

"Girl, you're tripping, for real," Nichelle said. "You still paint."

"But not like I want," I protested. "I was going to the 'Living Your Best Life' conference because I know there's more to life and I'm just trying to figure out what that is. I wanted to find a way to center my joy and it's like that dream was derailed because of my family."

"So is this about you missing the conference?" Roxie asked. "You're still mad about that?"

"It's deeper than that," I replied. I was getting frustrated. It's not that I expected them to understand. No one ever did. Not my parents, who pushed me in a different direction whenever I wanted to paint. Not the guidance counselor, who made me change my major. And not my family, who kept relegating my painting to hobby status.

"I have a gift that I've just been sitting on," I said.

Nichelle threw up her hands. "Y'all's friend has been watching too many *SuperSoul Sunday* episodes."

"Okay, maybe if you take some painting classes, you'll feel better, since that's what you love," Roxie said.

"Ooh, go paint some nude men." Nichelle waved her hand in the air and I was sure she was about to break out into a dance again.

Simone giggled. "I bet that would make you happy."

Roxie cut her eyes at Simone and Nichelle before she turned back to me. "Aja, I understand you feeling some kind of way right now, but you don't go visit another country and just up and decide to stay there."

I stood and started pacing the length of the dining table where just an hour ago, we'd been laughing and reminiscing about our trip. I didn't expect my girls to agree with my decision, but I at least thought they'd understand. "Look, I just have to stay so that I can figure some things out."

"Aja, this isn't making any sense," Roxie said. "You can't figure out what's going on in your own home, in your own bed, with your own husband?"

Before I could say a word, Nichelle sang out, "Ooohhh! I know what this is about." There was a glare in her eyes, but a smile on her lips when she pointed her finger at me. "You ain't fooling anyone."

All three of us frowned at Nichelle.

She said, "You slipped out and hooked up with some DR cutie, didn't you?" She nodded. "Uh-uh. That's where you went this morning. And it was probably that guy you were dancing with at the club all night. The one that looked like Marc Anthony. What did you do? Did you sneak out and go to his place?" She bobbed her head again. "Yeah, that's what happened. He rocked your groove and now you're ready to change your name to Stella."

Now Roxie wasn't the only one to roll her eyes at Nichelle. "No one has rocked my groove, whatever that means. I didn't even get that guy's name or number."

"Well, you should have," Simone said. "He was super-fine."

"No. She shouldn't have," Roxie said. She kept her eyes on me. "Because she has a husband who loves her like her life depends on it. She has a love people pray for."

"And," I continued, ignoring Roxie, "I would never make a decision like this over some guy."

"But, Aja—" Roxie began.

I interrupted her. "I just need some quiet time to get my head together. Maybe it took turning forty-five to make me realize that I need something more." I popped back down in my seat.

"We're all forty-five," Roxie said.

"Speak for yourself," Nichelle said. "I'm thirty-five. Aging backward. And it's all because of shots."

"Okay, Benjamin Button," Simone said. "And by the way, I'm forty-four, don't make me any older," she added.

"Whatever," Roxie said. "The point is, that's why we came on vacation. To get rejuvenated."

I stared into the faces of my friends. "Have any of you ever stopped to think, what if there's more to life than what we're doing?"

Roxie stood, circled around the table, then bent down in front of me. She took my hands. "Sweetie, I know we all get bored sometimes, but look at your life. You have a good life. No, let me correct that. You have an amazing life. With a husband and children who love you. Think about what Charles did for you for your birthday. We're all here because of him. He's wonderful."

I snatched my hands away from her grasp. "I know! Charles is so wonderful. He's Denzel, Idris, and George Clooney rolled up into one."

"No, Clooney cheated on his wife," Simone said. "We don't want him to be Clooney."

"That's not the point," I huffed. "I know how perfect my life is. The perfect husband, the perfect kids, the perfect everything. Well, what's not perfect is *me*. That's what I discovered on this trip. All is well on the home front, except with me."

"Do you know how many women would love to trade places with you?" Simone said, her mood completely shifting as my words settled in. There was such sadness in her voice, and I knew where that came from. And if I was in a different place, I would have stopped this conversation and hugged her. And prayed for her, because I knew her divorce was breaking her heart. She continued, "So many women would love to have a husband who adores them the way Charles adores you."

"That's part of the problem," I said, almost wishing we could focus on Simone's problems and not mine. "Everyone acts like I should be so grateful to have Charles. I love him dearly, but he's just as lucky to have me as I am to have him."

"Honey, no one is saying that you should be grateful. It's just hard to understand what you're feeling because of what you do have in your life," Roxie said.

"And this isn't making sense to us," Nichelle added.

"I get that. Because I don't completely understand it myself. If I did, I'd be able to explain it better to you." I sighed. "All I know is I need to stay and figure it all out."

The way my girls looked at me, then at each other, I knew that they heard me. Finally. Thank God.

"Fine, Aja," Simone said. "Ladies, we need to get rolling or we'll all be here with Aja."

"How long are you going to stay here?" Roxie asked.

I shrugged.

"I have a bunch of vacation days, plus I can take some personal leave for as long as it takes."

Simone shook her head as she walked over and hugged me. "Okay. Call us daily and let us know what's going on."

"I will. I promise," I replied.

Nichelle stepped toward me, reached in the messenger bag draped across her body and pulled out a travel-sized bottle of tequila.

"Here. This will help you clear your head while you're here."

I managed a laugh. "I'm good. Plus, I'm sure you'll need it for the plane."

She thought for a moment, then dropped the bottle back into her bag. "You sho right."

Nichelle hugged me, too, then moved aside as Roxie stood, looking like she wanted to cry.

"Are you sure about this?" she asked me. "You being here alone worries me. Maybe I should stay with you."

I hugged her. "Thank you, but no. I need quiet time to think."

"Fine." She sighed, then headed toward the door. "Call me tonight."

I watched as my friends reluctantly left, and then a silence blanketed the room leaving me with nothing but my thoughts.

Chapter 6

The silence engulfed me, and the magnitude of what I'd done felt like a boulder on my shoulders. But at the same time, it felt freeing. I'd gone against the grain, done the unexpected, and it felt exhilarating.

I was settled in a smaller hotel room, a single unit, rather than a three-bedroom suite. The bellman had looked at me with trepidation when he'd come back up to move my bags. His narrowed eyes, sideward glance, and pursed lips told me he thought I was up to no good. I guess even the help couldn't understand my decision.

My girls had texted and called until their plane took off an hour ago. And then I received the text that I'd been dreading. From Charles: *Can't wait to see you!* That had sent a pang through my heart. He was an understanding man, but how would he ever be able to understand this when I couldn't understand it myself?

It would have been much easier to wait a few more hours, build up some fortitude, and then wait for Charles to call me when he realized I wasn't on that plane. But I couldn't do that to him. He deserved more from me.

Leaning back on the bed, I pulled out my cell phone from my purse, scrolled to my Favorites, and stared at my husband's photo for a moment. Even in the thumbnail picture, his personality beamed through—the grin on his lips, the gleam in his eyes, his sexy, masculine cheekbones. I sighed as I pressed the photo, then listened for the few seconds of silence as the international connection went through. With each passing moment, my heart pounded harder.

Charles gave me no extra time to prepare; he answered on the first ring.

"Well, if it isn't the love of my life." I heard his smile. "Wait. Shouldn't you still be in the air? Or did you all land early?"

Tossing my legs over the side of the bed, I stood. This was going to be one of those "I need to move" conversations. I paced from my bed to the door, then back, wishing I had the space of the luxury suite where I'd spent the last four days.

"Hi, babe, how are you?"

"I'll be better when you get here. I'm so glad you had this birthday celebration, but we've missed you and can't wait to see you."

I stopped moving and had to resist the urge to roll my eyes. Since she'd been home from school, Anika had been spending all of her time hanging with friends. Kelli had gone on to her father's and Anika was constantly on the go. I doubted if she spent two waking hours a day at home. And Eric was the same. He had a girlfriend now and he spent all of his free time with her. He'd returned to school for basketball practice the same day I left. No, it wasn't the kids who missed me.

"We? The kids are both off doing their thing and your mother, well . . ." My stomach churned at the mention of his mother.

Charles chuckled. "Okay, me and the dog missed you. Bailey doesn't even want to come out of her kennel because she wants you to come home. So what time will you be here? Do you have your baggage yet?"

He didn't even realize that my plane wasn't due to land for another hour and a half. So, he hadn't figured anything out yet. I inhaled. Exhaled. Prayed that my husband would be understanding. "So, sweetie, I'm, ah . . . I'm not on the plane."

"Oh." He paused and I imagined him trying to figure this out. "What? The plane was delayed?"

"No, not quite. It took off . . . just without me. I'm going to stay a few days."

There was silence for a moment, then he said, "What?" as if he couldn't comprehend my words.

"Yeah, I, um, I decided to stay a little longer. Stay here in the DR."

"I'm confused," he said, his jovial tone definitely gone. "So all of you just decided like that to extend your trip? But what about—"

Before he could finish, I interrupted, "No, not everyone else, just me."

"Just you?" There was a pause as the words continued to compute in his brain. "Aja, what in the world are you talking about? You've been gone almost a week. It's time to come home."

There it was. That tone that had dictated my life for the past twenty years.

Painting is not a career, Aja.

You have a family. A job. You don't have time for that stuff.

That. Stuff.

I remember the first time I'd felt Charles stepping on my dream. He'd referred to my painting as *stuff* and it had settled in my core. Now, save for the few pieces I had on the walls at home, when I painted, I put my "stuff" in the closet.

As Charles continued talking about how I needed to return to my family and my responsibilities, I began pacing once again, my eyes now on the carpet. I needed something to focus on because Charles hadn't even started. Not really. He was going to go off when I told him that I wasn't coming back. Yet, anyway.

So as I moved, I turned my attention to the carpet, taking notice of the difference between this covering and what had been in the suite.

When he became silent, I said, "Charles, I've only been gone four days."

"That was the plan."

"And I didn't call you to debate. I just wanted to let you know."

"Aja, this is ludicrous." His voice went up several decibels before he pulled back. "Sweetheart." His volume was lower, his tone was gentler. "What's going on?" He paused. "Mother, may I have some privacy, please?"

Dang! His mother had been there the whole time, listening. This wasn't good. In the background, I heard his mother ask, "What's going on? Why isn't she coming home? What happened?"

"Mother, please," he muttered. Then he must've put his hand over the phone because his voice was muffled. Still, I could hear him say, "Not now, please."

Judy Clayton was that mother who thought her son could do no wrong. For the most part, I liked her and she liked me—until it became a situation that involved her son. Then she was a brutal mama bear that would maul anyone who dared hurt her boy.

Finally, Charles's attention returned to me. "Okay, let's get serious, Aja. Just stop playing and tell me what time I should be at the airport."

So this was how he was going to handle this. "I'm not playing. I need some time and I'll be home in . . . a few days."

"So you're serious. You need time for what? How long are you planning to stay there? Why are you staying? Was this your plan all along?" He pummeled me with questions.

How was I supposed to explain this to Charles? How was I supposed to say my life was in disarray? I couldn't tell him that. He'd look around and ask me again if I was serious. Because on the surface, everything appeared better than fine. It was what was inside me that was the problem. That was the part that I couldn't explain. I couldn't tell the man who tried so hard to be the light of my life that he'd extinguished my fire. "I'm going through some things and I just need some time to sort everything out."

"What kind of things? This isn't making any kind of sense, Aja, and you know what? I'm just gonna get on a plane and come to you."

"Don't be ridiculous. You can't come to the DR."

"I can if my wife is talking crazy about not coming home." He paused again like he'd just had a revelation. "Wait." He lowered his voice as if he didn't want to be overheard. "Is everything okay? Are you being held against your will? Say something like 'Did you mail the package' and I'll know that's code for call for help."

I pulled the phone away from my ear and stared at my cell for a moment. If this wasn't so serious, I'd laugh. Twenty-five years of working in the television business had given my husband an overactive imagination that had just run away from him.

"No, honey." I sighed. "I promise I'm fine. It's just, I just really need some time."

"Time for what?" He huffed his frustration. "It's one thing if you just wanted to spend more time with your friends, but you're saying that you're staying there alone."

I was starting to feel like we were going in circles. Charles had a way of wearing me down. My whole family did. They would pile on and on . . . until I gave them whatever they wanted, so I knew it was time to shut this conversation down. But I had to be careful. "Please, Charles, just try to understand, and if you can't do that, just give me time."

"No."

"No?" Before I could tell him that he couldn't say no to me, he added:

"I'm catching a flight there."

I stifled my groan. If this had been any other time, I would've jumped at the prospect of a few days in paradise with my husband. But this was now and I wanted, no, I *needed* to be alone.

"I moved hotels," I lied, "so you won't be able to find me." Through his moan, I said, "Please, honey. Just be patient."

"Aja, babe—"

Suddenly, there was rumbling and my mother-in-law's voice filled the phone. "Aja, what in the world is going on? What is this nonsense about you staying on vacation?"

I would never disrespect Charles's mother, but I deserved a medal for that. Because the number of times that she had imposed herself in our marriage . . .

Without missing a beat and keeping my tone even, I said, "Judy, how are you?"

"Not well when I see my son all frazzled and worked up. You've upset him, now what in the world is going on?"

I swallowed back the words that would have made it clear that she needed to mind her damn business, and said, "I'm just taking a few extra days of vacation. But this is between me and Charles."

"You've already been hanging out with your girlfriends for a week like you're back in college with no responsibilities."

I let out a long sigh.

"Aja, I have no idea what is going on with you, but Anika is home for winter break. You need to be here navigating her into womanhood."

Navigating her into womanhood? What was this woman talking about? "Judy, Anika goes back to college in three weeks. I'll be home before then."

"You need to come home now. I told Charles this trip was a bad idea. Charles, I told you that you shouldn't have let her do this."

Let me.

I groaned inside as she continued. "This is asinine." I could just picture her wagging her finger like she was scolding a child. "Husbands and wives need to take their trips together. That girls' trip is the work of the devil, trying to destroy happy homes."

"Can you please put Charles back on the phone?" I said.

"My son is stunned right now and trying to make sense of why his wife has abandoned her family just so she can frolic on the beach. I don't know what's going on with you, but mothers don't get to run away. They stay and take care of their families. That's God's calling for their liv—"

"Aja," Charles said. The way his voice sounded, I imagined that he'd snatched the phone from his mom. "Excuse Mother. This is just startling to me. To us."

"I know. Just please let me have this time."

A brief silence filled the phone before Charles asked, "Are you with someone?"

That caught me a little off guard. I'd been married twenty years and there had never been someone else. And while I would never say never, I was sure Charles had been faithful as well.

"Don't be ridiculous, Charles. Of course I'm not with someone."

"It's not ridiculous. What would you think if I went away and then called you, telling you that I was not coming back?"

"That's not what I said. I am coming back. In a few days."

He drew a sharp breath and I felt him suppressing his anger. "Fine. Do what you need to do. I'll be here once you finish 'figuring things out.'"

"I love you," I said, ignoring the sarcasm in his tone. I wasn't

lying. I'd loved Charles for almost half my life, since Roxie introduced us. He'd been a golfing buddy of Roxie's late husband,
Brian. And the minute Roxie found out he was single, she had
been on a mission to set us up.

"I love you, too, Aja." With that, he hung up the phone.

Chapter 7

I had contemplated turning my phone off so I could spend some time with me. I didn't know exactly what I was searching for and I didn't know exactly what I was doing. I just knew that I suddenly felt ill-fit for the life I had been living. Or maybe the life I had been living had been ill-fit for me.

Sighing, I glanced around my hotel room. It was as if it was just hitting me—I was on this island, now alone. Had I done the right thing by letting that plane take off yesterday without me? But then I tightened my bathrobe before I stepped onto the balcony and soaked in the sight of the ocean. I inhaled the tropical air that was sprinkled with a pinch of the ocean's salt. Then I closed my eyes, and the twin sounds of delight and glee settled into my ears as children romped and played on the beach.

Winter had spared the DR and I was loving every minute of it. Opening my eyes, for the first time since my girls had left, I smiled. Yes, this was right. And it was amazing. I was really doing this, and my smile turned into a chuckle as I thought about the hard time I always gave to one of my coworkers, Sophie. Sophie took at least one vacation every year, cruising everywhere, alone. I thought that kind of independence was the craziest thing ever. How could anyone travel by themselves and have a good time? But Sophie always returned to work relaxed and refreshed, and she'd laugh with me when I teased her. But whenever she did, there was this gleam in her eyes that always made me feel like the joke was on me.

I got it now. It wasn't until this moment, leaning on the rail of my balcony at the Barceló Bávaro Palace, that I now understood Sophie. There was so much joy in solitude.

I'd forgotten that. I'd been so busy filling my life with the wants and needs of others that I'd forgotten what it was like to be alone. I'd forgotten the tranquility of solitude. I'd forgotten the peace that came with the quiet. I definitely needed all of that to figure out how to fix this empty feeling that had settled inside of me like it was taking root and spreading.

From inside my bedroom, the sound of my cell phone broke through that peace, and I hesitated. I was just coming into the understanding of what being alone could do for me. Did I really want to interrupt that now?

But my curiosity was greater than my need for solitude—right now. So I rushed inside, grabbed my phone from the bed, and glanced down to see my sister's phone number in London. Now the second smile of the day consumed me. My solitude would have to wait for just a minute.

"Hello," I answered, hearing my smile go through the phone.

"Great day to you," Jada said in a faux British accent.

My sister had been in London since she graduated from Texas Southern University sixteen years ago, and though she was still a U.S. citizen, she'd become a dual citizen six years ago. I loved her living in London because Jada had been hit the hardest by our family tragedy, and London, with its world-famous theatre, world-class shopping, and world-renowned delicacies, had been therapeutic for her. I loved that city just for what it had done for my sister.

She had been the most broken of the three of us after what happened with our mother, and then when our brother, Eric, committed suicide, I was convinced there would never be light in her life ever again.

But the passing of time had been a blessing and a healer. She'd slowly improved over the years, and then moving to London had caused that light that had begun to shine in her to now beam.

"Hey, Jada, what's up?"

"I'm good, sissy," she said, reverting back to her normal voice. "How are you?"

"I'm doing great," I said with a bit of hesitation in my voice that she didn't seem to notice.

"Well, I called to see how the girls' trip went. Did you meet some cute DR dudes to show you a good time? I mean, I know none of those guys could hold a candle to my brother-in-law, but you can look 'cause you aren't dead."

I sighed. My husband should've been a 90s sitcom show called *Everybody Loves Charles* because I didn't think I had one friend or relative who didn't like him.

"I'm still in the DR," I said, hoping Jada would make an assumption that she'd miscalculated the days and then change the subject.

"Oh," she paused, "I thought you guys were going back yesterday."

Taking a deep breath as I fell across the bed, I said, "My friends did go back."

This time, a longer pause filled the phone.

"And you didn't." It was a statement. Like she already knew that—Houston, we have a problem. Even though we were thousands of miles apart, my sister and I were extremely close, so it didn't surprise me that she could read me through the phone.

Then she said, "Hold on one second, sis. Let me get rid of whoever is at the door; we need to talk," she said in a tone that sounded like she thought she was the big sister.

I rolled my eyes but smiled again. I was the oldest of the three, and because of that, I was the responsible one, wanting to take care of my brother and sister. But even with all that we'd been through, Jada was now just as strong, just as confident as I was. And right now, she had her life together while I was questioning mine.

As I waited for her to return to the phone, I settled onto the bed and shifted so that my legs were stretched out in front of me. My thoughts stayed on my sister and I shook my head a bit. There was a time when no one would have ever been able to convince me that we'd arrive at this day when she was ready to have a talk to try to help me.

It was amazing that we'd arrived here when I thought back to the night this all started, the night that had changed our lives and our souls forever.

My parents were fighting. Again.

My dad was drunk. Again.

And my mom was begging and pleading for him to "just go to sleep." Again.

But on this particular night there was something that was different. On this night, my thirteen-year-old brother said, "Enough."

Usually, we hid in either our bedroom or Eric's whenever our parents fought and we stayed until the screaming and the beating stopped. But on that night as I held my six-year-old sister while we were crouched on the side of Eric's bed, my eyes widened when Eric stood from where he'd been hiding, rushed to his closet, and grabbed his prized Hank Aaron– signed bat.

"What are you doing?" I whispered.

Eric didn't turn to me nor answer me. With a determina-

tion that I'd never seen in him, he moved toward the door, then marched his bony frame down the hall to our parents' bedroom.

"You stay here," I whispered to Jada before I rushed behind Eric. My heart pounded with my fear. What was my brother going to do?

I was just two steps behind Eric when we turned to my parents' bedroom and the sight made me want to scream, made me want to cry. The door lay on the floor and right away I knew now what that crash had been; my father had actually kicked the door down. But that wasn't the worst of it. It was the sight of my mother, hovered in the corner near the bathroom, gown torn, tears streaming, blood dripping from her nose. She trembled as she looked up at my father and I saw the same fear in her eyes that was in mine.

"Leave her alone," Eric hissed at our father.

"What . . . ?" Daddy muttered as he spun around and faced us.

I wanted to grab my brother's hand and pull him away. But I knew that he wasn't going to leave because this was as bad as our father had ever beaten our mother. Eric was going to save her.

But how was he going to do that? The difference between my father and my brother was jarring. Daddy had to be at least six four and he weighed as much as those big football players on TV. And my brother—he was taller than me, but I weighed more than him.

"What did you say?" my father slurred as he tried to focus on Eric. His hazel eyes were bloody red, the color they always were after he'd spent a night away from home.

"Come again." He edged closer to Eric, and though I took a step back, Eric stayed planted like a tree. Even though my father's shoulders were slumped and his shirt was torn at the sleeve, he still looked so ominous to me.

Drool trickled from the corner of his mouth. "What you goin' do with that bat, you little sissy?" He laughed like a madman as he towered over Eric.

"Eric," Mama whimpered from the corner, "please, go back to bed. I'm fine." As if she wanted to prove that she was, she tried to push herself up, but she struggled to just get to her knees before she fell back onto the floor.

"I said, leave her alone." Eric's voice trembled, but he still stood strong, still stood determined.

Inside my head, I screamed Eric's name. It was bad enough to see Mama like this, but I knew if Eric didn't turn and run now, our father would beat him down just like Mama, maybe even worse.

"Well, well, well. If the little piss-in-the-bed, sissy-ass son of mine ain't trying to have him some balls." Daddy laughed. "Boy, you'd better be glad I'm feeling good because I'm gonna give you a pass. If you know what's good for you, you'll put that bat down and get your ass back to bed before I break you in half."

I could see Eric's legs shaking, but still he stood, his fingers clutching the bat tighter.

"Oh," our father said, stumbling back just a little, "so I guess you gotta see to believe." Daddy lunged forward and punched Eric in his chest so hard, his body became airborne, flew into the hallway, and landed in front of the wall across from their bedroom.

I screamed, though no sound came out of me as Eric hit his head on an antique table, then slumped over like he was dead.

"Eric!" Mama screamed. She found her strength and scrambled from the floor.

But before she could take more than a few steps, Daddy reached back and backslapped Mama with the same force that he'd used on Eric. "Sit down!" he shouted as he knocked Mama back to the floor.

"Mommy."

Until I heard my sister's voice, I'd been frozen. But now, I tried to reach out and grab Jada before she sped by me and ran into their bedroom.

"Mommy," Jada cried again, "are you all right?" She clutched Mama's neck.

"Baby," Mama cried, trying to push Jada away. "Just go. Go back to your room." But as she tried to ease Jada away, my sister held on tighter.

Then Daddy grabbed Jada's neck. "Get back to your room!" He lifted her into the air.

Jada screamed, her arms and legs flailed. "Mommy! Mommy!"

"Shut up!" Daddy struggled to get his belt off with one hand. "I'll teach your little behind to mind!"

"Mommy," Jada screamed louder than I'd ever heard anyone ever scream.

"Gerald, please," Mama cried, "you're hurting our baby."

Mama struggled to move, though it seemed her legs were too weak. She stretched her arms toward Jada, and all I could do was cry.

I couldn't count the number of times I'd seen Daddy out of control in one of his alcohol-driven rages. But even though I was sixteen and had seen more than Eric and Jada, this was by far the worst. I was so scared. Mama had been beaten so bad, she couldn't move, Daddy had Jada hanging in the air by her neck . . . and I glanced down at Eric. I wanted to see if my brother was dead; he sure looked like it. But still, I stood, unable to move.

"Gerald, let her go!"

My eyes had been on Eric, but when I heard Mama's voice,

I turned to her. She sounded so different, a bit stronger now. My mouth opened wide and my eyes bulged in horror.

What was Mama doing?

"Gerald, let her go!" Mama repeated, her voice even a little stronger now. She wavered a bit before she stood, everything on her shaking. Her face was smeared with her blood and tears as she pointed the small black pistol right at Daddy. "Don't make me shoot you. Put my baby down."

Daddy dropped Jada onto the floor like she was a rag doll and then, he threw up his hands before he took a step toward her. "Has everybody in this house lost their minds?"

"Baby, don't." Mama's brown eyes softened as she pleaded with Daddy. She backed up but kept the gun pointed straight at his chest. "I don't want to use this. I just want you to go get some sleep."

"You pull a gun on me," he said moving toward her. He sounded as if he couldn't believe what was happening. "And then you tell me you don't want to use it?" He only stopped moving when he was standing right in front of her face.

I cried out again, but like before, nothing came out of me. The screams stayed inside.

"Go ahead, shoot me." He laughed as he placed his chest to the gun's barrel.

Tears rolled down Mama's face as she held the gun as firmly as she could. "Just go."

Daddy laughed again, but then I breathed when he pivoted and took steps away. He was still chuckling, but my hope was that he would just keep walking, go into the living room, fall down on the sofa, and sleep until morning.

But then suddenly, he whipped around, knocked the gun out of Mama's hand, and pushed her to the floor. In a motion that didn't seem possible since he was so drunk, he grabbed the gun with one hand and Mama's hair with the other. When he pressed the gun to Mama's head, I screamed, and this time, I heard the sound.

"Okay, Superwoman, who's bad now?" He laughed.

Tears slid down Mama's cheeks and I watched the man I had loved so much hold my mother's life in his hands.

My eyes were riveted on my parents. That was why I didn't see Jada push herself from the floor. That was why I didn't have a chance to scream out and stop her. That was why Jada raced toward Mama without anyone really seeing her until it was too late.

"Noooooooo," my sister screamed as she threw herself against our parents.

It felt like a slow split second. That's how much time passed between Jada's scream, the sound of the gun, and the splatter of Mama's blood . . . all over Jada's face . . .

"Helllllo!!!"

Jada's voice snapped me from the worst memory of my life.

"Oh, what? What did you say?" I asked my sister as I blinked myself back to the conversation and struggled not to cry.

"Where did you go?" Jada asked.

"Nowhere. I'm right here." I took slow, deep breaths. It had been years since I'd relived that memory. Years since I had replayed the moment that stole all of our innocence.

"No, you're not. I kept calling your name—you didn't hear me?"

"Sorry. I was just lost in thought."

"Obviously," Jada replied. "So what in the world is going on? First, you tell me that you've stayed in the Dominican Republic, and now you're drifting away in thought. What's up with you?"

"By your questions I guess that Charles didn't call you."

"No." I heard the frown in her voice. "Why would your husband call me?"

I sighed. Charles knew that I was close to Jada, so I'd wondered if he'd called her to make sense of what I was doing.

"Aja, what's going on?"

I'd never burdened my sister with any of my problems before. It wasn't that I didn't feel comfortable. It was that Jada had suffered so much after that night. So much that she had shut down completely, finding a safe place within her mind to survive. She refused to speak and was getting worse with our aunt, who she'd been sent off to live with. She ended up being institutionalized for a while. There were days when I wondered if my sister would ever recover from being right there when our mother died at our father's hands, so close that the last of the blood that pumped through our mother's veins ended up on her.

But she had found a way out, through a relationship with our father before he died eight years ago. He served thirteen years in prison before being released for good behavior. Thirteen years for our mother's thirty-eight years of life. I'd hated him for that. But at Charles's urging, I had made peace with him because he'd saved Jada.

So there was no way that I ever wanted to do anything that could take Jada away from the happiness that she'd found.

She said, "Are you going to answer me? Are you going to tell me what's wrong?"

"Nothing," I said, trying, though I had little hope, to steer my sister away from this discussion.

"Aja, this is an international call and I don't want to spend minutes going back and forth. I can hear it in your voice, so please just tell me what's going on?"

Pushing myself from the bed, I sauntered through the room, back to the balcony. When I inhaled, this felt like my own safe place. I closed my eyes and savored the light breeze that grazed my face. "I don't know," I said, finally answering my sister with the truth. "I'm just going through some things, feeling kind of down."

"During your birthday celebration? This is a happy time."

"It should be, right? But I just have had a funk I can't seem to shake. I'm trying, though. I'm reflecting on some things." I hesitated before I added, "I don't think I'm happy."

Then I braced myself for Jada's chastisement, expecting her to tell me my thoughts were crazy, just ridiculous when my life was perfect.

She said, "Then you need to get to happy."

Tears welled in my eyes and I pressed my hand against my heart. "Oh my God, Jada. You're the first person to say that to me; the first to understand what I've been trying to say."

"Are you painting? You know that's freeing for you."

"Not yet, but you know I brought my supplies to the DR," I said.

She laughed. "Of course you did. Do you remember how you used to sit up under Mama when she used to paint?"

That brought the nostalgia back. But this time, it was happy memories.

"Of course, I remember. I'm surprised that you do," I said. That's where I first developed my love of creating on canvas, watching my mother. I could sit at her feet for hours watching her paint. She'd bought me my first watercolor set and set me up on an easel next to hers. By the time Jada came along, Mama and I were painting together. I would start the picture and she would finish it. It was our mommy-and-me time, and I relished every moment of it.

And then Daddy had lost his job and Mama lost her joy. Daddy would rant about how "painting didn't pay the bills" and "we couldn't afford that stupid hobby." It wasn't long before Mama abandoned painting altogether. Our once beloved mommy-and-me activity had become just me—and I did it more and more as a way to escape the violence that set up permanent shop in our home.

"I just remember how utterly crazy you would get whenever anyone interrupted you guys," Jada said.

That made me laugh. If you wanted to see me go ballistic, try interrupting my mommy-and-me painting time. "Because once you and Eric came along, I barely got any time with Mama, so I didn't want the two of you to come intruding," I said.

My sister laughed with me, then grew quiet. "In the bad times, you know, with Daddy, you used to say painting freed your mind. That it gave you clarity on the life you wanted to build."

I responded with silence. During that time, painting had become therapeutic. That's when I first decided I was going to have a perfect husband, a perfect life. Completely different from what I had then. That's what I used to draw.

"So, maybe you just need to lose yourself in the canvas again and it can bring you some clarity," Jada added.

My baby sister understood me. That warmed my heart.

"You're right," I said. "I need to paint." I thought about being able to freely create without someone interrupting me to do something, find something, or deal with some crisis. That thought made me smile. "Maybe that will help me. I'm trying to figure out why I have this hole in my heart."

"Look, there are a couple of things I know. I may have never been married, though Von has some issues with that," she said, referring to her French boyfriend. "But I know this: We are designed to love and be loved. To love what we do and be able to boldly say we are living our best life. And if you're not walking in your happiness every day, you need to change the path."

Even though tears rolled from my eyes, her words brought a smile to my face. "When did my little sister become so wise?"

"When she chose to come out of the darkness and live in the light, when she decided life was worth living to the fullest," she said, causing more tears to fall. "I'm all about being happy. I know we make better decisions in our lives when we're happy. We're healthier, we'll live longer. That's what I want for you. I want you to search so that you can get to your happy, sissy," she said. "And the whole time, I'll not only support you but I'll be praying for you, too."

I was so thankful for my sister and her words. She was right. Now all I had to do was figure out how to get to my happy the way she told me to do.

Chapter 8

My eyes fluttered open and after a moment, I stretched, welcoming the new morning. I rolled over, facing the window. I hadn't closed the curtains last night. My room faced the ocean; no one could see inside. So I'd been awakened by the warmth of the tropical sun and the brightness of the cloudless sky.

There was nothing but contentment in my sigh. For the first time in a long time, I'd had a peaceful night's sleep. That wasn't something that came easy to me.

Over the years, memories of the night my mother died had eased, but I still had so many restless nights. My mind was always in overdrive on something I needed to do for the kids, Charles, or work. I don't know if I kept so busy just because that was the life that I'd become accustomed to, or if I was trying to block out the memories.

"Stop suppressing the memories, Aja. Embrace them and you will heal."

That was what the therapist I'd seen right after Anika was born had told me. It was that advice that had helped me forgive my father. Well, that and Jada had begged me, telling me that our father hadn't been in his right mind that night. At one point, when we were dating, Charles had even convinced me to go visit him in jail. Of course, that visit didn't go too well. But Jada had been right that once sober, my father had been devastated at what he'd done. Although he spent years in prison, my father tried to make amends with me and Jada. It wasn't until just before his death that I uttered the words I never thought I would say to him, "I forgive you."

That forgiveness had been so freeing for me. I had to thank my sister, but I also owed Charles for that. My husband had encouraged me in what Jada had been begging me to do. Charles was the one who'd taught me the true meaning of forgiveness and had helped me let go of the pain. Now I could only hope my husband would forgive me for what my heart was telling me to do. I hadn't verbalized it, not even to myself yet. But it was my baby sister's wisdom that had me thinking—how was I going to get to my happy?

Pushing myself from the bed, I stretched once again before I stood in front of the window. No matter what I ultimately decided to do, I needed this time and this new day.

As I showered, then dressed, I couldn't believe how content I was this morning. Even as I left the room and wandered down to the hotel's beachside restaurant, even as conflicted as I was, I felt more at peace than I had in a very long time.

"How many?" the hostess asked me.

I paused for a moment, wondering if I'd ever spoken the words I was about to say. "Just one." And then, as if I needed to say it for myself, I added, "I'm eating alone."

The hostess raised her eyebrow, but that was the extent of her judgment. Her lips curved back into her smile as she led me to a table that was probably meant to be an intimate setting for two, but I was grateful for one of the only tables that were right along the open side of the restaurant.

As I sat, I was greeted by the breeze and wondered if it was too early to have one of those fruity drinks with the little umbrellas.

"Are you going to have the buffet?" the hostess asked.

"Hmm . . . I think so."

She nodded. "Your waiter will be right with you for your drink order, but you can go ahead and help yourself with the buffet."

Within minutes, I had a feast in front of me: two waffles, a cheese and spinach omelet, a platter of fruit . . . and a mimosa. As I ate, I bobbed my head to the salsa beat from the music that piped through the speakers. And I smiled. This was a different type of experience, eating alone. Was this a step toward my happy?

I shimmied my shoulders just a bit, giggled, and then sat up straight when I heard:

"Well, if it isn't my dance partner."

Turning to my right, I glanced up to see the Marc Anthony look-alike from the other night.

"Hi," I said. My surprise turned my lips up into a smile.

"You're even more beautiful in the daylight," he said. "Mind if I sit?" He pointed to the empty chair across from me.

No! This is my solitude! My first time ever eating alone in a restaurant! But my protests remained in my mind because I didn't want to be rude. So I said, "Sure, go ahead and have a seat." Roxie said that was part of my problem. I was always worried about others—even to my own detriment.

He sat and then as he scooted his chair closer to the table, he extended his hand toward me. "I'm Don Juan."

Don Juan? Really? I wasn't sure if it was his name or the mimosa that made me giggle. "Come on; is that what your mother named you?"

He grinned as if he'd heard that question before. *"Sí, señorita."* He leaned in closer to me and lowered his voice. "It was also her favorite liquor."

I laughed. "Don Juan, I'm Aja."

"Ahh, like the continent?"

"Yes, but spelled with a 'j.'"

His dark eyes zoned in on mine as the tip of his tongue grazed his bottom lip. "Aja. Beautiful name for a beautiful woman. Anyone ever told you that you look like a young Whitney Houston?"

That was a first. I'd heard Diana Ross before, but never Whitney.

"No, I haven't heard that one," I said. "But it's been a while since anyone said I looked like a young anything."

"Ah, we're only as young as we feel." Now he shimmied in his seat. "And the way you moved on that dance floor the other night . . ." He laughed. "Where are your friends? Sleeping in?"

This time, it was the mimosa that made my lips move before my mind could stop me. "Oh, they returned home." By the time my mind caught up with my mouth, it was too late and I regretted my words. The last thing I needed to do was let some stranger named Don Juan know that I was alone in the Dominican Republic.

"Ah," his eyes got wide, "so you decided to stay?"

"Yes, I . . . I have . . . a . . . friend. Yes, a friend. I have a friend here," I lied. "So I'll spend some extra time here . . . with my friend."

"Male or female?"

"What?" I frowned.

"Is this friend a male or female?"

"My," I began, determined not to fall into his trap again. This time, I was going to think about what I was going to say. "Don't you have a lot of questions?"

He gave me a one-shoulder shrug. "You don't get answers if you don't ask questions."

I nodded, impressed with his candor. I thought for a moment, wondering which way I wanted this to go. "It's a female friend," I finally told him.

He flashed a grin that made me wonder if maybe I should have told him the opposite. "Would you like a male friend?"

My stomach fluttered, and that made me want to slap myself. Not because I ever thought I was going to do anything, even if Don Juan oozed all kinds of sexiness. But in the middle of my time of solitude, in the middle of me needing to focus on how I could get my happy back, the last thing I needed was some hot and spicy man messing up what I needed to do. "I'm sure you make an amazing friend, but I am very much married."

"And very much alone," he added without hesitation as if he'd said these same words dozens of times before.

Don Juan. I said, "But I'm still married."

Again, he shrugged with just one shoulder. "What happens in the DR stays in the DR."

"I'm flattered, Don Juan, but no." I shook my head.

He feigned a pout. Then he grabbed a napkin, removed a pen from his pocket, and said, "Okay, but here's my number," he scribbled digits onto the paper, "just in case you change your mind. Or maybe we can go dancing later." He held up his hands. "No strings attached."

He held the napkin out for me, and it dangled in the air. It felt like we were in some kind of face-off; who would blink first.

I took the napkin from his hand. He smiled before he stood, then turned and walked away. I waited until he was out of my sight before I tucked the napkin into my purse.

<hr />

I opened the door to my room just in time to hear my cell phone ringing. I didn't even realize I'd left it in the hotel room. That, in and of itself, was huge. The DR had to have been working its magic if I'd just spent the last two hours not even missing it.

I grabbed the phone and looked down to see my daughter's smiling face on my screen.

"Hello," I said.

"Mom," she exclaimed without bothering to say hello. "I've been calling you! I was starting to get worried. What's going on?"

"Hello, sweetheart. How are you?" I set my room key on the table and removed my shawl, throwing it across the bed.

"Horrible. Dad said you weren't coming home. That you're extending your vacation," she whined.

The peace that had just begun to seep into my soul was being pulled away from me just by Anika's tone. She knew that I couldn't stand to hear a nineteen-year-old whine. But all my chastising never did any good.

"Yes. I'm taking some extra time," I said, keeping my voice as even as I could, her hint to do the same.

"But why?" she said, sounding as if she were two years old.

"Because I need it," I replied, sitting on the edge of the bed.

"Dad's upset. He wants you to come home," Anika said.

I knew this conversation was necessary, but I simply wasn't ready to have it with my child.

"I'm not trying to upset your father, or you, for that matter. This is something I need to do."

"Oh my God," she said as if she'd just seen a building on fire. "I've heard stories about this. Women travel off to some island and meet a young pool boy. Am I going to have a twenty-four-year-old pool boy as a stepfather?"

That was a joke, right? Except that this was Anika, so I knew that it wasn't. This girl should've majored in theater instead of international politics because she was a drama queen. I rubbed my temples at those ridiculous words from my dramatic child. I was two thousand miles away from home, but I could picture her wide-eyed, her curly auburn natural curls bouncing as she paced her bedroom near hysteria.

"Mom," Anika shouted. "Oh, God. Are you there?"

"I'm here. First, you don't have to yell, and no, I have not met a young pool boy, so please calm down. How are things going, anyway?" I asked, trying to change the subject.

"Horrible," she cried. "I miss you."

Oh! My daughter missed me. Maybe . . .

"I need you, Mommy."

Oh! My daughter needed me. Maybe I should . . .

"You have to come home to get all my stuff ready for me to go back to school. There is so much that I need because you know they moved my room to a single so I want to completely redecorate. And you know at Spelman, I have to be on point with everything and . . ."

Her words were like a reality bolt of lightning, deafening me for a moment. This was exactly why I had stayed here. "Sweetie," I broke into the conversation she was having that I wasn't listening to, "I made sure you had everything you needed prior to my leaving, but I promise to be back in more than enough time to take you back to school. Your dad bought the plane ticket weeks ago."

"But what if I need something before then?" she cried.

"Then . . . you'll walk down the hall to our bedroom," I began, slowing my cadence, "tap on the door, and tell your father what you need. He is quite capable of handling anything. Or . . . your grandmother is there and you can go to her. She would love to help you. Or . . . you'll get in that Jeep Wrangler we bought and you'll drive to the store and get whatever you need yourself."

She sighed like none of my suggestions would ever work and I was the one being difficult. "Mom, you know I don't want to be bothered with all of that stuff. That's your thing, not mine."

I pulled the phone away from my ear to stare at it for a second. Then I told her, "It's my thing only because it's the only way anything will get done. But you know what I discovered? I have an intelligent family who are more than capable of taking care of everything themselves. And you're part of that family who needs to start doing these things for yourself."

"Mom, what in the world am I supposed to do?"

"You created those monsters."

"I already told you, and so I'm going to end this call now," I said, wanting to return to that space of peace.

"But, Mom—"

"I'll be home in a few days, sweetheart."

"But Mom—"

"Goodbye, Anika. I love you." I tapped the screen, ending the call.

"You created those monsters."

Roxie's words played in my head again. She always said that, always told me that I was creating monsters instead of eagles who wanted to soar. She'd told me that by doing everything for them, I was stifling their growth. That I wasn't preparing them to fly; I was just clipping their wings.

As I thought about Anika's call, all I could say was that she was this way because of me. She whined because of me, she didn't shop for herself because of me, she didn't even go to her father because of me. Both she and Eric hadn't even been pressed about getting their driver's licenses because I took them everywhere they wanted to go. My family was more than capable, but I'd crippled them.

I bounced up from the bed. I wasn't going to just sit in this bedroom and think about all the things I was trying to get away from. But even as I changed into my swimsuit and went down to the beach, thoughts of my family stayed with me. Even as I found an umbrella on the beach and laid my beach towel beneath it, I couldn't stop thinking about how all that disturbed me had been caused by me. I'd built this house over the twenty years that I'd been married.

"I didn't come out here to think about this," I whispered to myself as I leaned back on the towel. But even as I pulled out the novel I was reading, my thoughts returned to home and what my life had been like for all of these years.

"Mom," Anika's voice came into the kitchen before she did. "Did you wash my volleyball uniform?" Anika asked, pressing against the island where I stood.

But before I could even answer her, my son dashed in and jumped in front of Anika as if she wasn't there. "Mom, I don't feel like going to school today." He grabbed his neck and released a pitiful cough. *"My throat hurts. I think I have Ebola."*

My son was only ten, yet in his mind, Eric had had every disease known to man.

"You didn't have Ebola last night when you were up playing Nintendo."

"But really, Mom," he coughed again, "I'm dying. My throat. Are you gonna let me just die?" He staggered backward as if he were about to fall out.

I reached into the basket in the center of the kitchen island. "Here." I tossed a tin of Sucrets to him. "Take one of those and go finish getting dressed."

Eric sucked his teeth but turned and left me alone with his sister.

As I reached for the loaf of bread, Anika said, "He's so rude. But, Mom, what about my uniform? I can't find it. Please don't tell me that you forgot to wash it again."

My hand was inside the bread loaf and it froze right there. I gave my eight-year-old a hard stare, but she didn't back down. "When have I ever not washed your uniform?"

"Remember that time?"

I held up my hand. "Anika, I'm not going to do this with you. Your uniform is in your bedroom."

"But I can't find it," she whined. "I need you to help me look for it."

I tossed the bread onto the plate in front of me. "Really, Anika? You want me to stop making your lunch and help you do something that you can do alone?"

"But, Mom . . ."

I inhaled, but before I could say another word, Charles strolled into the kitchen. "Babe, this tie or this one?" he said, holding up a red and a navy tie.

"The red one," I said, as I slapped turkey onto two slices of bread. "Red is a power color."

"*I knew that.*" *He paused.* "*But wait, you don't like this one?*"

I didn't miss a beat as I spread mayonnaise on the other two slices. "*I love it, but haven't you noticed that whenever you ask me, I'm always going with the power color?*"

"*Mom, my uniform.*"

"*Okay, Anika,*" *I said as I dumped her sandwich and Eric's into baggies.* "*I'll help you find your uniform.*"

"*Thanks,*" *she said, as she ran out of the kitchen.*

"*Thanks, babe,*" *Charles said before he kissed my cheek and walked out behind our daughter.*

I sighed. A moment of peace, until . . .

"*Mom!*" *Anika screeched.* "*Bailey peed on the floor.*"

I sighed as I reached into the pantry for two bags of chips. "*Then clean it up, Anika. Bailey is your dog.*"

"*Ewww, you want me to go to school smelling like dog pee? Yeah, no.*"

Instead of arguing, I packed their lunches, then even though I was already wearing my dress for work, I snatched a paper towel, crouched down and wiped up the dog pee, then grabbed the Swiffer WetJet and ran it over the floor.

"*Mom!*"

I dashed upstairs and in three seconds flat showed Anika where I'd hung her volleyball uniform in the front of her closet.

"*Oh wow, I didn't even see it. Thanks, Mom.*" *Anika hugged me.* "*You're super.*" *She giggled.* "*Get it . . . Supermom.*"

As I rushed into my bedroom to get my shoes, my cell phone rang and my supervisor's name popped up. I contemplated ignoring it, decided against it, and pressed Talk.

"*Hey, Karen,*" *I said as I slipped into my pumps.*

"*Good morning, Aja.*" *She sounded her usual stressful self. I used to think it was her being extra, but after twelve years on the job as a social worker, I got it; I was stressed most days,* too. "I need you to go by the Martins' house. There was an incident last night with their foster child."

I sighed as I motioned for the kids to come on. "I hate going over there," I said as I grabbed my purse, kissed Charles's cheek, then rushed into the hallway. "I thought when I got promoted, I wouldn't have to make home visits anymore," I said, trotting down the stairs. At least one of my children was downstairs, though the way Anika was slouched on the sofa, playing some game on her phone, it didn't look like she had any plans for school. I pointed toward the garage and mouthed, "Let's go," before I turned my attention back to Karen.

"I know, but you know, budget cuts," Karen said. "You know we're down and there's nothing we can do."

"Mom, I don't want to wait in the car. It's gonna be a long time 'cause Eric went back to sleep." Anika pouted as she stomped toward the door.

"I have to go, Karen. I'll handle it right after I drop my kids off."

"I really need you to get over there," she said. "Your husband can't drop them off for you?"

Inside, I laughed and I wanted to fill Karen in on the joke so that she would laugh with me. Yeah, my husband was a great father, except when it came time to run our kids around. He'd insisted on private school, yet I was the one who had to take them and pick them up—even though we both worked full-time. But that was another thing Roxie said was my fault and that I should make Charles carry the burden of child-rearing, too.

But I just felt like it was my job, so I told Karen, "I got it. It won't take much time at all. I'll drop the kids and will be at the Martins' in less than an hour."

"Thanks. Girl, I don't know how you balance it all, but I give you major props."

I opened my eyes and peered into the sky that was bright with the sun that was rising to its high noon point. Reaching for my bottle of water, I took a long sip, but that didn't clear my mind. All I could do was think about how many of my days were like the one I'd just remembered. Roxie used to call it the Clayton Chaos, and she warned me that it would get old at some point.

"You're going to break sooner or later."

I'd always laughed her comments off. But it seemed that she'd been right. It seemed my sooner and later had finally arrived. Even though the chaos wasn't of the same magnitude, I was broken.

It seemed crazy that I'd waited until the kids were out of the house to finally reach this point. But though they were grown and gone—yet still demanding—it seemed like Charles had picked up that slack. He seemed even more helpless:

"Honey, where's my other shoe?"

"Baby, did you drop my suits off at the cleaners?"

"Sweetheart, can you call the dealership and find out when I can take the car in for servicing?"

All of that on top of working at one of the most demanding and depressing jobs in the world, a social worker for the Harris County Department of Human Services and Child Protective Services. I knew they were probably losing their minds at my absence, but that had been the first thing I decided I couldn't worry about.

Though my family knew how stressful my job was, when it came to taking care of home, no one seemed to care. It was as if everyone just expected me to effortlessly balance it all. I used to find balance in the solitude of painting. Like my time with my mother. That had been my "me" time. But I guess when you have a family, "me" becomes "us."

Painting and sketching had been a love of mine since I was ten years old, but it was a discarded dream, a gift that I hadn't used— because I needed a stable job to take care of my siblings since our father had gone to prison. Then I'd gotten married and had kids, and everything that they wanted, all of their hobbies, had become more important than mine.

"Aja, sweetheart, Anika is crying for you."

I had just sketched the outline of a little girl being pushed on the swings at the park and was looking forward to filling in the picture with the most vibrant colors of paint when I heard the door creak open and the wails of my four-year-old daughter. I inhaled and turned to my husband, who had just walked into my converted art studio. Anika was on his hip. He set her down, and she came scurrying over to me.

"Mommy, I wanna go to the park!" she cried, as she jumped into my lap and knocked over the easel and the tray of paints. I cringed as an assortment of paints scattered across the picture I'd spent the last three weeks outlining.

"Anika, sweetie, be careful. Look what you did to Mommy's stuff," Charles said.

I took a deep breath as I helped her get settled in my lap. "Charles, I thought we agreed that you would keep the kids out of my art studio," I said.

One of the things I'd loved most about this house when we first bought it was the mother-in-law suite. Not because I had any intention of my mother-in-law coming to live with us, but I saw it as the perfect place to set up a studio so I could get back into painting. The oversized window provided the perfect natural lighting. I'd decorated the room with plants and modern decor. Inspirational messages were framed and hung on the walls. My eucalyptus scented candles added the perfect touch to finally get the room to be my place of solitude.

Only every time I came in, my family wasn't far behind. I'd had this conversation with Charles on multiple occasions, but it never seemed to make a difference.

"I told Anika she couldn't come in here but she kept crying

and whining. I tried to explain to her that it's raining and we can't go to the park." He knelt down and started picking up the items Anika had knocked to the floor. "The problem is these kids need some place to play," he added.

"Why can't they play in the den?" I asked.

"Because I'm trying to watch football." I wanted to tell Charles to watch the game on the TV in our room since he'd insisted on that fifty-two-inch in our bedroom, but we'd had that discussion once before and he was adamant that watching sports on the eighty-inch in the den was a completely different experience than the TV in our room.

"Anika, come sit over here and draw," Charles said, pulling our daughter off my lap and arranging a blank piece of paper and some paints on the floor next to me. "You can sit here and paint with Mommy."

Before she could get settled, Eric came in with his basketball and Anika jumped up and said, "Basketball, brother. Throw me the ball!"

"Do not dare throw that ball in the house," Charles said, and massaged his temples before turning to me. "See, this is just ridiculous. There's just nowhere for them to play when it's raining." He looked around my studio. "You know this would be the perfect playroom, with all this open space and natural lighting."

"Playroom? Yes!" both of my kids squealed in delight.

"Mommy, can we make this a playroom? Please, pretty please?" Eric said. "I can put my video games over there." He pointed to the back wall.

"And I can put my dollhouse right there," Anika said, excitement all over her face. "I'm gonna go get my dolls."

I looked at my family, preparing to protest, when Charles shrugged and smiled. "I guess it's a done deal. The things we do for our kids." Then he had the nerve to lean down and kiss me. "Going back to finish watching the game."

That next day, after dismissing my complaints, Charles had begun the process of converting my art studio into a playroom and as I watched my children's eyes light up, I decided that my art could wait if it meant giving them immediate joy.

As they got older and stopped playing, I thought maybe I could change the room back. But my mother-in-law had moved in, and all hopes of a studio moved out.

In recent years, I'd been able to do a bit more sketching and painting, even giving a few away as gifts. But it was nothing of the magnitude of what I would've loved to do.

Just thinking back over the last two decades of my life had me exhausted. That day when my studio became a playroom was the day my dream had been officially squashed. That's when Aja ceased to exist and mom and wife became my existence.

With each passing day, my family leaned on me more. Somehow along the way, all three of them became people who ran me ragged simply because they could. And to hear Roxie tell it, because I let them.

Chapter 9

"Doing me" had taken on a whole other meaning these last few days. I'd spent time doing the things that I enjoyed. Not what anyone else wanted to do. Just me. I'd had daily massages—stone one day, hot wax the next. I'd watched the sunrise from my balcony, taken part in yoga, and yesterday, I'd taken a salsa class.

I had never spent so much time alone in my life. I had never had a week where it was all about me, and it felt refreshing to finally have that.

As I reconnected with my passion on this beach, I knew this was what I wanted to do. What I *needed* to be doing.

Today, I was sitting at the poolside bar, painting a portrait of a young man dribbling a basketball in the sky. My therapist had told me that I never properly grieved my brother's death and, therefore, had been unable to completely heal. I'd been thinking more and more about Eric and I thought maybe painting a portrait of him would be therapeutic. But sitting here, at the oceanside bar, putting the finishing touches on a painting I'd started just two days ago, sent my mind spiraling back to the abyss.

"Aja."

I yawned, turned over, and looked at the alarm clock, wondering who was on my phone at six in the morning.

"Aja."

It sounded like a man crying.

"Eric, is that you? What's going on?" I sat up when I heard a baby screaming in the background. "Eric? Eric? Talk to me. What is going on? Is that Madison screaming?" That could only be my niece, but why was she wailing? Where was Elise, Eric's girlfriend? No way would she let the baby wail like that.

"Aja . . . Aja . . . Aja."

My heart started racing. "I'm here, Peanut, talk to me," I said, calling my brother by his nickname, hoping that would get him to break out of whatever trance would only allow him to say my name over and over.

"Eric!"

A sob, then, "She's dead. I killed her . . . I'm just like him. He's in my blood. I'm him, he's me . . . I couldn't stop him, but I can stop me."

I swung my legs over the edge of my bed and jumped up. "Eric, what are you talking about? Who's dead? Elise? Oh my God! Where are you? Are you at home?" I looked at the Caller ID and saw his home phone number.

My brother battled demons. He had a temper like our father and he hated himself—and our father—because of it. I'd tried my best to protect him from himself, that's why I was half dressed and heading toward the door.

"Just hang on, baby brother, I'm on my way."

"I loved her, Aja. I loved her with all my heart," Eric said. I could barely understand, he was sobbing so hard. "It was an accident. Don't let Madison hate me like we hate him. Please. I love you."

The despair in my brother's voice sent chills through my spine.

"Eric, wait . . . wait."

And then I heard it. I heard it like I was in the same room.
A single shot.
   "Eric, nooooo!"

"If it makes you sad, maybe you should paint something else."

I shook away my thoughts and looked up to the voice that had thankfully pulled me from that tragic path down memory lane.

"Excuse me?" I said.

Don Juan was standing over me in a button-down Hawaiian shirt and khaki shorts. He handed me a napkin. "You're crying. As you paint, you're crying. Paint things to make yourself happy. You're too pretty to be sad."

I took the napkin and dabbed my eyes as I managed a smile. "Sorry, didn't realize I was crying."

"Hold on." He darted over to the bar, while I quickly put up my paints and removed my painting from the easel. I didn't want Don Juan to ask me any questions about what I was painting. That whole situation was painful. Eric's girlfriend Elise hadn't died. She'd survived, but Eric's death had taken its toll on her and she cut herself off from us for a while. Eventually, she had remarried and moved to Australia, so we seldom got to see Madison. Nothing about my brother's story had turned out right.

I kept my eyes on Don Juan at the bar. It looked like he was ordering drinks. A few minutes later, he returned and handed me a margarita. "Here, tequila for breakfast. This will make you feel better. It will wash away your tears."

I managed a smile as I took the drink—only because I'd watched as the bartender made it.

"Thank you," I said, taking a small sip. "Though it's crazy to be drinking margaritas before noon."

"Crazy by whose standards?" he said. "You're on vacation, *chica*. Enjoy!"

Don Juan had a point.

"So do you live here?" I asked, trying to ease the heaviness that often accompanied thoughts of my brother. "Or work here since you're always around?"

He leaned in and whispered, "My sister is the bartender. So I come and have free drinks and fun. I do have a pay-the-bills job, but this is my happy space." He motioned around. "This is where I come to live."

"Yes, you really look like you have a lot of fun." I laughed. I'd never met anyone like Don Juan. Though he flirted, it wasn't overbearing. He really did seem like he was just a guy enjoying life and inviting others to his party.

"Try it. You might like it." He took a sip of his drink. "Did you ever catch up with your friend?" He gave me a knowing smile.

I replied by taking another sip of my drink.

"May I offer a suggestion?" he asked.

Somehow I felt like that question was rhetorical. I knew I was right when he continued with, "Finish the painting, then put it away. Let the last stroke wipe away the sadness."

I don't know what made me say, "It's my brother. He died a while ago."

Don Juan nodded in understanding. "And I'm sure that he would want you to live."

The sounds of salsa music began filling the air as the band began playing. The beat immediately sent Don Juan's hips to swaying. "Ay ay ay," he sang.

He shimmied, twirled, and dipped around my table. "I make it a point to dance every day like no one is watching." He stopped a passing waitress and twirled her. Several patrons around the bar area laughed. "And I put a show on when they are."

His enthusiasm was infectious, as several other people started dancing with him. "If you find nothing else here, find your fun side," he told me as he twirled someone else. "And you come find me if you want to have fun. There's a party here at the resort tonight." He two-stepped away from my table and on to dance with someone else.

As I watched Don Juan party like he didn't have a care in the world, I wondered what it must be like to have that kind of joy. To put your stresses on the shelf and just enjoy life. I didn't know, but watching Don Juan, I knew that I wanted to find out.

Chapter 10

The irony wasn't lost on me. I'd balked at partying with my friends of more than two decades, yet here I was, partying like it was 1999 with a perfect stranger.

"Play that funky music white boy . . ."

I laughed as Don Juan mimicked playing a guitar as he belted the lyrics like he was on stage at an arena.

"What do you know about Wild Cherry?" I asked, referring to the 1970s band that sang the song.

"I feel the vibe, *chica*. Everyone knows that song." He leaned and whispered in my ear. "Anyone ever told you how sexy you are?"

I was a little surprised at the fluttering I felt in my stomach. I'd had my share of compliments over the years, but no one had ever been this close. . . . especially when I felt so free.

Don Juan took my hand and spun me around as the music changed to one of my favorite songs by Sam Smith.

"Look what you made me do," Don Juan sang.

"Is there any song you don't know?" I laughed.

"I know them all." Don Juan was telling the truth when he said he liked to "dance like no one is watching and give them a show when they are." He was straight putting on a show. And I was loving every minute of it. And before I knew it, I was joining in with him. Unlike the first time we danced, I pushed aside all thoughts of anything except the here and now, and it felt so good.

Finally, Don Juan was the one to say, "Okay, I give."

I shimmied and playfully teased him. "What? The party animal is partied out?"

"Yes, time out. I need a time-out." He staggered back over to the table. And instead of following him, I danced with two other men who had danced over to me. Don Juan watched me from the sidelines as I tossed up my arms and danced like no one was watching.

By the time I rejoined Don Juan at our table, he said, "I thought you would go all night."

I was shocked. I couldn't remember the last time that I'd been out this late. "I can't believe I've been out there dancing so long," I said with a satisfied grin. My feet didn't even hurt. I was operating on pure adrenaline.

After a solo dinner at a seaside hotel a couple of blocks away, I'd returned fully ready to go to bed. Then I thought about Don Juan's invitation and ended up here at the resort bar, which had been converted into a nightclub.

Don Juan looked at his watch. "Almost an hour and a half. But I like it." He motioned for the waitress. "Two more mojitos, please."

Instead of protesting, I said, "Can you add an extra shot to mine?"

"To both," Don Juan added with a grin.

The waitress nodded and scurried off. Don Juan kept his eyes on me.

"What?" I finally said, bobbing to the salsa tunes.

"I love a woman who is so free."

That made me smile. "Free is the last word I would ever use to describe myself," I said.

"Sexy and free," he added. "When I first met you, I thought

you were a little on the prudish side, but I could really have some fun with you."

My smile faded just a bit. I hoped that I wasn't sending the wrong message.

"Um, Don Juan, thank you for the compliment, but I should reiterate that I'm very married," I felt the need to say. "So I have no interest in an island fling."

"And you feel the need to tell me that again, because?"

I paused as the waitress set our drinks in front of us. "Because, I mean, well, I don't want to give you any ideas."

He sipped his drink and chuckled. "Can't a man just pay you a compliment without wanting anything? I wasn't trying to get you into bed. You made that clear earlier and I know that you may have heard things about Latin lovers, but we know that no means no." He flashed a grin.

I was embarrassed by my assumptions. "Oh, ah, I'm sorry. I just . . . I . . ."

"It's fine," he said, saving me from fishing for an explanation. "As I told you, I love living, so I recognize all of God's beauty, and that includes beautiful women."

"My apologies." I took another sip of my drink, wishing I could rewind the conversation.

"What do you do, *Mrs.* Aja?"

"I'm a social worker."

"Hmmm, you don't strike me as a social worker. I would've taken you more for the creative type, especially after seeing you paint the other day."

I nodded in appreciation. "That's what I'd like to be doing."

"Then do it." He shrugged like it was no big deal.

"Hmph, that's easier said than done."

"No, Nike was on to something when they said, 'just do it.' Would you do your social work job if no one paid you, if they stopped giving you a paycheck?"

I couldn't get the 'no' out fast enough. Back when I first started, maybe. But today, no way.

"Absolutely not," I said.

Don Juan shrugged. "Then that isn't what you're supposed to be doing."

"Yes, I'm coming to discover that while I'm here on vacation," I replied.

"Yeah, people make jokes about how much time I spend at the resort bars, but I believe you have to find what makes you truly happy, not just happy enough. My heart has to sing, and being here, mixing and mingling with the guests and dancing, gives my heart the music it's been looking for."

I wanted to comment that Don Juan's career equated to nothing more than being a party animal. But there was no disputing the look of happiness on his face, so I guess it worked for him.

"Well, I kind of made my bed, so I've been lying in it," I said.

He shook his head like I was a lost cause. "Put that bed on the curb and make a new one. It can be anything you want it to be. Other people won't understand or won't care to understand why you're making a new bed. They'll wonder what was wrong with your old bed. But they're not the ones who have to sleep in it." Don Juan stood and downed the rest of his drink. "I've enjoyed talking to you, but I have to run. Think about what I said. The woman who's been out on the dance floor all evening, she seems like a wonderful person. Let her out."

He dropped a twenty-dollar bill on the table. "I wish you all the luck." He took my hand and kissed it. "And for the record, if you had said yes to sleeping with me, I would've done it in a heartbeat."

He winked and was gone before I could say a word.

Chapter 11

I was back in the marketplace in search of Jewel. I'd been in the DR by myself for almost a week now, and in that week I'd gotten more clarity than I'd had in a very long time. Still, I needed to be sure that following my gut was indeed the way to go.

I'd come to the marketplace twice, hoping to see Jewel, but each time her booth had been empty. None of the other vendors had any idea where she was or when she would return. It was as if she'd disappeared. If I hadn't known better, I would've thought she was sending me a personal message—that I had to figure all of this out on my own.

Even still, since I was leaving tomorrow, I wanted to try her one more time, though I wasn't convinced this was the perfect day. This was the first day since I'd been in the Dominican Republic when there were far more clouds than sun.

I almost tiptoed around the corner, not wanting to be disappointed, but as soon as I made that turn, I smiled. There was Jewel, finally. She was sitting behind her table, but her head was down so she wouldn't see me approaching. It looked like she was polishing her wares.

I felt my smile widen as I moved toward her. "Hello," I said as I got closer. "Remember me?"

She rose her head slowly, and at first, her stare seemed blank. But after studying me, a smile filled her face.

"You're almost there," she announced.

I stopped moving. Wow! She knew what I'd been thinking? What I'd been doing? She could read me that well? That kinda creeped me out; this woman didn't know me. But I pushed my apprehensions aside. It was clear that she had some kind of prophetic insight. So I stepped even closer to her. "Almost," I said in response to her statement. "Is it okay if I sit and talk with you a bit?"

Her smile dipped a bit as she glanced around the marketplace and hesitantly replied, "Well . . . I'm working, and you would be taking me away from that . . ."

With the overcast sky, there weren't even ten people mulling about the marketplace. It wasn't like she was going to lose out on any sales by talking to me. Even still, I understood that this was her place of business and even one missed customer would be one too much. So, I said, "How about I buy some of your rocks to take back as souvenirs for my family?"

She nodded her approval and winked at me. "I like the way you think."

I pointed out the rocks I wanted—not even sure that I would give them to anyone, then handed her a fifty-dollar bill. "You can keep the change," I said.

She beamed as she took the money. "The generosity of Americans. I love it." She pushed the money down into a pouch around her waist and then pointed to a small stool in her booth. "Sit."

I did as she instructed.

She adjusted her long, Mexican-print skirt, and without looking at me said, "Have you found what you're searching for?"

I shrugged. "I'm not sure. I think I have. But I'm wondering if I need more time here. I'm supposed to be going home tomorrow, but I'm thinking of extending my stay again."

"Really? You don't have to go back home?"

"I do." I sighed. "It was hard because we're in a crisis situation at work, but we're always in a crisis, so I took vacation and personal leave and really could stay another week, though my daughter wouldn't be happy because I'm supposed to be taking her back to school."

Jewel shook her head, her long plaits swinging with emphasis. "No, staying is not the answer. What you need is not here. At least not anymore. You needed time to get a clear head, reconnect with your calling, and now that you have it, you have to face all that you've discovered. You can't run from your problems."

I nodded, no longer surprised at her ability to read me. "It's just, it's my marriage. It's my life."

She tilted her head. "It usually is."

"I have a good husband." I wanted to make that clear for some reason.

"But?"

"But . . ." I inhaled, then released the next words when I exhaled. "I feel crazy saying this, but I'm just not happy."

Now she tilted her head the other way. "Why is that crazy?"

"Because I'm supposed to be happy with a life like mine. My husband has loved me unconditionally and as far as I know, has been faithful to me for over twenty years. He can be a little controlling and dismissive, but the good in him far outweighs the bad. Financially, we're great, and even though my children are demanding, they're really good kids." I threw my hands up. "All of that should make me the happiest woman in the world."

"And yet?" She gestured with her hands for me to continue.

I'd been thinking these thoughts for years, here and there. I'd never connected them to the emptiness that I felt inside. That's what the DR had given me.

I opened my mouth and released words I'd never spoken before. "I feel like I slipped into my husband's world and created the life *he* wanted. Not the life I wanted."

"What life did you want?"

I thought about her question for a moment, then said, "One that was different from the one I had growing up."

"And from what you say, it seems like you got that life."

I nodded. "I did. And for a while, I thought it was enough. I thought I wanted this—the perfect husband, the kids, the dog, the house, cars, all of it. But somewhere along the line, I asked myself wasn't there more to life than being a wife and mother."

Maybe I was comfortable saying this to a woman who didn't know me because I was too ashamed to say it to anyone who did.

With a nod of understanding, she leaned in and took my hands. It startled me a bit. Not just her touching me that way, but the feel of her hands. They were wrinkly and weathered, like she had lived on this earth for dozens of decades.

But once she began to speak, I forgot about the touch of her skin. "Sometimes, the price of entering his world is losing yourself." She shook my hands as if she wanted me to get the next point. "Often we are so intent on being our mate's everything that nothing else matters until, one day, we wake up and realize we no longer know our own purpose."

This was so eerie how she was reading me without knowing anything about me.

"But what if my purpose is to be a good wife and mother?" I said. Even as I uttered the words, I knew they weren't true.

"If it was, you wouldn't be here searching for something more," she replied, releasing my hands. "What is it you feel about your family?"

"I love them," I replied without hesitation.

"No, beyond that," she said. "What do you feel in terms of the role they play in your achievement of your dreams?"

I shifted my weight as I weighed my answer. "I think I'm starting to feel some resentment because I didn't get to follow my dreams."

"And whose choice was that?"

"It was mine, but . . ." I was getting frustrated. "I'm just saying, as I told you, my passion is painting, but every time I try to really get into it, something happens. Everything ends up taking precedence over what I want to do."

"And whose fault is that?" she asked.

Though I was getting worked up, her voice remained calm, in turn, calming me. "I guess it's mine."

Her silence said that she agreed with me. Finally, after a moment, she said, "People, including those who love us, only do what we allow them to do. They only suck up the energy we give."

"So because my life took a detour, I need to just accept the way things are as the way that they're meant to be?"

"A detour is not a derailment," she said.

I sighed.

"It appears that your husband became your purpose. So the reason you got out of bed, the reason you got dressed, the reason you did everything was for your husband. Even your job—if it's anything other than your passion—is for your husband . . . and your children, of course. It seems that your family has become your entire world, and that can be detrimental." She talked like her words were coming from experience. Or wisdom. Or both.

I choked back my next words, took a deep breath, then released it. "My heart is telling me to leave my husband." I paused, not believing that I'd said that. "I sound crazy, don't I? I mean, what kind of sense does that make?"

She released my hands, though she appeared unfazed, completely unsurprised by my declaration. "The hardest part of a journey such as this is recognizing that we are lost," Jewel continued. "We strive for so long to be one with our partner: one mind, one voice, and acting as one. But while oneness can be wonderful, it is not always the best."

"But Charles really is a good man. We have a good marriage."

"And yet you feel the need to run away." She paused to let her words sink in. "Do you want a new life?"

Jewel was reading me like a novel. Over the past week, that question had gone from an inner whisper to a roaring siren.

"All I can tell you for sure is that the life I'm living no longer feels like enough."

She continued, "Your intuition always knows what's right for you. The only reason you're hesitating is that you're not accustomed to listening to your instinctual voice." She leaned in and narrowed her gaze. "Your emotions tell you everything you need to know about what's right and what's wrong for you. So, in essence, *how you feel is everything.* Your emotions are always guiding you along your life's path, but be aware . . . that path might be different from the one you're currently on. I think that's what you're finding out."

I sat there for a moment, letting her words settle inside me, and I felt tears welling in my eyes. "But we've been together more than twenty years," I said, dabbing at a tear that seeped from my eye. "How do I just throw that away?"

"Just because you have traveled a path doesn't mean that you are meant to be on that path forever. That path is only useful to you as long as it retains its ability to support your growth. You can only hold on to something that you've outlived for so long before the universe will take it away from you."

"What does that mean?" I asked.

She paused and flashed a smile at a customer who had stopped at her booth. "Good afternoon, those make great gifts for your loved ones."

The woman flashed an uninterested smile and said, "Just looking."

I expected Jewel to break out into her sales pitch, but she simply nodded and turned her attention back to me, even before the woman walked off. She lowered her voice and said, "I can always tell the ones who are a waste of time." She clasped her hands together and leaned back in. "As I was saying, you can voluntarily

stay in a relationship that leaves you feeling unhappy and unsatis-
fied, but don't expect the universe to comply with that destruc-
tive pattern," she said matter-of-factly. "If it's not in your best
interest to continue coupling with your partner, then the universe
will arrange convenient circumstances in which to help you separate."

I weighed her words and wondered how much I believed what
she was saying. Her new age mentality didn't mesh well with my
solid Christian upbringing. But while she spoke of the universe, I
looked at that as God. I didn't want God to make something happen so that I'd be pushed into my true purpose. I wanted to begin
my new chapter on my own terms.

"I feel that it's time—I feel that I'm being set free to find my
purpose. But honestly, I'm terrified to walk forward alone," I
said.

She nodded. "Stay if it feels like growth; leave if it feels stuck,
or worse—if it feels like you're going backward. The only thing
that's important for you is to allow yourself to continually grow
and evolve as a human being. If you can do that within your current relationship, then you are in the right place. If not, it might
be time to find your place."

"So you agree that I should leave?" Why was I asking this
stranger her opinion on my marriage? It was bad enough that she
didn't know me, but she'd never met Charles.

But again, I felt like she had some abilities. It was as if she were
an angel sent to help me find my peace.

"That is a decision only you can make," she replied. "But it's
always better to be alone than to be in a relationship that has outlived its purpose. When you're alone, you can live your life on
your terms. It will definitely be scary at first, especially if you've
never been alone."

I nodded, thinking back over the number of times I'd been
alone in this last week. I'd done more alone this week than I had

my whole life. Jewel was right. It had been scary and exhilarating at the same time.

But the thing about having breakfast or lunch or even a drink alone down here was that I had a husband waiting for me. My solitude wasn't permanent. But with what I'd been thinking . . .

There were knots in my stomach and now, even more questions in my head. Was my relationship with Charles really a wrong relationship? "Am I being selfish for wanting, or even thinking about wanting, to end this marriage?" I asked.

"You are not selfish for ending a marriage. You are selfish for holding on to it for the *wrong* reasons. This is what you must understand . . . a relationship isn't good because it lasts a lifetime. A relationship is good if it gives you the wisdom of a lifetime."

Those words were beautiful, but that wasn't why tears sprang to my eyes. It was because with those words, I knew. It was time to go home and rewrite the ending to my story.

Chapter 12

It was hard to say goodbye to the DR. But Jewel was right; I couldn't hide out forever. Not only was it childish not to face my challenges, but staying in the Dominican any longer than I already had wasn't fair to Charles.

Charles. The thought of my husband made me grip the arms of my first class seat—which he had paid for. He'd made sure that I had luxury in the sky both ways. But I didn't enjoy it as much on the way home for all the obvious reasons. For the entire time, I felt sick, refusing the first class meal, the first class drinks. All I did was look out at the clouds, and tried to sketch a few, as I imagined that I was flying through heaven.

Once the wheels touched down on the tarmac, I knew I was far from any kind of utopia. My stomach did more than rumble, it tumbled over and over. But I knew this was nerves—all because I knew what I had to do. I knew what I *needed* to do.

"Welcome to Houston, where the local time is 6:35 p.m."

As the plane rolled toward the gate, I wondered what Charles was doing. Was he at work? Had he stayed late there or was he already home, wondering when I was coming home? I hadn't told my husband the exact time I was landing because I knew if I had, he'd be at the airport waiting with dozens of roses and as many kisses. I wouldn't have been able to handle that—not when I knew what was to come.

I closed the sketch pad I'd been doodling on the entire ride. Just as I did that, the man to the right of me leaned over the console between us. "I don't mean to be nosy, but that's a beautiful sketch. If I hadn't seen you start with a blank slate, I'd swear that you'd purchased it from somewhere."

I chuckled. "Thanks, but it's just a hobby." I silently rebuked myself. I'd started referring to my painting as a hobby just like my family.

The man stood and raised the overhead bin to get his bag. "Sometimes God gives us our gifts and we sit on them." He winked. "And that's a shame. You're very talented. When your desire becomes greater than your resistance, I look forward to seeing you among the greats. You have a nice day."

I stood and trailed behind him through the jet. Even once I'd claimed my bag and then slipped into an Uber, I thought about his words: *"When your desire becomes greater than your resistance . . ."* I still heard him as if he was sitting right next to me.

Why am I thinking about this so much?

That thought consumed me for the twenty-minute ride home; it filled my thoughts so much that I'd forgotten how sick I'd been feeling. That feeling didn't rush back to me until the Uber rolled to a stop in front of my home.

"Thank you." My voice was soft as I thanked the driver when he handed me my roller bag from the trunk.

"Have a good day."

I stood on the curb until the Uber driver sped away. Then, after a deep breath, I made my way up the walkway to the front door, feeling like I was walking the longest mile. I turned the key in the lock, stepped inside, and when I was all the way in the foyer, I turned to my right. Charles, Anika, and Judy were all sitting there—at the dining room table.

"Mom!" Anika jumped from the table and hugged me the way she used to do when she was a little girl. "Oh my God. You're finally home. I'm so happy to see you."

"Finally," Charles said. He stood to take my suitcase from my hand. "We missed you." He kissed my lips, and when he hugged me, I felt relief permeate through his body, almost like he was scared that I wasn't going to come back home.

They were acting like I'd been gone for months when in reality it hadn't even been two weeks.

"I'm so glad you're home."

Before I could respond to my husband, my mother-in-law asked, "Is this still even your home?" She was sitting at the end of the table, not even trying to hide her disdain.

"Mother, don't start," Charles warned.

"Grandma's pissed," Anika said in a whisper as she leaned in.

With the anxiety that I'd been feeling, I didn't have the energy to deal with my mother-in-law. The only great thing about my timing was that Judy was leaving on her own trip tomorrow. Funny, right? She was going on a cruise, and I hoped that she'd extend her time away from home.

"Why didn't you let me know you were coming in?" Charles said, trying to break the tension in the room. "We would've picked you up."

Judy scoffed and banged her fork on her plate as she continued eating, but Charles, Anika, and I ignored her.

"I just caught an Uber so I wouldn't bother anyone. It was no big deal."

Judy dropped her fork again, then pushed herself up from where she sat. She glared at me when she said, "So, you don't feel you owe this family an explanation?"

"No disrespect, Judy, but I talked with my husband." I bit my bottom lip, stopping myself from saying anything more that would definitely have been disrespectful.

"So you think he's the only one you owe an explanation?"

I folded my arms and raised my eyebrows. That was supposed to be enough to get her to sit back down and be quiet. But it didn't work.

She shot back, "And I've been here with my son. Trying to help him make sense of your nonsense. It's pure foolishness when a wife abandons her family."

"I didn't abandon anyone," I said, filling my voice and my temperature rising.

"You know what?" Charles said, kissing me again. "You're here now. And that's all that matters."

Anika hugged me again. "And I am so glad. What's this?" she said, taking my portfolio and unzipping it. "You took your art stuff on vacation? Really, Mom?" She pulled out the canvas. "And you actually painted?"

"Good," Charles said. "You got to do some relaxing stuff."

Anika looked at the picture and frowned. "Is he playing basketball . . . on the beach? That's crazy."

Judy tsked as she sipped her iced tea. "So, you couldn't come home because you were off dabbling on a canvas like some hippie with no care in the world, huh?" she said.

Charles took the painting from Anika. "I think it's nice, babe."

I almost smiled, until he set it down on the floor and leaned it against the wall, then turned back to me.

"We're just glad you're home," he said.

"For real," Anika said. "We have less than two weeks before I head back to school. I need you to get my new bedspread and all the other stuff."

I wanted to be upset at the scenario that had just played out, but I was used to it by now.

"Anika," I started as I removed my jacket, "I just got home. Haven't you done some of the shopping?" Anika had lucked out and gotten a resident assistant position, so she was moving into her own room at Spelman.

"No," my daughter said, sounding appalled. "Why would I do

that? I was just waiting for you to do it," she said as if I should have known that.

"Sweetheart . . ."

"I know, I know, Mom. I know what you're going to say. I'm an adult and it's time for me to do things like this on my own. But what sense does that make when you're so good at that stuff." She kissed my cheek, then almost skipped back to the dining room table as if she really was glad to see me and her words were the end of the discussion.

"Are you hungry?" Charles said, motioning toward the spread on the table. "Mom made smothered pork chops."

"Somebody had to," Judy mumbled, as she resumed eating.

"No, you guys finish dinner. I'm going to go upstairs and shower."

I ignored Judy's piercing glare as I passed by her and moved toward the staircase.

Inside the bedroom, I said a silent prayer of gratitude. I was so thankful that Charles hadn't followed me, giving me more time to work this all out in my head. But really, I didn't think there was enough time on earth for me to prepare for what I had to do.

I stripped, tossing everything onto the bed, then stepped into our double-headed shower. The warm spray of the water soothed me, brought me back just a little to that place of peace that I felt so many of the days while I was away. But it wasn't enough to soothe my stomach.

As I stepped out of the shower, Charles poked his head inside the bathroom, and I almost felt the need to hide. But I didn't and he smiled as he watched me dry off, then begin massaging my body with the stress relief aromatherapy lotion that had become a staple in my beauty routine over the years.

With just a few steps, Charles was by my side. He took the lotion bottle from me, dabbed a bit onto his hand, and began to massage it into my back.

"I really am happy to have you home." His voice was thick as he kneaded that long stretch of skin along my spine.

I said nothing as he continued his massage. His touch was so gentle, so loving. Our first kiss flashed through my mind. The first time he made love to me. The last time he made love to me. I closed my eyes. That was my weapon to fight the tears that were rising. Oh, how I loved this man. I really did.

When Charles finished, he kissed the back of my neck, what had always been my sweet spot. Only this time, his kiss didn't arouse me. It just made me sad.

Charles rounded his way until he stood in front of me, then he sat on the edge of the tub. Looking up, he said, "You ready to talk to me? Tell me what's going on?"

I blinked, to hold back my tears, my emotions, my words.

"Is this some kind of I'm-feeling-some-kind-of-way-because-I-just-turned-forty-five?"

"Kind of." Turning away from him, I moved to my walk-in closet and reached for a maxi dress. I slid it over my head before I returned to the bathroom.

Charles was still perched on the edge of the tub.

Standing in front of him, I said, "It's not forty-five per se, because I feel great. I'm happy about getting older because there is an alternative."

"Then what is it, babe?" I didn't say anything and Charles took my hand. "Talk to me," he said when I didn't continue. He peered into my eyes as if he really wanted to know, as if he really cared.

I released a long sigh. Part of me wanted to just do what I normally did—just tell my husband that nothing was wrong and forget about all that I'd discovered in the last two weeks. If I said nothing, we could just go on about our lives. But I'd stayed an extra day in DR just to get up the strength that was needed not to back down or back out. I'd made that promise to myself. I owed this to myself and I was going to do it.

Finally, I said, "Charles, I feel stagnant. Like I'm missing out on the life that I'm supposed to be living. Professionally." I paused. "Personally."

Right away, he released a long breath that made it sound like he was relieved. "Oh my God. Is that all?" He laughed. "Oh my God. Whew. Do you know what I was thinking?"

I shook my head. That wasn't the response I was expecting, but it's one that shouldn't have surprised me.

"I thought you were going to tell me that you'd fallen in love with somebody else or something." He released a relieved chuckle.

"Fallen in love?" I asked. "Don't be ridiculous. No, I'm just not fulfilled at work . . . in life . . . in general, and it's taking its toll on me."

"Half of America is working in jobs they don't like. Whew." He blew out another breath before he stood, leaned in, and kissed me. "I'm so glad that's all it is. As for the life part, you probably just needed that little vacation to rejuvenate yourself. Now I'm really glad you took the time to get that jolt you needed." Charles hugged me. "Oh, and before I forget, Eric has a basketball game next weekend. I told him I can't go because I have plans, the play-by-play for the James Harden all-star charity game. But I told him you'd be there and you'd take Anika, if she doesn't have any other plans. Mom won't be able to go, remember she'll be on the cruise. But at least he'll have you and maybe Anika in the stands cheering for him. He needs that."

I sat in awe as my husband planned out my schedule as if he hadn't heard anything I'd said. Or maybe it was worse. Maybe he had heard and it didn't matter to him. His schedule was still more important than mine. Hell, what he was saying was that even Eric's basketball game was more important than anything I had to do.

"Did you hear anything that I said?" I asked.

He kissed my forehead. "Yeah, baby. You're unfulfilled," he said in a tone that sounded like he was just telling me the temperature. "But that happens sometimes. You'll get over it." And then he had the nerve to blow out another "whew" as he walked toward the bathroom door. He paused long enough to say, "I'm so glad this is all that's wrong."

I turned and followed him because I just couldn't believe what he was saying. Inside our bedroom, he plopped down on the bed. "You've been gone almost two weeks and I missed you something fierce." He patted the bed next to him. "Come show your husband just how much you missed him."

I blinked, but I didn't think that it would be enough to hold back my tears this time. Turned out that it was enough.

"Come on, babe," Charles said again. "I missed you. I missed my wife."

I stared at him for a couple of long moments and then, even though I'd discovered myself while I was in the Dominican Republic, within one hour of being home, I lost myself once again. And so I did what any dutiful wife was supposed to do. I walked over to the bed and made love to my husband.

Chapter 13

I was back on the grind, on my way to work and feeling worse than before I'd left for my birthday celebration. It was because I had no courage. All the powerful advice I'd gotten from strangers this past week—Jewel, Don Juan, even the man on the plane—and nothing. It had been two days since I'd returned and I'd yet to get up the nerve to tell Charles I wanted out.

I was so mad at myself for breaking my promise. And not only that, I'd slept with Charles, and that had been a big mistake. I had never felt so empty after making love, and afterward, as a single tear had trickled down my cheek, Charles kissed it and said, "I missed you, too, baby."

Still, I had remained silent, because I had no courage to hurt the man who loved me so much.

"You are not obligated to stay in a relationship that has outlived its purpose."

I wished that I'd asked Jewel for her telephone number. Not that I was sure she would have given it to me or that she even had a phone. But if she did have one and if she'd given it to me, I would have been calling her right now, getting all the encouragement that I needed to do what I had to do.

A car honked, snapping me out of my thoughts, and I realized that I had drifted into the next lane.

"Sorry," I mouthed and held up my hand, apologizing to the driver, who sped past me with a growl on his face. His lips moved and I imagined that he was calling me all kinds of names that I didn't want to hear.

I sighed. I wanted to curse out my own self. But I couldn't keep thinking about what I needed to do at home. I had to work, and I needed to get my head in the game. Signaling, I exited the freeway, then made a couple of more turns before I slowed my car to find the number of the house that I was visiting. Just as I edged my car to the curb, my cell phone rang.

I needed to get inside, but when I saw Roxie's number, I answered.

I said, "Hey, girl. It's about time that you called me back."

"Really? You just texted me five minutes ago."

We laughed together; she knew that I was kidding. "So, how was the real estate convention?" I asked.

"It was great, *chica*, but I want to talk about you. I'm glad you came to your senses and finally came home. You know I was worried sick about you. Nichelle and Simone, too, especially when you wouldn't answer our calls or return any of our messages."

"I texted you."

"And you better not have been driving." She laughed, but only because she knew I didn't have a car while I was in the Dominican. But any other time, she would not have been kidding. Roxie was like the text police, and that had brought on too many clashes with my friend. Being in the car with her was hell for both of us. But I got her concern. Her husband, Brian, and their only child, my godson, Brendon, had been killed by a distracted driver fifteen years ago. So Roxie hated all things that took your attention off the road. I knew it was not safe, but I had mastered the ability to keep my eyes on the road while texting.

"Anyway," she continued, "a few texts weren't good enough. We wanted to hear from you."

"I know, I'm sorry. It's just that I didn't feel like answering any more questions because I really didn't have any answers."

"You know I had to keep Simone from getting on the plane and coming back down there."

"Actually, I'm surprised you didn't get back on the plane yourself."

"I thought about it, but this convention had been in the works for a year. Besides, I've known you for how long now? I knew you wouldn't do anything stupid. I could tell you had to work some stuff out." She paused. "Did you?"

I leaned over to the passenger seat to peer at the rickety old gray house. It had been a while since I'd visited this family, and all the houses were beginning to look the same to me.

"I'll have to fill you in later. I just pulled up to my client's house for a home visit."

"Wait, you just texted me," she replied. "You better have been at a stoplight."

I shook my head. "Can I get this lecture later?" I asked. "I need to get inside."

"Fine. Call me as soon as you leave. Before you begin driving," she added.

We said our goodbyes, but still, I had to summon up the strength to go inside. This was the part of my job that I used to love so much—the home visits. I loved sitting down and speaking with families, guiding them, helping them to get their lives together so they could be better parents to their kids. I loved saving kids and repairing families. But after twenty-two years of the same grind, the same sob stories, the same heartbreaking situations, this had long gone past the point of old. This was ancient.

I'd celebrated my promotion almost twelve years ago that had taken me out of the field and put me into an administrative position. But just like Karen told me all those years ago, it was budget cuts and short staffing that had me in the field once again. The only saving grace was it wasn't every day because I still had my administrative responsibilities.

I took a deep breath, fought off my disdain for this part of the job, then suppressed thoughts of my mangled personal life as I slipped out of the car, and hit the remote to lock it . . . twice. I walked up the pathway that was half dirt, half paved and knocked on the front door.

"Who is it?" a male voice yelled from the other side.

"It's Aja Clayton with the Department of Human Services and Child Protective Services."

"Bitch, get away from my door."

I gritted my teeth. I assumed that was the voice of Mr. Ozell Jackson. He hadn't been home on any of my other visits in the past few months, but judging from his file, he was not someone who was going to make my job easy. "Mr. Jackson," I began, keeping my tone even, "please don't make me call the police."

First, the sound of heavy footsteps, and I imagined a burly man, an ex-football player type. But then the door swung open and a straggly-looking man whose skin was barely hanging on to his bones stood at the door. He had no shame standing there in a once-upon-a-time-white wife beater and plaid boxers. A red Solo cup was in one hand and a cigarette dangled from between his fingers in the other.

"What?" he snapped.

"Good morning, Mr. Jackson," I said as if he hadn't just called me out of my name. "We had an appointment today."

"I don't know nothing about no appointment. Come back later. We busy."

As he moved to slam the door, I moved closer to the threshold, putting my hand out. "Sir, you know I have to do a family inspection."

"Well, my wife ain't here."

"I understand that," I said, keeping my voice at a normal level even as he shouted. "But I still have to do the inspection. It's been on the books for three months."

"I don't give a damn about your books," he said.

The stench of liquor emanating from his breath, from his skin, caused my nose to twitch. It was just eleven in the morning and this man smelled like he'd been dunked in a bucket of cheap whiskey. I wondered what he'd smell like by noon.

"Mr. Jackson, is Juwan here?" I pushed the door aside so I could get a better look inside. Mr. Jackson jumped in front of me, blocking my view.

Now my volume got a bit louder. "Do I need to call the police to help me? I need to see Juwan."

He huffed, flicked his cigarette on the front porch, gave me a long glare, and then finally stepped aside to let me in.

The moment I stepped in, I wondered if I could count it as a home visit if I saw Juwan on the porch. The house was filthy. No, the better word was disgusting. There were empty bowls of molded milk where I guessed Juwan had eaten cereal, sitting at the coffee table in the living room. But it was as if a bowl was never washed—there were a half a dozen of them stacked there. Next to the bowls were cartons of take-out food and frozen dinners. It seemed like whenever someone finished eating, they just got up and left everything there—for days.

I guessed they ate in the living room because the kitchen wasn't an option. Even from where I stood, I could see the table completely covered with beer cans, pizza, bottles, and . . . clothes.

I squealed as a roach, and a few of his friends, scurried across the floor toward one of the empty cartons, and when I glanced up, Mr. Jackson smirked.

Karen and I were going to have a talk. Budget or no budget, I couldn't do this anymore.

Then I spotted Juwan and my eyes narrowed. He was to the right of me, sitting legs crossed, facing the corner. "Juwan." I called out his name, but he didn't turn around. "How are you today?" Still, there was no reply. "Can you turn around and talk to me?"

He slowly turned around and right away, I saw the fear in his eight-year-old eyes.

"Are you okay?" I asked him. A too-small T-shirt clung to his small frame and he wore no pants—only a pair of dingy underwear.

Juwan's eyes darted from me over to his father, and with his father's eyes still on him, Juwan nodded.

His father said, "I told his little bad ass to get somewhere and sit down. He wants to play with that stupid truck."

"Because that's usually what kids do," I replied.

"Well, they don't play in my house."

Because it's such a beacon of perfection, I wanted to say.

Moving closer to the child—I had to step over a half-filled trash bag—I asked, "Are you excited about going back to school next week?"

He still didn't part his lips, so I reached for his hand. "Come on, Juwan, let's go sit and talk," I said, really having no idea where I was going to sit and talk to him. But that thought left my mind when I touched Juwan's elbow and he winced. I knelt to get eye level with him. "Juwan, are you okay?"

He blinked, fighting his tears and he shifted and pulled his arm closer to his body.

"Juwan," I said his name softly, "do you mind if I take a look at your arm?"

His glance rose above my head, but I didn't turn around. Not even when Juwan began to whimper. I imagined his father glaring at him, but I wanted Juwan to see that I wasn't afraid.

"I mind," Mr. Jackson said over my shoulder. "You inspected. Now get out my house."

Standing slowly, I rose all the way before I turned my glare to him. "You do know I have the authority to examine him, right? And if you need to be reminded, I can have the police here in just under five minutes." Now I wished that I'd called for the police in the first place. I should have done it the moment he called me a bitch. And now, the way his bottom lip curled, I really regretted my decision. I'd seen this look before—a few years ago an irate father had dang near broken my arm when I tried to remove his kids.

But it didn't look like I was going to have an issue this time. Mr. Jackson huffed, but he backed up. I gave him a "smart move" nod, then turned back to Juwan. Crouching again, I slowly raised up his arm. He flinched; it was tender, but it didn't seem like he had any broken bones.

"Turn around," I told him. "I want to look at your back."

He gave his father a long glance, but finally, he did what I said.

"I'm going to raise your shirt now," I said, wanting to inform and assure him at the same time.

He shivered when I lifted his shirt, and for the second time since I'd stepped into this house, I released a sound that I couldn't keep inside. This little boy's back—it was like someone thought he was a canvas and had painted black and blue marks all over him. There was hardly an untouched spot. I had to breathe deeply to hold back the bile I felt rising at the thought of what this boy had gone through to have this as the result.

When I stood again, I faced his father. "What happened?" I shot him a piercing glare.

"He fell down." He spoke so casually before he took a swig of whatever was in that red cup. "I told you he was in here playing. It ain't enough room in here for all that. A kid is bound to hurt himself." Then he had the nerve to grin and shrug.

"All these bruises wouldn't be caused by falling down."

When I pulled out my cell phone from my purse, the smirk faded from Mr. Jackson's face. "What are you doing?" he asked.

I ignored him, then shifted a bit so that he couldn't see what I was doing. Let him think that I was calling the police, though, I was dialing my office. Before I could finish punching in the number, Mr. Jackson whisked over and slapped the phone out of my hand.

I jumped back in shock and fear.

"I wish y'all would stay y'all nosy behinds up out my business," he spat. "This me and my family's business. That boy right there is my son, and ain't no damn gov'ment gonna tell me how to raise him."

As if I didn't have a snippet of fear inside me, I casually reached down, picked my phone up, then held my hand out to the little boy. "Juwan," I said, now gripping his hand in mine, "I need you to come with me."

"Bitch," he put down the cup, "if you don't get your hands off my son." Reaching around me, he grabbed the little boy and Juwan screamed. Mr. Jackson pushed me so hard I fell to the filthy floor. I jumped right up and my first instinct was to fight. But that wasn't the best of ideas. First, Mr. Jackson was stronger and drunker than I was, and I'd already been hurt by one violent parent.

So I took my purse and spoke to the little boy only. "Juwan, I'll be right back." I gave Mr. Jackson a look that I hoped let him know that he shouldn't have messed with me. And then I scurried outside. This was a job for the police.

———————

"Um," I heard my husband's hum over my shoulder from where he stood at the entrance, "is there a reason you're drinking at five in the evening?"

I turned to face Charles. I'd been so out of it, I hadn't even heard him come in. My thoughts were still on what had just happened hours before.

The police had shown up within ten minutes, looking like they were ready for a fight. And Mr. Jackson had given them one, getting into a three-hour standoff with police. When Mr. Jackson fired two shots from his house, I just knew Juwan would be the one to end up dead and it would be my fault.

It had taken SWAT going in through the back of the house and safely removing Juwan before the police took his crazed—that's the only adjective I had to describe him, with the way his eyes bulged—father into custody. Mr. Jackson had spewed obscenities at everyone within hearing distance, especially me, vowing that he would make me pay if it was "the last thing that he did."

"Sleep with one eye open, bitch," he'd shouted right before an officer pushed him into the back of a cruiser.

Once I made sure Juwan was safe, I'd called Karen.

"You have no idea what I've just been through." I told her about the last few hours and ended with, "I'm resuming my personal leave."

"Wait, you just got back."

"I know. I'm resuming my personal leave." I'd made that decision after the first gunshot.

"You won't be paid, Aja. You know that, right?"

"I know, I'm resuming my personal leave," I said again, wondering how many times I was going to have to say this to her.

She sighed, but all she could say was, "Okay." There was nothing else she could do, and the job had become too much for me. I'd rushed home, opened this bottle of tequila, and been drinking ever since.

I was a little surprised to find out that it was only five. It felt like I'd been drinking for so many hours.

Charles lifted the bottle sitting in front of me and frowned. "Tequila? Really?"

"Yes, tequila." I snatched the bottle back. "Because after the day from hell I had today, I need this and then some."

"What happened?" Charles asked, sliding in the seat across from me at the dining room table. There was so much concern in his voice, I knew he cared. I knew he would listen, too; Charles always listened. I just never knew when he heard me.

"Baby," Charles said when I didn't answer, "talk to me. What happened? What's going on?"

I took the bottle from him, poured another shot, sprinkled the salt on my finger, then turned the shot glass up. I grabbed a lime from the slices I'd set up, then sucked on the wedge.

"Baby . . ."

I set the shot glass on the table, dropped the lime wedge in the glass, and said, "Charles, I want a divorce." My breath caught in my throat and my eyes widened. *Did I really just say that? Oh my God. I didn't want it to come out like that.*

My heart beat in anticipation as a heavy silence filled the room. And then it was interrupted when Charles burst into laughter.

Chapter 14

My husband was still laughing, and not only was he messing up my buzz but I was getting pissed.

"Divorce?" He cackled as he stood and walked toward the kitchen. "You're funny. Lay off the tequila, babe."

Now I was suddenly sober. "Charles," he paused and turned to face me, "do I look like I'm kidding?"

He blinked.

I continued, "You've been asking what's wrong for weeks now. What's wrong is that I want a divorce."

His eyes narrowed as he studied me. "Wait. Are you for real?"

I nodded.

Charles eased back into the dining room and slid back into the chair. "A divorce? What in the world? Where is this coming from?"

I shrugged.

"Is there someone else? Have you met another—"

Before he could finish, I said, "No." Now I really regretted the way I'd let this come out. I rubbed my temples, mad at the tequila but grateful that I had finally found courage, even if it was at the bottom of my shot glass. "I promise you, this has nothing to do with anyone else. This is just about me. All about me."

His eyes stayed on me as if he was trying to determine if he should believe my words or if he should just chalk this up to my being drunk. It was as if he was *hoping* I was drunk. "So"—he stopped, a long pause—"you're not happy with me?"

"I'm not happy with *me*," I said. "This has nothing to do with you. It's me."

My husband leaned back in his chair. The shock on his face told me that he had made the determination that yes, I was drunk, but I knew what I was saying. He believed me. He blew out a long breath. "You're going to have to explain this to me, Aja. A divorce? That doesn't make any sense."

His voice was eerily calm, and I almost wished that he was the opposite. I would be able to handle him screaming, but this?

I took a breath before I said, "I told you I felt like something was missing in my life. That I was unfulfilled professionally and personally."

"Yeah." He squinted as if he didn't understand. "But you said the vacation helped."

"No, *you* said the vacation helped. You listened to me, but you didn't *hear* me, so you came up with your own solution—the vacation. I never said that."

He blinked as if he were trying to recall. "Okay, so the vacation didn't help. Do you need another one?"

Really? "No, I don't. A vacation isn't going to fix this."

"But a divorce will?"

I sighed. "I just need to do something different with my life."

"So your definition of different is divorce? You just decide that you're going to abandon your husband and kids?" he said, now echoing his mother's sentiments.

"I'm not abandoning anyone. Our kids are grown and you'll be fine. Don't you understand, Charles? Aren't you listening to me? I'm trying to save *me*." I felt my voice cracking.

"Save you from whom? From what?" The shock was beginning to wear off and the anger, though he was trying to hold it back, was seeping through. "I'm sorry, I didn't realize you needed saving from me."

"See, Charles? You're doing it again. I never said you. I've been saying me, me, me."

"And maybe that's the problem. Because when you're in a marriage it can't be just about you."

I stared at him as a mist covered my eyes and the tequila headache intensified.

"But at some point it has to be about me. To this point, it's been about everybody except for me, and I'm drowning and there is only one lifeline."

He nodded, but I could tell he didn't understand. "Let me ask you something."

"Okay."

"Have I ever cheated on you?"

The mist turned to full-fledged tears.

"Have. I. Ever. Cheated. On. You." He yelled when I didn't respond.

"No," I whimpered. "But . . ."

He moved in closer and leaned over me, placing his palms on the dining room table. "Have I ever put my hands on you?"

"No. Can you just—"

He lowered his voice an octave. "Have I ever emotionally or verbally abused you?"

"No. I just want—"

"Then help me understand why the hell you'd want a divorce!" He slammed his hands on the dining room table, causing me to jump.

Maybe I didn't want to see his anger verbalized after all. I kept my voice even, hoping it would soften my words.

"I'm trying to tell you, but you're not listening. I just do. I just want out. I have to get out so that I can get up again."

Charles stood and paced across the dining room floor. "I'm

not understanding this. I have loved you for over twenty years. I spend each day trying to make your life better. I think about you all the time. And now you sit here and tell me you want out? That this is about *you*. After all I've done, this is about *you*? Are you freaking kidding me?"

"Charles . . ."

It was like he was talking to himself now. "Do you know how many women approach me?" he asked, though he wasn't looking at me at all. "Women come on to me all the time. I know how I look to them. They know who I am, they know I have money. So I'm rich and good looking and just a damn good catch. I can walk through the mall, or let me speak somewhere, and women throw their freakin' panties at me like I'm a Hollywood celebrity. And not once, never, ever once have I said anything besides, 'No, sorry, I love my wife. I'm faithful to my wife. I'm not interested.' That's all I say, no, no, no. For twenty years, I've said no, no, no and you come at me talking about you want out because . . ." Now he stopped moving. Now he looked at me. "Because, why again?"

My bottom lip trembled. I knew I didn't have an answer for him. All I could say was, "I just do."

He leaned his head back and released a laugh, a maniacal sound that I'd never heard come out of him before. "That's right. Because you just do. Twenty years down the drain because *you just do*. I've been faithful to you and this is how you repay me?"

I wanted to protest. I wanted to tell him he didn't get an award for being faithful, but I figured now wasn't the time for that debate. "Charles, this has nothing to do with fidelity."

"Fine. Let's push aside the fact that I could have had any woman I wanted out there." He paused as if he wanted me to hear his words. As if he wanted the words to hurt. When I didn't blink or flinch, he continued, "Let's just focus on the fact that I was *good* to you, was I not?"

"Of course you were," I said, feeling and hearing the weariness in my voice.

"Then help me understand." He took a deep breath, trying to calm himself down. "Help me understand this, Aja, because I really and truly don't."

Tears streamed down my cheeks. "Charles, I don't have anything more to add. You're a good man, but . . ."

"But good guys finish last." He let out that crazed laugh again. "Maybe if I had beaten your ass, called you out of your name, treated you like dirt, you'd be okay with me. Maybe if I had been an asshole husband, that would've turned you on and you wouldn't be sitting in the dining room of our six-thousand-square-foot house that you just *had* to have, at a three-thousand-dollar imported table that you wanted, telling me you want a divorce."

Now, those words hurt. Because Charles was right about all of that. He'd worked hard to give me all of those things. If it had been up to him, we would have been living much more modestly. But I'd wanted the house that was probably three times what we needed; I'd wanted the designer furniture, some pieces imported from places that I couldn't even pronounce; I'd wanted art pieces that sometimes cost more than many Americans earned in a year. It was all me, and Charles had worked hard to grant my every desire.

"You've worked hard to give me everything that I've wanted, Charles, and I will always be grateful to you. You've given me that life, but the problem is none of that filled the void that has been inside me, probably since I was a child. I don't think I even realized the void was there, but it was, inside me, growing and growing."

"Yeah, that void that started because of your dysfunctional family," he snarled. "I tried to help you, tried to make up for all the craziness you had to go through with your folks, and now you want to leave me?"

I took slow, deep breaths, appalled and hurt that he would go there.

"Charles, I understand you're mad, but you do not need to talk to me crazy."

"Why not? Isn't that what you come from? That's what you want so you can feel complete? Somebody to treat you like your daddy did your mama," he spat. This side of my husband, the mean-spirited angry side—was something that I'd never seen. "Isn't that all you understand? Abusive-ass men who hurt their families?" But then right away, he sighed, and I could tell he regretted his words. "I'm sorry," he said after a moment of angry silence. His shoulders slumped as he stood up straight. "I'm so sorry for that," his voice lowered, "but I don't know what to say, Aja. Am I supposed to just look at you and say, 'Okay, cool'? You want me to agree to tossing away twenty years just because? You tell me how I'm supposed to reply to this news."

It took me a moment to respond because of the stone in my throat. The stone that had risen there just from hearing the pain in Charles's voice. In all our years of marriage, he'd never said such vile and hateful words about my family. But then, I'd never blindsided him with a request for a divorce.

"I don't know how you're supposed to respond," I said. "This is difficult for me, too."

More silence filled the room as we just looked at each other.

Then, "Nah." Charles stood erect as he shook his head. "I don't receive this. You're talking crazy because you're going through some kind of midlife crisis. Well, I get that. That happens to people every day. But we aren't getting a divorce. For better or for worse, remember? Until death do us part. You recall that part? That's what we will be doing. You're not going anywhere."

His words, his stance sent a chill through my body as I recalled those same words coming from my father once when my mother threatened to leave. "Is that . . . is that a threat?" I asked.

Shock blanketed his face. "What? Have you completely lost your mind? Hell no. I don't threaten women. I've never in my life threatened you." He exhaled again and threw his hands up in frustration. Then he slumped down into the chair. "I don't know what to do with this, Aja. If you really don't want to be here . . ."

He paused as if he was giving me a chance to change my mind. When I said nothing, he continued, "I don't want you in a marriage that you don't want to be in." Another pause, another chance for me to plead insanity. When I said nothing, he sighed. "But maybe, maybe we just need a separation. Or rather, maybe *you* need a separation because I was fine."

"You've been fine. You *are* fine. Please know that this problem is me, all me." I had to inhale, I needed courage again. "I don't want a separation. I want a divorce. I want out." Those words made me choke. "I *need* out."

He stared at me. For the first time since his father died, Charles's eyes filled with tears. "Aja, why are you doing this?"

I lowered my eyes because if I kept looking at him, I'd jump up from my chair and try to kiss his tears away. "Because I'm dying inside," I said, my voice quivering.

"Wow," he said, leaning back in the chair as if I'd taken a sledgehammer and rammed it into his stomach. "Being married to me is killing you? Just wow."

I buried my face in my hands and sobbed. "I wish there was a better way to explain this to you. But I don't have the words. It's not just the marriage. It's everything. It's us, my job, my life," I cried.

He stood, turned and stumbled toward the window. "I have no words."

Silence returned and hung from the rafters. Finally, I said, "I'm sorry, Charles. Since your mom is here, I'll leave. I can go stay with Roxie."

"Yeah, you're right, you'll leave. You want out, you leave," he said, his back still to me. His tone was filled with anger, tempered by his shock.

I bit my lip, then continued, "Anika leaves for school this weekend. I would rather we just let her go on back and tell her and Eric after they both get into the semester. Maybe over spring break."

After a moment, he turned, faced me, and said, "You're making all the decisions about this family now. Do whatever." He stomped past me. "Do whatever you want, Aja," he said as he moved toward the door. "Tell them whatever you want. I'm out of it."

I flinched as he slammed the door so hard, if it had fallen onto the floor, I wouldn't have been surprised. When I heard the roar of Charles's Corvette, I pushed the almost empty tequila bottle aside, then lay my head down on the table and cried.

Chapter 15

My husband very rarely got angry, and when he did, he hardly ever verbalized his anger. But those who knew him well could definitely tell when he was angry. And right now, Charles was beyond angry; he was at the highest level of pissivity.

His lips were pursed, his stare was hard as he looked straight ahead on the road. He navigated onto Interstate 85, and I wondered if he was going to remain this way all the way to Spelman.

It may have been a sunny seventy degrees in Atlanta, but a January chill was definitely filling the car.

I don't know how I expected Charles to react to my desire for a divorce, especially since it had only been three days since I had dropped that bombshell. I definitely didn't think he'd take this trip to Spelman with me and our daughter. But he loved Anika more than he hated me, at this moment, and he didn't want to disappoint her.

I looked back over my shoulder and took a quick glance at our daughter. She'd slept the entire flight from Houston, and now, with AirPods in her ears, she was oblivious to the silent discourse. How could she notice when Drake screamed through her headphones?

I turned my attention back to Charles, whose eyes were still in the same place.

"So," I began, and then searched for words to follow. I said, "What do you think about Eric's new coach?" I was desperate to fill the car with some type of conversation.

That was a reach, I knew, because he'd raved about the coach when he was first hired a few months ago, but what else was I supposed to talk about? I was sure that Charles hadn't said five sentences to me over the past few days. The only saving grace was that Judy was still on her cruise. I couldn't imagine what life would have been like if she had been here.

I'd managed to deal with the deafening silence by staying in the guest room—I'd told Anika that her dad had been snoring badly lately—and just keeping my distance from my husband.

But this—this was brutal. Being this close to him for these hours was difficult. I knew this trip would be hard, but I hadn't envisioned it like this.

My eyes were still on Charles, but he only glanced at me for a moment before he returned his eyes to the road. I sighed as I just turned to stare out the window. There was nothing else left to do, but wait this trip out.

I wanted to raise my hands and shout "hallelujah" when we rolled through the gates of Spelman's campus. We'd hardly moved a block when Anika said, "Wait, Daddy! Stop!"

Charles hit the brakes and both of us turned to Anika, startled. "What's wrong?" I asked.

She opened her door. "There's Kelli and Rachel and Andrea," she said as she bounced out of the car.

Our eyes followed her as she ran to Kelli, the art major who had come to our house to visit, and two other girls I didn't know. They squealed as if they hadn't seen each other in years. Then the girls ran over to us and leaned into the car, hugging both of us.

"Jump in," Anika said, and the four of them piled into the back. "Y'all can help me carry up all this stuff."

"You weren't here to help us," Rachel said, and for some reason that sent them into a fit of giggles.

"Have you done any more paintings, Mrs. Clayton?" Kelli asked, before turning to her friends. "You guys should see some of her work. It's, like, totally amazing."

That made me smile. "As a matter of fact, I have—"

"Oh my God, is that Danny, Mr. Morehouse?" Anika said, tapping on the window and cutting me off. She was pointing to some young man, standing and talking to a group of women. "He cut his dreads!"

And just like that, all interest in my art was gone as the girls started talking about Danny and his dreads.

I was actually glad to have the girls in the back seat, their chatter filling the car with delight. And once we pulled up to Anika's dorm, their chatter continued as her friends helped us unload the car.

With the girls' help, it took less than thirty minutes to unload and then just a couple of hours to get her settled into her room.

When she was all unpacked, Anika said, "Mom, I hope you guys don't mind, but we're getting together with a couple of our friends at the cafeteria. I know you guys wanted to go get something to eat, but I really—"

"No, go right ahead," Charles said. "Go and enjoy your friends. Your mom and I will head on to the hotel."

"Are you sure?" she said, looking at me. She cocked her head a little bit. "Are you okay, Mom? I just noticed, you've been awfully quiet."

I faked a smile. "Yes, sweetheart. I'm fine. How could I say anything with all of you Chatty Cathys around?"

That sent Anika and her friends into more laughter.

"Okay. Well, thank you all for everything," Anika said before turning to Charles. "Daddy, did you put some money in my account?"

That put a genuine smile on his face. "Of course I did. You know I'm not going to let my baby come up here with no money."

"Yes!" she said, throwing her arms around his neck. "Okay, let me walk you back to the car."

I had to trot to keep up with her. Anika was back in college mode and she didn't have much time or room for her parents. Outside of the dorm, she quickly hugged me, then Charles.

"Okay, bye. I'll call you guys later. Maybe we can have breakfast tomorrow?"

"We have the parents' meeting, remember?" I said. Both Charles and I had done more than send our daughter off to college, we'd been active members of the Spelman Parents Association.

"Oh yeah, that's right," Anika said.

"So we'll do lunch or maybe dinner. We'll be here for a couple of days anyway," I said.

"Okay. See you!"

"Be careful," I called out to her as she ran to catch up with her friends. "Love you."

She turned around and blew kisses before she rounded the corner out of our sight.

Charles and I stood in an awkward silence before he said, "Are you ready?"

I nodded and then moved to the SUV that we'd rented. Charles unlocked it with the remote and I opened the passenger door, something I hadn't done in the years of our being together, but something I'd done on this trip.

"Did you still want to get something to eat?" I said once we were in the truck.

Charles took a deep breath, turned over the ignition, then looked over at me. "I'm not good at faking the funk, Aja. You want out of our marriage, yet you still want to pretend that we're this big happy family."

"I'm not trying to pretend anything, Charles. We have to eat." I released a heavy sigh. "I just want to do what's best for our children." I paused. "Can I ask you a question?" He didn't respond, but I continued anyway. "Do you think we'll ever be able to be amicable? Be friends?"

He released a convoluted laugh. "I don't want a damn friend. I got plenty of those. I had one wife," he snapped.

I wanted to remind him that really he didn't have a lot of friends and that might have been part of our problem. Instead, I just said, "For the sake of our kids, I want us to get along."

He shook his head and turned his attention back to the freeway. "When do you plan on telling them? I think we should just do it now. I don't want to pretend until spring break," he said, his voice rife with enough ice to fill the Antarctic.

It was interesting that he now wanted to tell the children. I didn't have the feeling that he wanted to do that before. Maybe he needed everyone to know in order for it to feel real to him.

"I don't know when we should tell them. Like I mentioned before, I was thinking I didn't want to mess up the holidays. But I wanted to talk with you about that. I just want the kids to get settled into this semester."

"Why wait?" he asked. "I think you should've told Anika now. Let her know that you're trashing our family right before she went bouncing off with her friends. Let her know that all of a sudden, after twenty freaking years, we're no longer good enough for you."

I knew this was Charles's anger speaking. I just didn't know how to respond to it.

"Whatever," he continued. "When are you moving out?"

"Again," I swallowed, "I wanted to wait until Anika was gone."

"She's gone." He waited for me to say something, but I didn't want to cry so I kept my mouth closed. He continued, "So you can get out as soon as we get back. I changed our tickets. We're leaving tomorrow afternoon."

My heart hurt because I didn't think I'd ever seen Charles like this. It felt mean. But what else did I expect? "Leaving tomorrow? We can't. Anika thinks we're staying for a couple of days."

"She'll be fine," he said without a bit of emotion. "Or you can stay if you want. I'm out."

I knew it would be futile to argue. "Fine. We'll leave tomorrow and I'll move out when we get home."

"Good," he said, though it didn't quite sound like he meant it.

I fought back the tears as we continued toward the hotel, once again in silence. At the Buckhead Marriott, Charles pulled up to the valet.

"Good afternoon, welcome to the Marriott, are you checking in?" the valet asked as he opened Charles's door.

"Yes," Charles replied. "One night."

The valet gave Charles a ticket as he took his keys. "There are two bags in the trunk," Charles told him.

By the time another attendant opened my door, Charles was in the lobby. I followed Charles inside, stunned that he hadn't bothered to wait for me. I arrived at the desk just as he was handing the clerk his license and credit card.

"Mr. Clayton, we have you all set in a king suite," the front desk clerk said.

"Would it be possible to change that to two separate regular king rooms?"

The woman looked from him to me, then said, "Of course." She tapped on her keyboard. "I'm so sorry, I have two king rooms but they're not on the same floor," she said.

"That's perfect," he said.

I swallowed, struggling to suppress that stone that now seemed to want to live in my throat. I needed to help Charles work through this; I wanted to help him handle his hurt. But honestly, taking care of him only was how we got to this place. I needed to focus on me.

The attendant checked us in, then said, "Here are the keys, Mr. Clayton." She handed both keys to him.

Her glance turned to me and her eyes were filled with sympathy. But when she glanced back at Charles, she gave him a long smile.

And when he gave me one key, then turned back to the attendant giving her the same smile, I spun around, grabbed my luggage, and made my way to the elevator without turning around to see if Charles was following me.

By the time I got to the elevator, I realized that he was not.

Chapter 16

I rolled over again, then again, once again. Finally, I sat up, and in the darkness, I leaned back against the headboard. Pulling my knees to my chest, I wrapped my arms around my legs. Maybe that would keep me in place. Keep me in this room so that I wouldn't do what I really wanted to do. And that was to go to Charles's room. I wanted to knock on his door, make him let me in, then hold him and comfort him and tell him that I was so sorry. Let him know that I never wanted to hurt him. My mind raced back to the last time that I'd hurt him. That had been the only time he'd ever been mean to me. Well, until now.

I took a deep breath and summoned up the strength to do what I needed to do. We'd been together less than six months but I knew this relationship wouldn't work.

"Charles, honey, we need to talk," I told him as I entered his luxury apartment. His sports anchor salary definitely had him living a life I knew nothing about.

Charles closed the door and walked to his recliner to sit down. "Okay, what's wrong now?" He kicked back in the chair and muted the TV.

I sat down on the sofa across from him and immediately started fumbling with my purse strap.

"Look, I've been thinking about us."

"Good things, I hope." Charles leaned forward and flashed a smile.

"Please, Charles, you're not making this easy."

Charles stopped smiling. "Aja, what's going on? Not making what easy?"

"I've been doing a lot of thinking. And I just think . . . well . . . I just believe . . . I don't think things are working out between us." I fought back tears but was determined not to cry.

"What? Where did this come from?"

"It's just not working."

"Aja, this is crazy. You come to me out of the blue with this crap. Does this have anything to do with Candace?" he asked, referring to his ex-girlfriend, who had tried to cause trouble with us.

"No, it doesn't. It has to do with us. You and me. It's just I don't think I should be focusing on a relationship right now. My sister's getting better and she needs my attention. Then there's Eric."

"What?" Charles rubbed his temples. "You've got to be kidding me! Where did this come from?"

"I'm sorry, Charles. I knew I should've never gotten involved in the first place. I knew I wasn't ready." My voice was soft as I spoke. But that didn't stop his from rising.

"Wasn't ready?" Charles shook his head like he was trying to process what was going on. "I don't understand you, Aja. One minute things are great between us and the next you come at me with this BS."

"It's not BS. You never have understood my relationship with my brother and sister, how important they are to me." I knew I was grasping at straws, but I didn't know what else to tell him.

Charles stood up and started pacing. "I don't believe this. I

*have been there for you and your family, put up with your histri-
onics, your lack of trust in me. Here I am talking about a future
and you're telling me you don't think things are working?"*

"I'm sorry."

*Charles spun around, his face fiery with anger. "You're
sorry? Is that the best you can do? You're sorry?! No, you
know what, Aja, I'm sorry! I'm sorry I got involved with you!
I'm tired of dealing with this. You women are always holler-
ing about finding a good man and you get one and don't know
what to do with him!"*

"Charles . . ."

*"Don't Charles me." He lowered his voice. "I'm tired of this
indecisive crap. You got issues, Aja. And I can't deal with 'em.
Maybe you're right. Maybe we weren't meant to be."*

*"I was hoping we could handle this like adults and stay
friends."*

"Friends? No thanks, I got enough friends."

"Charles, please."

*"Aja, go. Just go." Charles turned his back. I could no
longer hold back the tears. I reached in my purse and pulled
out a tissue.*

*He turned around and glared at me. "What are you crying
for? This is what you wanted."*

"You don't have to be so mean."

*"Mean?" Charles laughed, then turned to face me. "You're
the one who came over here with this out of nowhere. Mean?
No, Aja, I'm not mean. I'm tired, tired of trying to make you
love me, of always coming second and pretending like it doesn't
bother me, tired of watching you make your life miserable over
your damn brother, tired of you blaming yourself for something
that happened fifteen years ago. I'm just tired." Charles
walked over and opened the front door. "So I'm through. You
got your wish, I'm through."*

Charles held the door open. I slowly stood up. My face felt full and swollen. "Charles, can we talk about this some more?"

"Goodbye, Aja." I wanted so badly to tell him the real reason that I was breaking up with him. I thought he'd cheated with his ex-girlfriend so I'd cheated with my ex-boyfriend. When I found out his ex had been lying, I was devastated. I had made some screwed-up choices in life. But I felt I was doing the right thing by setting Charles free.

I just looked at Charles, then walked outside. I stopped and turned to face him. "I do love you."

"You have a hell of a way of showing it." Charles slammed the door.

The memory of that night made me shiver. Charles and I had gotten back together after that because he was there for me after Eric died. But rebuilding the trust that I wouldn't hurt him again had taken some time. And I'd kept my word to never bring him that kind of pain again.

Until now.

I wanted desperately to go to Charles, tell him how sorry I was, convince him how sorry I was. But I couldn't do that. Because that would only complicate our situation and we didn't need that. So I sat up, holding my knees until I was exhausted. Then I lay down and turned and tossed. Then tossed and turned.

Finally, I just lay on my back and stared at the ceiling. And in those quiet moments, I realized something—while I really wanted to comfort Charles, I wasn't questioning myself. I was doing the right thing. I was doing what I had to do.

My cell phone buzzed and I frowned as I glanced at the clock on the nightstand: 3:17.

In the few seconds that it took for me to reach for the phone, my heart pounded. Was this Anika? Was something wrong with my daughter?

Meet me downstairs at 8. We can go to the parents' meeting, say goodbye to Anika, and get back to Houston.

I stared at the message for a moment. Charles couldn't sleep either. But there was nothing I could do. I slipped back beneath the covers, closed my eyes, and prayed for peace on this night and all the nights to come.

───※───

I yawned as I stepped off the elevator, then rolled my bag down the long hallway to the front lobby. It was only a little after 7:30, but I'd wanted to come down early, grab a cup of coffee, and wrap my brain around all that was going to happen today. We were going to say goodbye to our daughter and then fly home before tonight, when I'd say goodbye to my life as I'd known it.

My mouth stretched into another yawn, and when I made my way around the corner, I stopped. There was Charles, sitting in one of the round booths, reading a *USA Today*.

"Oh," I said as I approached him. "Good morning."

"Morning," he replied. He folded the newspaper, took a sip from the coffee cup in front of him, then he stood. "Are you ready?"

His tone, his demeanor was so cold. He hadn't even asked if I wanted coffee or anything. But again, how could I blame him? It was jarring, though. So out of his character.

Rolling my bag behind me, I followed him through the revolving door, then outside where our car was already waiting. The valet took our bags, I slipped into the car—once again opening the door myself—then waited for Charles to get in.

This time, I didn't fight the silence. I just let it be and settled into my own thoughts. Of how Charles and I had spent twenty really good years—at least for him.

We parked in the lot of the student services building and then signed in for the parent meeting. As we sat in the auditorium, I wondered if Charles was listening because I wasn't. Oh, I was putting on a good enough act, nodding and pretending that I was interested in Anika's classes and the changes coming to the campus. But I was thinking about today and how different my life would be in twenty-four hours.

When we left orientation, we headed in silence to Anika's room. I knocked on her door and a moment later, she answered.

"Mom. Dad." She threw her arms around me, then her father. "Come on in. You're just in time. Cynthia arrived last night and her parents are here," she said, referring to her friend. "And guess what? She has a private room right next to me."

"We just wanted to make sure you got settled," Charles said. "Our flight is actually in a couple hours, so we're not going to be able to stay long."

Anika frowned. "What? You're going back? Why so soon?" she asked. "I thought you were staying through the weekend."

I pressed my lips together. This was going to have to be Charles's lie.

"We were," he said. "But something . . . uh, important . . . came up at work."

Anika pouted. "But I wanted to spend more time with you."

"I'll tell you what," Charles said. "I'll put some extra money in your account and then you can do a little shopping at Lenox Square."

That wiped the pout right off her face and instead, she squealed again. "Oh, Daddy. You're the best." She kissed his cheek. But when she stepped back, she added, "But still, you have time to meet Cynthia's parents." She opened the door before we could reply and stepped out into the hallway. "Oh, here they are now. Mr. and Mrs. Greene, come meet my parents," she said.

I turned and watched the Greenes walk in the room. Cynthia and Anika had been roommates first semester, but although I'd spoken to her mother on the phone, we hadn't had the chance to meet, even though they lived in Kingwood, a suburb of Houston.

"Hi!" Anika sang.

"Oh, Mr. and Mrs. Clayton," Cynthia said as she stepped into the room. She hugged us before she turned to her parents. "Mom and Dad, these are Anika's parents."

I would've definitely mistaken the Greenes for sister and brother. I don't think I'd ever seen a couple that looked more alike.

We exchanged greetings.

"Mr. Clayton," Cynthia's father leaned in and shook Charles's hand. "I'm a big fan."

"We both are," Mrs. Greene said. "Nice to meet both of you finally." She extended her hand and shook mine. "We've had lots of phone calls, haven't we?" Her laughter filled the room with warmth. "I'm sorry we haven't connected. I always tell Greg it's like we don't even live in Houston, we live so far out."

"Well, we're meeting now," I said, managing a smile.

"And I'm just thrilled," Mrs. Greene continued. "Cynthia just adores the two of you."

"We adore her," I said.

We really did. Anika was lucky with her roommate, Cynthia, a sweet girl she'd met on Twitter their senior year of high school once they'd discovered they were both attending Spelman.

"Well, I really wish we could stay and talk, but I have to get back to Houston," Charles said.

"Okay, well, we're walking out, too," Mr. Greene said. "We just came up to meet the two of you."

So with the girls behind us, we walked through the hall. The men chatted as Mrs. Greene and I followed with the girls.

Outside, Anika hugged us again. "My parents are relationship goals," she said as she hooked her arms through ours.

I felt like a deer caught in the headlights.

"This is what I want when I graduate from college," she added.

Mrs. Greene laughed. "Isn't it wonderful to have a child who admires you so much?"

"I admire you and Daddy, too, Mom," Cynthia piped in.

"Oh, of course, sweetheart. I know you do. But it's always nice to see another wonderful family," Mrs. Greene replied.

"That's what we are," Anika gushed.

I didn't even want to glance Charles's way.

"You know," Mrs. Greene began, "I'm a freelance reporter, and right now, I'm working on an article for *Essence* and I would really love to include you two in our black love edition. I'm doing a story on the secrets to longevity in marriage."

That deer that I thought I was now wanted that oncoming car to just hit me. Take me out. What were the chances of this?

It must have been the twin expressions on our faces that made Mrs. Greene back up. "I mean . . . I know how private you are." Her eyes darted between the two of us.

"But it's *Essence*." Anika beamed. "Oh my God. That would be so totally cool."

I had to save all of us. "Why don't I take your number and give you a call about it?" I said, trying to get the words out quickly. Trying to get ahead of either Anika noticing me and her father or him saying something.

"Take the picture now," Anika said. "The picture for the article. You'll have to have one, right?"

"Yes, but . . ."

"Well, if you take it now, I can be in it," Anika said.

"Now you know your brother would blow a gasket," I said, looking for any out just in case Mrs. Greene was considering it.

Mrs. Greene laughed. "Well, I'm just a writer. We'd have to send a staff photographer, but I have a great one in Houston, so when we get back I can set that up. But," she paused, then proceeded, "I'd love to interview you. It's a simple article; I'm just speaking with several couples, getting tips on how to make a marriage last."

The way my daughter was beaming, all I could do was take Mrs. Greene's information and figure it all out later.

"Here's my contact information," Mrs. Greene said, handing me a business card. "Please give me a call when you get back."

I nodded, not wanting to speak my lie out loud.

"Well, we need to get going," Charles said, turning to Anika.

The ends of her lips dipped. "I hate to see you guys go, especially since I expected a few more days." Anika was a daddy's girl, and it gave him immeasurable joy to make her happy.

"Oh, I'm sure you have your plate full," Charles replied. "And remember Lenox Square?"

"Yeah, that'll help," she said, trying to contain her excitement about a Daddy-sponsored shopping spree.

"And then there's the Omega party at Morehouse tonight," Cynthia said.

Anika gave her friend an exasperated look and Cynthia said, "Oops," before they giggled.

"Morehouse, huh?" Charles said.

"Daddy, it's just a party."

"Mmm-hmm. Don't have me come back to Atlanta with my shotgun."

"You don't have a shotgun." Anika laughed.

"I'll go buy one," he said.

And when they all laughed and Anika and Charles hugged, the moment squeezed my heart. We would no longer have family moments like this.

"If you need any suggestions on what kind of shotgun to get, let me know. I stay locked and loaded," Mr. Greene said, and he and Charles bumped fists.

While they laughed, I stepped back. But when I glanced at Mrs. Greene, her eyes were on me. Her journalist's eyes.

Yeah, she knew something was up. And she had probably figured it out. But of course, she had far too much class to say anything—at least not now.

I wondered if she would still bother to call me or expect me
to reach out to her. Probably not. She'd figured out that on the
subject of a long, happy marriage, I was definitely not the one to
talk to.

Chapter 17

I don't know how I thought this was all supposed to go. I hadn't had an ugly breakup in my life, so, I dang sure didn't know how a divorce was supposed to play out. All I did know was that it broke my heart to see my husband walking around alternating between depression and anger.

We'd gotten home from Atlanta late last night after several plane delays. Charles had retreated to our bedroom. The only thing he'd said to me was, "Let me know if you need any help carrying your suitcases out." And then he disappeared. I often heard about divorced couples who led productive friendly lives with one another. I hoped that one day Charles and I could get there, though I really didn't see how.

I groaned at the sight of my mother-in-law standing in my doorway watching me as I pulled a suitcase on my bed. "So, you're really going through with this?" she asked.

My stomach had tightened when we returned home last night and saw her car parked in the driveway. I suddenly wished that her cruise had been one of those two-week Alaskan cruises instead of the six-day Caribbean cruise out of Galveston.

I ignored Judy as I walked over to my dresser and pulled some more clothes out.

"When Charles told me about this this morning, needless to say I was dumbfounded. Just like him."

I kept ignoring her.

"He thinks there's someone else because that's the only thing that makes sense." She paused. "Is there someone else?"

I was so sick of people asking me that question. Like the only reason I could possibly leave the great Charles Clayton was for another man. "Judy, there is no one else. It's just me."

She folded her arms and glared at me. "My son has sacrificed so much for his family."

"So have I," I said, stopping and matching her glare.

"I hope you know what you're doing. I hope that this isn't some midlife impulse. I hope that whatever it is you're leaving your family for brings you happiness since you're sacrificing everything."

I couldn't tell if she was being sarcastic or if she really wanted me to be happy. Regardless, I wasn't going to waste one moment trying to figure out which it was.

"Well, I better get going," I said. I zipped my suitcase, then stood, inhaled, and glanced around the room that I'd shared with my husband for the past two decades.

"Are you going to stay with him?" Judy asked.

"There is no *him*," I yelled. I took a deep breath and calmed myself because my outburst actually startled her.

"There's just me," I repeated. I grabbed my suitcase off the bed and headed down the stairs. Charles stood with his back to me looking out the living room window, a glass of bourbon in his hand. I stood for a moment, not knowing what to do or say.

"Charles," I said. My voice was soft as I approached.

His shoulders tensed to let me know he heard me. But he didn't turn around.

I shifted, fighting the urge to go hug him. "I'm sorry," I said. "I really am."

I had expected him to turn around and plead but he didn't say a word. His body just remained stiff. I glanced back up at Judy, who was standing at the top of the stairs, her arms folded, her lips pursed, hatred oozing from her pores.

I walked over and touched Charles on his shoulder since he wouldn't look at me. "I'll always love you." And still, he didn't move. I took another deep breath, and this time without looking at Judy, I turned and walked out of the room.

Chapter 18

I stood at the door of my friend's apartment, a bag of mixed emotions. You'd think that I'd be filled with remorse. But while I was sad, I wasn't remorseful.

Roxie opened the door, stepped aside, and let me in. I was greeted by Al Green belting a sorrowful tune about mending a broken heart.

"Please help me mend my broken heart and let me live again."

I cocked my head at Roxie.

"Sorry," she mumbled and raced over to change to something more upbeat.

I know Roxie had a ton of questions, but like the good best friend that she was, she'd been content with waiting on answers. She eyed my suitcase, then took it from my hand.

"Come on in. I made martinis," she said, setting the suitcase by the door. "Have a seat. I'll be right back."

I entered her spacious loft condo and sighed at the beauty of the waterfront view from the floor-to-ceiling windows. As a real estate agent, Roxie had a knack for finding rare and amazing properties, and this penthouse was no exception with its open floor plan and modern décor.

I settled on the sofa and in just a few minutes, Roxie returned with two martini glasses.

"Dirty martinis."

I took the glass, turned the entire drink up, then handed the glass back to her. Instead of saying anything, Roxie handed me her glass.

"Take this one slow," she said.

She returned to the kitchen, refilled her glass, and then walked back in the living room. She sat on the other end of the sofa.

"Do you want to talk? Or just sit here?"

"We can talk." I had called Roxie last night and told her that I needed to come stay with her for a while. I didn't get into details, but I know she assumed this was all behind a fight.

"Okay, let's start with you telling me what kind of fight would lead you over here with that." She pointed at my suitcase. "In twenty-plus years, you've never so much as spent one night away in anger."

I shrugged, a little surprised that I had no tears. "Nothing really left to say. Charles and I didn't just have a big fight. We are divorcing."

Her eyes bucked and she grabbed her martini glass like she had to keep it from toppling over. "What? Divorce?"

I nodded.

"Where did this come from?"

I took another sip of my drink. "I asked him for a divorce." I downed the rest of my drink and set the empty glass on the table.

Roxie sat forward in shock. "Oh my God. Don't tell me he was cheating. I just knew he was the last good one."

"No, it has nothing to do with another woman. There is no one else."

Roxie hesitated, frowned, then said, "Um, are you cheating?"

"No. I repeat, it has nothing to do with anyone else." It was a sad testament that people automatically assumed any couple breaking up had to be because of a third party.

I debated whether I should pour myself another drink, but my head was already pounding from how quickly I'd downed the first two drinks.

She looked at me in confusion. "Okay, if it's not someone else, then I really don't understand. Do you guys have some financial problems? With the financial gurus you both are, I would find that hard to believe, though."

I shook my head. "No, it's not that either."

"Then what in the hell . . . ?"

"It's complicated."

"Obviously." She sighed, then set her drink down. "Okay, sweetie. What's going on? What's wrong?"

I stood and began pacing across her living room floor. I needed to check my Fitbit because with the amount of pacing I'd been doing recently, I knew I had to have broken some kind of steps record.

"Well, you know how when we were in the Dominican," I began, "you guys kept asking what was wrong."

"Yes, and you stayed behind to get your head together."

"Well, I did."

"And?"

I let out a long breath. "It's just a lot."

"Okay. What's a lot, Aja? You know this isn't making sense." Roxie was getting exasperated. She scooted to the edge of the sofa.

"I told Charles I wanted out." I stared out of her floor-to-ceiling window. Maybe I could see if Roxie could find me a place like this—once I got my life together.

"But why? Why do you want out?"

"Do I have to have a why?"

"Yes," she exclaimed. "You don't throw away twenty years of marriage without a why. So you gotta help me understand this."

"You yourself have said that I lost me in them."

"When did I say that?"

"You always say that. Maybe not in those exact words, but . . ."

"Okay, maybe so. But I meant stop doing everything for them.

Pull back. I never said leave. Oh, God, if I had anything to do with you leaving Charles . . ."

I turned to face her. "This has nothing to do with you. All I know is this is something that I have to do. So can I stay here until I work this out?"

She sighed and it looked like she wanted to cry. "Of course you can, that's a given. I mean, it's a long way from your job, but if you don't mind the drive, it's cool with me."

"I'm quitting my job," I announced. I'd made that decision after the SWAT standoff with Mr. Jackson. Roxie was the first person that I'd told about my decision. If I was recharting the course of my life, I might as well go all the way.

She blinked. Sat in stunned silence for a moment. Then she blinked again.

"What do you mean, you're quitting your job? Quitting to do what?"

I released a long sigh. The dirty martinis had won. "My head is throbbing. Can I just lie down and we talk about this later?"

Roxie blew an exasperated breath. "Okay. Fine. Go lie down. Maybe when you wake up, you will have come to your senses."

⇒●⇐

I heard the voices before I opened my eyes.

"You think she caught some disease that messed with her mind? One of those bacteria diseases or something?"

"No, I think that voodoo rock lady put some kind of mumbo-jumbo spell on her."

"It's the eggplant."

"The what?"

"That fine Dominican dude that she was dancing with on her birthday. I saw the bulge in his pants. She snuck off and got some. That's what happened."

"I can hear you all," I said, groaning as my friends stood over me, whispering.

"Well, get your behind up so we can stage an intervention," Nichelle said.

I squinted, then forced back my headache. I didn't know how long I'd been asleep, but I opened my eyes to see my three friends standing over me like I was some sort of scientific experiment.

"Really?" I asked. "What time is it?"

"Nine o'clock. You've been asleep almost five hours," Roxie said.

I sat up in the bed, stretched, and looked over at Roxie, who was standing in the corner, worry all over her face.

"You called them?" I asked.

"Girl, she put out a mayday call, one of those test of the emergency broadcasting system alerts," Simone said.

"This is some serious stuff," Nichelle added. "She needed to call us, and once we get you back in your right mind, we're going to kick your behind for not telling us yourself."

I swung my legs over the bed, stood, almost lost my balance, caught myself, and then headed to the living room. "Guys, it's really not that serious."

All of them followed me.

"If you're talking about divorcing Charles, this is definitely a serious matter," Simone said.

My head wasn't pounding as much, but I knew I probably should've just had some water or something. But as I looked into the faces of my friends demanding answers, I knew water wouldn't cut it.

"You guys want some wine?" I asked. "Roxie, do you have any Stella Rosa?"

"No, we need a male for this drama. Something along the lines of Jack Daniel's or José Cuervo or something," Simone said.

"You don't even drink whiskey," I replied.

"Well, I do," Nichelle answered, heading to the cabinet where Roxie kept her liquor.

"Well, we need something strong," Simone said.

"I have tequila; I'll make some margaritas," Roxie said, moving Nichelle out of the way. "Those martinis should've worn off by now, so you'll be okay mixing drinks."

"Have a seat," Simone said, pointing to the sofa. I didn't bother to protest because I knew no one was getting out of there until I gave some answers. I plopped down on the sofa. "Okay, tell the truth," Simone continued. "Is Nichelle right? You got a taste of some eggplant from someone else's garden and you lost all good sense?"

"Don't be disgusting." I looked over to see Nichelle sifting through my purse. "Um, why are you going through my bag?"

"I'm trying to see if someone gave you some kind of drugs while you were in the DR. Some weed, some ecstasy, one of those drugs that make you think you're being attacked by mutants."

I jumped up and snatched my purse from her. "There is nothing wrong with me, other than I've just been reflecting."

Simone took a seat on the sofa. "Ooh, so this is a midlife crisis you're going through? I saw something about this on Oprah. They were talking about how men in the middle of a midlife crisis go buy cars or motorcycles. You need to go buy a Harley or something."

"No, I saw that episode," Nichelle said. "They said women get Botox or something like that when they go through a midlife crisis."

"Well, if she gets a Harley she better use it to ride her ass back home to her man," Roxie said, handing us all our drinks.

"Why?" I asked.

"Because he's a good man," Simone replied.

"Yes, because he's a frigging great man," Nichelle echoed.

"And I'm a good woman. That doesn't mean we're good for each other," I said, exasperated.

Simone shook her head. "Aja, women would kill—"

"I know," I said, cutting her off and rolling my eyes. "Women would kill to have a man like Charles on their arm. I'm so sick of people telling me that. Those women can have him."

"You're just saying that," Roxie said. "You would be sick if someone came along and was living your life."

I took a sip of my margarita and savored the liquor as it eased down my throat. It dawned on me that I had drunk more this past month than I had all year. "I don't mean to be ungrateful. I appreciate everything Charles has done and I love him. But I'm not in love with him anymore. I'm just existing. It's like Jewel said—"

"Who is Jewel?" Simone asked.

Nichelle's eyes grew wide. "That's that old voodoo lady from the Dominican. I told y'all she put some kind of spell on her."

"Nobody put anything on me," I said. "All she did was help me to reflect."

"So, leaving your husband is that crazy woman's idea?" Roxie said. "You're really going to let some kook talk you into throwing away twenty years?"

"No, she helped me to look inside to try and get to the root of what was wrong with me," I said.

"So is that why you stayed there?" Roxie asked.

"I stayed to get my head together, to make sure this wasn't a decision I was making off the seat of my pants," I replied.

"I know what it is," Nichelle said. "It's because you've lost yourself in your kids and husband. We've been telling you that for years. You do too much for them. You know how when kids are little, they would rather be pushed in their stroller, even though they know how to walk? That's your kids, and you're just tired of pushing." She nodded her head like she had just solved some great world problem.

"You may be right," I said.

"And you fix it by taking some 'me' time," Simone said. "You don't fix it by divorcing your husband."

"What did Charles say about all of this?" Roxie asked.

"He's not taking it well."

"Do the kids know?" Roxie continued pummeling me with questions.

"No."

"Good, then don't tell them," Nichelle said. "Maybe you'll come out of this madness and there won't be any point in telling them."

"Charles is understanding," Simone said. "He'll understand you're going through a midlife crisis and take you back."

"I don't want to go back." I paused, then let a revealing smile spread across my face. "I feel free," I said.

All three of my friends looked at me like I had lost all good sense. "The divorce isn't all she's lost her mind about. There's more," Roxie said.

"You mean it gets worse?" Nichelle said.

Roxie nodded like she still couldn't believe it. "She's leaving her husband *and* her job."

"What?" Nichelle and Simone said in unison.

"Are you seriously quitting your job?" Simone asked.

"I'm unfulfilled all the way around, and so what I'm trying to do is rid myself of the things that don't bring me joy."

"She's been watching Iyanla," Nichelle said, standing and heading toward the kitchen. "I told you we needed Jack for this conversation."

"Oprah is paying Iyanla's bills. Who's going to pay yours?" Simone asked. "What will you do for a living? Texas is a non-alimony state. Your kids are over eighteen, so you won't get child support. How in the world will you survive?"

"I'm going to paint," I announced.

"You already paint," Roxie said.

"No, I'm going to open a studio and really paint, just lose myself in creating. I've been thinking about this, and maybe I'll open a gallery to display some of my work; maybe even the work of other artists." Just the idea sent a flutter into my heart.

"You know you sound crazy, right?" Simone asked.

"What's crazy about finally deciding to follow my dreams? I've thought this through."

"Do paintings have calories?" Roxie asked. "I'm just wondering if that's what you plan on eating since you're quitting your job and all. And I haven't met a landlord yet who would take a painting in lieu of rent."

I hadn't thought all of that through. I had a nice savings, plus my retirement from CPS, so I had some time to try and figure everything out.

"Maybe I can teach classes until my paintings start selling."

Nichelle returned with a bottle of whiskey and an empty glass. She started pouring as she spoke. "So, let me get this straight. You're going to leave your secure job with direct deposit, your wonderful husband, your awesome life to go sit somewhere and paint?"

"Yep."

"That's the dumbest shit I ever heard." Nichelle sipped her drink.

"I don't expect you all to understand," I said, getting exasperated with my friends.

"Your painting is something you do on the side to relax," Roxie said. Her tone was soothing now, like she was trying to reason with a two-year-old.

"Only because it was relegated to a hobby. But it's my passion. Plus, you bought a piece," I said, pointing to the abstract painting of a woman playing the violin hanging on Roxie's dining room wall. She had paid me $750 for that painting.

"Because you're my best friend and I was trying to support you," Roxie said.

My lips turned up in shock. "So you don't think it's good?" I asked.

"Of course it's good. We all think you're very talented," Roxie said. "But dreams aren't always meant to become reality."

She pointed to the painting. "How much do you realistically think you can get for that? Enough to pay the note on that Range Rover?" She pointed to my purse. "Enough to buy more Chanel bags like that?"

They didn't understand. I would let all of this "stuff" go if it meant inner peace.

"So where are you going to live while you . . ." Nichelle made air quotes, "pursue your painting passion?"

I looked over at Roxie.

"Of course you can stay here as long as you need," Roxie sighed. "But painting, Aja, really?"

"It's the eggplant. I'm sure of it," Simone said, shaking her head.

"I'm about to look on Google how to get rid of spells," Nichelle added, picking up her phone.

"You don't have to accept it; I just ask that you support me," I said.

They all stared at me for a few minutes. Finally Roxie said, "Fine. You know that we have your back. We love you, and when you can't pay your bills in three months, we will take up a collection to buy you some groceries."

That made us all laugh.

Chapter 19

This had been both the best week and the worst week of my life. I felt more at peace than I had in years. But hearing the pain in my husband's voice kept me from fully rejoicing in my newfound freedom.

The melancholy tone of his voice on his call last Saturday had haunted me.

"I'm praying God will bring you back to me, but for now, I am going to honor your wish and let you go," he'd said. He hadn't even given me time to respond, just said, "I love you to infinity," then hung up the phone.

Five days and he'd held true to his word. Five days and I hadn't spoken to Charles. My husband was hurting and it broke my heart.

But I'd never move forward if I kept thinking about his pain. I was on the verge of getting all I ever wanted, and that needed to be my focus.

I pledged that I was going to have a shift in thinking as I pulled into the parking lot of the building I'd come to see. My girls had been right. I needed more of a plan than just going somewhere to paint. I'd done some research and the idea of opening a gallery was seeming more and more plausible. So for the past two weeks, I'd been scouting properties and this one was it. It had been love at first sight when I saw the listing online. And seeing it in person two days ago, it was love at second sight. The owner had been out, but her assistant had shown me around, and the minute I stepped foot inside, I knew this was it.

It was an old quilting shop. I saw beyond the mountains of yarn and took in the aged hardwood floor. I'd do a special coating to keep paint from messing it up. It was spacious but cozy at the same time. Plus, the location was perfect, near the Galleria, but off away from the congestion of traffic. That's when I shot Roxie a text.

Can you look into this property for me? This will be perfect for me! I want to put in an offer!

I sent her the address and phone number, and within seconds she was sending back to me a reply.

Perfect for what?

My business, I typed.

So, you're serious? she replied.

I am. And I sent a smiley face image.

It took a moment, and then, finally *OK* popped up on my screen.

Roxie had done her job, negotiated a lease-to-own because I wasn't in a position to outright buy just yet, and taken the first step to make my dream come true.

I'd made it a point to drive by daily because it had become a source of inspiration. Today, though, as I stared at the building for the umpteenth time, I started to question myself.

Could I really do this? Could I really follow my passion?

I inhaled and then exhaled the negative thoughts. Not only could I, I was going to. I smiled and started the car up and continued the trek to my house.

I purposely waited until Charles was gone so that I could go and get some more of my things. I knew at some point we'd have to sit down and work everything out. I wasn't completely crazy. I couldn't give him everything, but I was going to be more than fair and only request enough for me to survive on. As long as Anika and Eric were taken care of, I was happy. Not that Charles wouldn't take care of his kids, but I had heard horror stories about men doing complete 360s after their divorce.

I pulled into my driveway, grateful that Judy's car was gone as well.

As I stepped inside, I took a moment to glance around the house. I saw the marks on the dining room door frame where Eric tracked his growth spurt. The summer he turned fourteen, he'd grown four inches in three months. I looked at the crack in the end table that Anika had done when she was bouncing a ball in the house, and that brought a smile to my face. Then my eyes made their way up the wall, to Anika's and Eric's photos from preschool, to middle school, to graduation. So many memories. I'd spent more than fifteen years here, but yet, suddenly it didn't feel like home.

I dropped my keys and purse on the end table and made my way up the stairs, halfway expecting to see all of my stuff already packed and sitting in a corner. But the room was just as I had left it. I opened the closet and pulled out one of my Tumi suitcases, wheeled it into the bathroom, and started loading some of my toiletries in. A part of me knew that Charles hadn't touched any of my things because he had hoped I would come back home.

After I'd gotten most of my things loaded into my suitcase, I paused at the photo on my nightstand. It was from the night Charles received an award for his reporting. The night that he'd proposed. A night that I'd always thought was the greatest night of my life.

"And for his special report, 'Rockets Revealed,' the Peabody Award for Outstanding Sports Reporting goes to Charles Clayton with KTRK, Channel 13." The announcer held up the gold statuette as Charles stood and made his way to the podium. The audience erupted in applause. I was beaming with

excitement. I glanced over at Mrs. Clayton, who looked like a proud mother hen. Roxie and Brian sat on the other side of me, along with some people from Charles's station. Everyone rose to their feet clapping until Charles finally accepted the award. I felt like crying. But this time, from joy. Charles had put a lot of work into that story, which chronicled the lives of four Houston Rockets players from boyhood to the NBA. He had won three Emmys before, but this was his first time winning the prestigious Peabody Award.

"Thank you." Charles's voice quieted the audience, and they began easing back into their seats. Charles gave a quick speech, then cleared his throat.

"Before I go, I have to thank the special person in my life who encouraged me to fight to get this story told. Aja James, will you please stand up?"

I looked around nervously. What was Charles doing? I hadn't expected to become the center of attention and felt frozen in my seat.

"Girl, stand your behind up," Roxie whispered.

I eased out of my chair and forced a small wave at the crowd. I was going to get Charles for this. I tried to slink back down in my chair, but under the table Roxie hit me in the leg.

"Don't sit down yet," Roxie muttered.

What is going on? I wondered.

"Let me first apologize to everyone," Charles continued. "I have talked with Jim and the other organizers of tonight's event, and they've given me the go-ahead, so I'll ask that you bear with me for a minute."

Charles cleared his throat, then began walking toward me. The spotlight followed him as he made his way back to our table. I turned toward Roxie, a bewildered look on my face. Roxie just shrugged and started stirring her coffee. Charles stopped in front of the table and kissed his mother on the cheek. She gave him a reassuring smile as he handed her his *award. Charles turned toward me and looked me straight in the eye. The room was silent and all eyes were on us.*

"Charles, what are you doing?" I whispered.

"Be quiet, girl. You talk too much," Mrs. Clayton said, but with a genuine smile.

Charles quickly shot his mother an admonishing look before turning back to me. He gently took my hand, then eased down on his left knee. When the reality of what he was about to do set in, I felt my heart begin to race.

"Oh my God," I muttered.

Charles ignored the trembling that had suddenly taken over my hand. "Aja, you satisfy me mentally, emotionally, and spiritually. I believe God has a divine plan for all of our lives, and a special person he wants us to share that plan with. Someone to complete our purpose on this earth. You are my completion." Charles reached in his jacket pocket and pulled out a small box. He opened the box to reveal a glistening three-carat pear-shaped diamond ring. "Aja Jenine James, will you marry me?"

I fingered the ring that had seldom left my finger for the last two decades. Charles had been a dream then. He'd been the reason that I'd begun the task of forgiving my father.

"I don't deserve you."

I'd broken it off with Charles and yet, when my brother died, he was right by my side.

"You know that's crazy, right? If anybody deserves happiness, it's you."

"That's the same thing Roxie said." I managed a weak smile. We'd just put my brother in the ground and it had been the hardest day of my life.

"Well, Roxie was right." Charles took my hand again. "Aja,

I don't want it to be over. I love you with all my heart. I just want you to love me back."

"I do, but—"

Charles put his index finger to my lips. "See, it's that 'but' part that I have a problem with. But—you can't give me all your heart."

"I—"

"No, let me finish," Charles interrupted. "You can't give me all your heart because it's too filled with hate. You can't love me because you can't love yourself. You can't forgive yourself or your father. Aja, you were sixteen. What could you have done?"

I felt the tears welling up. I stood and moved away from Charles. "You just don't understand."

Charles reached up and took my hand to pull me back down on the bed. "I do, Aja. That's what you don't understand, I do. Eric fought for your mother, Jada fought for your mother. And you have had a lifetime of guilt because you didn't. But if you had, it wouldn't have made a difference. I don't ever want you to let Jada or the memory of Eric go, but I want—no, I need—for you to let the past go. Let it go, so we can move on."

"If only I could've been the woman you deserved," I mumbled as I slid the ring off my finger and put it on Charles's nightstand. One day, I hoped that he could forgive me. I would always be grateful for his love.

That was my last thought as I closed our bedroom door—and the door to our marriage.

Chapter 20

"Aja!"

I heard what sounded like screaming. I couldn't tell from the blaring music but I turned around anyway and saw Roxie standing in her living room, staring at me like I was crazy.

"Hey, Roxie," I yelled over the music.

She walked over, picked up my iPhone, tapped the screen, and the room went silent.

"Barbra Streisand. Really?" she said.

I laughed. "I happen to love this Barbra Streisand song."

"I see, and you love it at seventy-five decibels as well." She glanced around her apartment at all my empty canvases and various containers of paint that were strewn about. I had been testing out some new color patterns and was just about to start a new painting.

"So, three days ago when I left to catch my plane to Dallas, you were sad because you moved out for good," she continued. "Now you are in here jamming Streisand and dancing around my living room, having your own private party. You want to tell me what's going on?"

I flashed a smile. "I'm painting."

"Yeah. I see that." She looked around some more. Her apartment had probably never been this messy. I'd lost track of the time or I would've cleaned up before she returned.

"Where's the weed?" Roxie asked. "You know I don't like drugs in my house."

"What?" I asked. "What are you talking about?"

"I was just wondering if you were in here getting high or something," she said.

I chuckled. "I'm high on life," I told her.

"Okay. No drugs." She looked over at my wineglass sitting on the coffee table. "How many of those have you had?"

"That's my only one."

"Well, have you been drinking coffee? Are you pumped up on caffeine?" she asked.

"I hadn't had coffee since I left home," I announced.

"What?" She looked at me in disbelief. I was a coffee addict, so I knew that caught her by surprise.

I shrugged and started picking up some of my mess. "I don't know. I just went cold turkey, and it's like I don't need it."

She must have realized that she was still holding her designer duffel bag because she finally set it down and tossed her keys on the bar.

"Wow, this is a real change from just a few days ago," she said.

I stopped cleaning and turned serious. "I'm not going to lie, I feel awful about what I did to Charles. I never want him to feel like I didn't love him. I did and I do. But I'm loving myself more than I love anyone else right now, you know what I mean? I had a pity party for about twenty-four hours after you left, but then I decided to put on my big-girl panties and toss the guilt I was feeling. I mean, I hate everything going on in my personal life, but once I let go of the guilt, I have never felt such peace."

She stared at me for a moment and finally said, "Wow. And I have to admit that I've never seen you look more peaceful."

My hand went to my heart. Roxie had no idea how it felt to hear her say that. "I'm glad you get it."

She nodded. "I didn't, but I do now. I've never seen you like this."

A huge smile spread across my face again. "I've never felt like this, Roxie. I can't explain it. I know that I'm going to have to break it to Eric and Anika and I know that's going to be difficult, but I'm prepared. And I know filing paperwork and all of that is going to be heartbreaking, but this is what I need." I swung around à la Mary Poppins. "I feel free."

"Well, more good news," she said. "I heard back from the owner of the quilting shop. Everything is a go, and if you're okay, I'll email you the papers tonight to sign and you can wire the deposit.

"You know I've been thinking about this," Roxie continued. "When Eric died, I worried so much about you. You poured yourself in him and you know I told you I don't think you ever properly grieved, but I was thinking about this. Not only did you not grieve, you jumped from pouring into him to pouring into Charles."

"Exactly," I said. "Then it was the kids who got all of me. I just want to now finally pour into me."

She gave me a hug. "I'm sorry for trying to talk you out of this. I just want you to be happy."

I squeezed her and said, "And I am. This makes me happy. My gallery will be my happy place."

She shook her head. "I'm still not with this whole gallery idea, but you do you. If you're happy, I'm happy."

"Thank you."

She picked up the bottle of wine off the bar.

"Let me pour me a glass of wine so we can really get this party started."

Chapter 21

My foot pressed down gently on the accelerator. I didn't want to take the chance of going any faster than forty miles per hour or else I was sure that my head would throb even more. I didn't feel all that well; I was nursing a wine hangover after Roxie and I polished off two bottles of Moscato last night. But while my head pulsed, my heart sang. It was because of our talk. Now that I'd had the chance to explain all of my plans to Roxie, it was great to have my best friend's unwavering support, even though she didn't agree with all of my decisions. She was down with me leaving Charles, but she wasn't so sure about quitting my job.

"I'm all for you pursuing this new life, but I'm telling you that direct deposit is the truth. You need to keep getting that paycheck while you work on your dream."

"But if I do that, I'll be treating my painting like a hobby and it will stay that way. No," I told her, "I'm either in or out. I'm going to do this or I'm not. I have money saved. I'll be okay. I figured I can make it a year at least before the gallery turns a profit."

In the end, my passion trumped her good sense, and she came to believe that I would be able to make it work on my faith alone.

As I exited the freeway, I smiled through the pain of my throbbing head. For the first time since this ordeal began, I was genuinely excited about what was to come—as uncertain as it seemed to be right now.

First up—my job.

That was my thought as I turned into the parking lot of my office complex.

"Hello, Mrs. Clayton," the security guard said as I slowed my car at the gate. "I haven't seen you in a while."

"Hey, Darryl, I've been on leave," I said, flashing a smile as he approached my car. I had to divert my eyes from his belly because his buttons on his two-sizes-too-small uniform were screaming for my help.

"Everything okay?" He peered into my car, standard procedure now that the crazies had started coming up to our offices. "I heard about the SWAT standoff that you had to go through last month."

"Yes, that situation could've definitely ended badly for me. But by the grace of God, it didn't."

"Yes, ma'am." He nodded at my mention of the Lord. "God definitely protects his angels. Well, you have a nice day." He waved me on through.

I weaved up and down the aisles. With all the cars in the parking lot, anyone walking in here would have thought that we had more than enough caseworkers to handle our load. But we'd have to triple our workforce to ever meet the needs of all the foster and abused children in Houston.

After finding a space, I sat in my car for an extra moment. What I was about to do was huge, and I was bursting with this news. But since I respected Karen so much, I hadn't told anyone else outside of my girls. I didn't want anyone in my workplace to know this news before I told my boss that my personal leave was about to turn into permanent leave.

As I took the path from the parking lot to my building, then to my office, I tried to remember every step of this last mile. In the threshold of my office, I paused and took in the sight that had been my home for more than two decades. The first thing that everyone noticed were the photos. Just like at home, pictures of Eric and Anika at every stage of their lives adorned my desk and bookshelf. But after the photos and a few plants, this office was all about work. There were folders upon folders of family cases sitting on top of my desk and filling the file cabinets. Some of the folders had happy endings; most did not.

Walking inside, I settled into my chair and swiveled around, taking in the 360-degree view. When I'd taken this job, my hope had been to save the world. I hadn't done that, but I'd been able to save lots of children in Houston. The only challenge was that this place, like my marriage, had sucked the me out of me.

"No more," I mumbled as I took a deep breath, pushed myself up, then grabbed the envelope from my tote before I made the march down the hall to Karen's office.

Her door was open as she tapped on her computer. I rapped on her door twice, then said, "Hi, Karen."

She looked up and grinned. Her shoulders relaxed as if she were happy to see me. "Hey, Aja. Welcome back. Come on in." She waved to me, then turned back to her keyboard. "Give me a minute. Just finishing this report."

I walked in and took a seat in front of her desk, which was just as cluttered with folders as mine.

"Is this something quick?" She glanced at me but continued typing. "I don't want to keep you sitting here. I know you're ready to jump right into work. There's a lot waiting for you."

It probably would have been better if I waited for Karen to finish, but then I asked myself why? I had come into the office so that I could get out. So after another breath, I said, "I'm sorry to do this to you since I know how short-staffed we already are, but . . ." I reached inside the manila envelope, pulled out a piece of paper, and slid it across her desk toward her. "I am regretfully submitting my resignation."

She stopped, her fingers frozen in midair. She swiveled her

chair toward me slowly, giving me all of her attention now. "Your resignation?" she asked. The shock was in her voice as she picked up the paper.

While her eyes scanned the document, I said, "I have been a social worker for twenty-two years, and it's just time for me to try something new."

"But," she shook her head, "you're one of the best directors I have. I mean, you're next in line for my job," Karen exclaimed.

If she thought that was a motivator, she just didn't know. The thought of that alone made my stomach turn. Karen didn't even want her own job. "I understand that," I told her, rather than telling her "hell no." "But this job is no longer what's best for me. My heart is simply not in it anymore."

She sat for a moment, looking at me, then looking at the letter, then back at me, then back to the letter. It was like she was searching to understand. "Do you have a new job?" she finally asked.

"I don't," I replied. "I mean, I don't have a job working for another company. I plan to open my own business." Then, with an extra bit of pride, I added, "An art gallery."

I couldn't be sure, but it seemed like a flash of envy crossed her face. "Wow."

"I know people really don't buy art like that anymore," I continued, "so I don't want to solely do that. But I'll showcase some of my work, others and various kinds of art."

Her eyes widened a bit and now, her blue eyes looked green for sure. "Wow. I thought that painting thing was just a hobby."

I nodded. "It's never been a hobby for me. I just never had time for it."

She nodded. "Must be nice. You gotta have a rich husband for that."

There were lots of things I could have said, but I just smiled. Karen was a friend, but I wasn't about to let her in on my business like that.

"So I know I'm on personal leave for another week and I still have about a month of vacation and sick time that I've accrued, but if you need me . . ." I let my words trail off because I really didn't want to come back for any reason. But I wanted her to think that I wouldn't leave her out there like that.

She leaned back in her chair and waved her hand. "Girl, I wouldn't do that to you. This workload," she gestured to the files on her desk, "isn't going anywhere."

I breathed with relief.

Then she added, "I can't say I'm surprised. I imagine that it was hard for you to even consider coming back after that SWAT standoff."

"I'm okay. But you're right. That day was definitely kind of the final straw for me."

"Well, I understand." She slid my letter back into the envelope and placed it in a bin on her desk. She sighed. "I don't like it, but I understand."

When she smiled, we stood and hugged. "Thank you for understanding."

"Here's to the next chapter of your life."

I gave her another quick hug. She just had no idea.

I was on Cloud Ten because Nine just wouldn't do. Turning in my resignation had been like the final chain that I needed to break free. And for the first time in years, I felt so happy that I almost skipped back to my office.

Right when I was packing up my office, the owner of the quilting shop called me back and said my leasing application had been approved and she really wanted to meet me. I felt like the universe was aligning all the stars. Now I knew what Jewel was talking about, because as I walked through the building with the owner, I finally felt like I had a purpose—for me.

"So, isn't this property great?" she asked.

"It's perfect," I said to the petite white-haired woman who was showing what I hoped would soon be my happy place.

"I'm retiring and moving across country to be near my grandchildren, so I'm excited about closing this deal."

"I remember passing this place two years ago and thinking it was in a perfect location," I told her, though I left out how I had quickly nixed that dream then because I was a social worker who had let her dreams die.

"I know you're going to be very happy leasing this building," she continued, then her eyes glanced down to my wedding ring. "Do you need to schedule a time to bring your husband back?"

That thought gave me pause. For twenty years, I'd discussed everything with Charles. I didn't make a decision without Charles's input. But this was all on me.

"No, I talked with my real estate agent who told me it was a great property and an awesome deal, hence the reason we quickly put the application in."

"That it is," she said with a smile. "I stand by that."

I returned her smile. "So then, how can I let it go?"

She studied me for a minute, then said, "You can always find the level of someone's joy by looking in their eyes. Your eyes sing with joy. I'm hoping when I get down with my grandkids, I'll have that."

My smile faded just a bit. "I'm still working on it."

"Well, I wish you all the best." She handed me some papers. "I'm old-fashioned. I know this stuff is all digital now, but I'm not up with the times, so take these and have your Realtor look over them. And if everything is in order, you can wire the deposit to my accountant because I don't fool with that stuff. And then you can pick up the keys next week."

I held the paperwork close to my heart. "This is a dream come true."

"You'll have to send me pictures of the place when you're up and running. I'll be in Florida enjoying my grandkids."

We shook hands and I had to struggle to contain my excitement as I floated on air back to my car. Inside, I shouted, then revved up the engine. Before I backed out, I cued up Lil Duval's "Living My Best Life," set it on repeat, then blasted the song through the speakers. Satisfied, I pulled out of the parking lot, my mind filled with all the things I would do with the studio.

As I pulled onto 610, I was filled with such excitement, I just couldn't wait to share this news. I was really doing it, this was happening. And I couldn't wait to tell . . . Roxie! She would want to know I had paperwork in hand.

Gripping the wheel, I bobbed my head and sang, "Living my best life . . ."

I grinned as I began my text: *I did it!* Then, I looked up. All safe. The next part: *The gallery . . .* I glanced up again. The midday traffic was light, so I finished my text: *is coming.* Glancing up again, I was about to toss my phone back onto the passenger seat, but then, I looked down and added three exclamation points.

That made me laugh out loud as I tossed the phone onto the passenger's seat.

Then . . . I looked up.

And a black SUV was in my lane, at least half of it was, right in front of me, cutting me off.

"Ah!" I screamed as I gripped the wheel and swerved to avoid the collision.

The SUV clipped the front of my car, sending me spinning, spinning, then crashing into the guardrail.

"Oh, God," I screamed as the car took flight and time . . . slowed . . . down. I floated, or maybe the better word was glided in the air, though it was amazing that I was having all of these thoughts. In this split second of time, in the air, I opened my mouth to scream, but tears filled my throat.

Then . . . my car bounced.

And flipped and flipped, then spun and spun until finally . . . it came to a stop.

I was dizzy in the quiet, felt delirious in the stillness. I blinked and tried to lift my head to see where I was.

And that was when I saw it . . . a royal blue Mustang speeding toward me. It slammed into me—sent me spinning again, and I felt myself careening off the embankment and onto the feeder road. It was too late to scream, too late to cry, it was even too late to have any real fear. I only had time to close my eyes and pray that when I opened them again, I'd see the face of God.

Chapter 22

*W*ould *God be calling me sweetheart?*

"Hello. Sweetheart, can you hear me?"

That's strange. I always imagined God's voice to be deeper.

"Sweetie, please wake up."

That wasn't God. That was . . . Charles. I battled to blink, struggled to move. Everything on my body ached.

"Please, baby. Please come back to us."

There was a desperation in Charles's voice. I heard whimpering and crying, which had to be my children. I'd know those cries anywhere. I tried to move to let my family know that I could hear them. I willed my eyes to open, but it was as if my brain couldn't connect the message to my body.

"Doctor, it's been . . . it's been two weeks. When will she wake up?"

An unrecognizable voice said, "As I've told you every day, she's lucky to be alive at all. That accident would've instantly killed most people, but Mrs. Clayton appears to be a fighter. Her vitals are stable and the worst is over. Now we just have to be patient."

I heard more sobbing and crying and I made out Anika's voice. "But, Dr. Hubbard, what if she doesn't wake up?"

Dr. Hubbard said, "Look, I know this is difficult but what your mother needs now is just your support. She's going to pull through this. I'm very encouraged by her vitals."

I was still struggling to connect my brain to my vocal cords and it took all kind of energy, but I felt the grunt that came out my mouth. "Ugh."

"Oh my God. Mom. Mom."

"Mrs. Clayton," the doctor said as I kept fighting to open my eyes. "Mrs. Clayton, can you hear me? This is Dr. Hubbard, your internal specialist." I felt someone lifting my arm. "If you can hear me, I need you to squeeze my hand."

He put his hand in mine, and once again it took effort, but I was able to squeeze it.

"Oh my God. She moved," I heard Anika say.

"Yes, she did," Dr. Hubbard replied. I could hear the smile in his voice.

I felt my eyelid open and a light filled my eye.

"Yep, her pupils are dilated," Dr. Hubbard said. "I'd say your mother is on her way back."

"Thank you, Jesus," Charles said.

I felt arms wrap around me and I finally willed my eyes to open. "Ugh," I said again. "Wh-what h-happened?" My voice was hoarse and sore, like someone had taken sandpaper and just run it up and down my throat.

"Honey, you were in a bad accident," Charles said, stroking my hair as everything slowly came into focus.

"We thought we'd lost you," Anika said, lying on my chest and sobbing, though not as hard as before.

"Yeah, Mom, we've been scared you were gonna die." Eric eased up behind his sister.

I blinked as visions of the black SUV and the royal blue Mustang filled my head . . . then careening off the embankment. My God. I couldn't believe I was alive.

"I-I'm okay?" I managed to ask. I must've sounded funny because Charles lifted a glass and straw to my mouth and I took a sip, though it seemed to be the hardest thing I'd ever done. But my mouth immediately felt better.

"Yes, you are just fine," Dr. Hubbard said, placing the stethoscope against my chest. He listened for a moment, then stood back. "Nice, steady heartbeat. Wonderful." He checked the machine and nodded his approval. "Well, I'm going to give you a moment with your family. Then I'll come back so we can run some tests. But, Mrs. Clayton, you're a very lucky woman."

I struggled to sit up but Charles stopped me. "Here, I'll raise your bed but don't move." He pushed a button that lifted my torso, giving me a better view of my family.

Anika's eyebrows furrowed as she clutched my hand as if she never wanted to let it go. "Mom, the police said you were texting and driving. You fussed at us about texting and driving since we first got our license."

"I know," I said, the memories racing back to me. "It . . . it was just a second."

"That's all it takes," Anika said, repeating my mantra throughout their high school years.

I looked over to see Judy in the corner of the room. I don't think that I'd ever seen her look so worried.

"Hello, Aja," she said, easing up on the side of my bed. "How are you feeling?"

"Like I was hit by a Mack truck," I managed to say.

"You were hit several times, so this is nothing but the grace of God." The gentleness in her words surprised me, but I welcomed them.

My voice was slowly returning and it was less of a struggle to speak. "How . . . how long have I been out?" I tried to sit upright again, but the pain immediately stopped me.

"No, no, baby," Charles said, coming to my aid. He gently pushed my shoulders back down. "Just lie there and rest."

"Yes," Judy said. "We have everything taken care of. You just recover."

I fell back against the pillow. "How . . . how long have I been here?"

"Two weeks. It's been the worst two weeks of my life," Charles said.

"All of ours," Eric repeated.

My son was the spitting image of his father. He'd grown into a handsome young man, but right now, he looked like a scared little boy.

"Why aren't you," I had to pause to catch my breath, "you . . . two in school?"

"Really, Mom?" Anika said. Her eyes were puffy like she'd had two weeks of nonstop crying.

"We were scared we were going to lose you. How were we supposed to concentrate on school?" Eric added.

"Eric . . . basketball . . ."

"Basketball will be there," he replied, taking my hand. "I wouldn't have been able to concentrate anyway."

The thought of what my family had been through the past two weeks broke my heart. I can only imagine the fear they must've been feeling.

Charles stepped up. "Well, your mother is out of the woods. So you both need to get back to school."

I could see them both about to protest, but luckily, Charles continued. "We'll talk about it later. Right now, we just want to get your mother home, nurse her back to health, and return our lives back to normal."

That's when it dawned on me. Home wasn't my home anymore. My normal was different. What in the world was I supposed to do now?

I had to figure this out. I managed to sit up, but then a wave of panic swept over me.

"Oh, Jesus," I cried, my eyes widening in horror.

"What's wrong?" Charles asked.

I looked up at my husband, my heart racing as I said, "I can't feel my legs!"

Chapter 23

The day that I couldn't feel my legs turned into a month without feeling—the most grueling month of my life. I watched the winter weather give way to spring sunshine and my body refused to return to normal.

What Dr. Hubbard and my family hadn't told me that day I came to in the hospital was just how bad off I had been. I had shattered my vertebra in the accident, and pieces of it had been embedded in my spinal cord. I also had a ruptured bladder. The pain—from the waist up—was unlike anything I'd ever felt.

"At best, you'll probably spend a year in the wheelchair. I wish I had better news, but we have to be realistic. You may not ever walk again," Dr. Hubbard had told me the day I'd been discharged to the inpatient rehab facility. "Honestly, your spinal cord is seventy percent compromised, and individuals with that diagnosis typically spend the rest of their lives in a wheelchair."

The rest of my life. The life that I'd been trying to reinvent.

I'd cried for days—refusing to get out of bed and participate in rehab. But when the therapist had told me I would have to leave so they could give my spot to someone who really wanted to get better, I had dried my tears and tried to figure out how to become the exception to his rule. I'm glad the therapists wouldn't indulge my pity party because within two weeks, I'd learned to roll over, get in and out of bed, and maneuver myself into and out of my wheelchair. I'd surprised the doctors and, though I was borderline depressed, I stayed committed to pushing myself.

It was hard to stay motivated, though, because despite the hard work, I still couldn't walk.

"Just be patient," Charles had told me. He was there with me every single day. He'd taken a leave of absence from work and often slept on the hard pullout in my room. I don't even know how he finagled that because guests weren't supposed to spend the night at the rehab facility. I was sure Charles had flashed his award-winning smile to get the nurses to look the other way.

But it was easy for him to urge me to be patient. He wasn't the invalid.

It's crazy how we take the little things for granted. Never in my life did I think that I would be unable to walk.

I did get feeling back in my right side, but not enough to propel one foot in front of the other.

I was back home now, and supposed to continue my physical therapy, but being here, the place I'd run from, had made me lose all motivation.

Right now, though, all I wanted was to walk across this bedroom, get my toothbrush and toothpaste, and brush my own damn teeth. I stood and demanded my legs propel me toward the bathroom. My legs didn't listen, and I plopped back down in the wheelchair. I hated this wheelchair. In my dad's final days, I'd seen his anguish about having to be in a wheelchair. I didn't spend a lot of time with him. Jada had been his caregiver when he got sick from prostate cancer, but when I was there, I felt his frustration. I had no idea it was this bad.

"Damn," I said, hitting the door frame as I tried to navigate the chair through the guest bathroom door. It had taken a full-fledged temper tantrum to convince Charles to let me stay in the guest bedroom, but I couldn't take his constant words of encouragement. It felt like all talk. I knew he meant well, but I was throwing a certified pity party and positivity wasn't welcome.

"I need you near me," he'd said when I first told him that I wanted to stay in the guest room.

"This just makes more sense. It's downstairs and more accessible for me," I replied.

I also didn't want to complicate things by going back into our bed. Though, according to the doctor, this disability was my life, I hadn't resolved that just yet.

"The guest bed is just more comfortable," I added, hoping he bought my excuse. Thankfully, he did and stopped fighting me on it.

I was up this morning trying my best to get up and move. I know that I had come a long way from the day I left the hospital. But still, navigating our non-handicap accessible house had proven to be difficult. Today, however, for some reason, I was determined to brush my teeth on my own.

It took me about eight minutes, but I managed to stand from the wheelchair.

"Yes," I mumbled. I had started trying to give myself verbal reinforcement. I massaged my right leg. The feeling had come back there before I left the hospital, so I had been able to strengthen it. The left side, however, had no desire to keep up and I remained weak.

I gripped the door frame and dragged my nonworking leg as I navigated my way over to the sink. I wanted to cry tears of joy when I finally reached the sink and toothbrush. I took a deep breath, surprised at how tired I was just from that small effort. I managed to get the toothpaste and was just squeezing it out of the tube when I lost my balance. I wobbled, willed my legs to work—to no avail—then hit the floor. Tears streamed down my face because no matter how much I tried, I couldn't get up.

"Charles," I called out. "Charles."

Anika came running in first. She and Eric had gone back to school, though both had wanted to take a hiatus for the rest of the semester. They both still worried me daily with calls. I was glad they weren't here. Charles's doting was smothering enough. I didn't mean to be ungrateful, but I was mad at myself for being in this position. I knew better than texting and driving. Roxie preached to me about it. I preached to my kids about it. And yet, I hadn't practiced what I preached.

Though she'd returned to school, Anika been coming home every other weekend since my accident. I could only imagine what our travel bill looked like. "Mom. Oh my God. Are you okay?"

"Yes. I just fell," I said.

"Dad!" she screamed.

It sounded like a one-bull stampede as Charles ran down the hall. "Oh no. What happened?" he asked as he burst into the room.

"Mom fell," Anika cried. She stood over me like she was scared to touch me, then finally knelt down and slid her arms under mine.

"Ow," I said as she struggled to lift me up. Charles came over on the other side, and together the two of them lifted me up and back into my chair.

"Aja, what are you doing? What were you thinking?" Charles said. His voice was filled with panicked worry.

"I just wanted to brush my teeth," I cried.

"You know you're not supposed to be moving without somebody here," he said.

"I told you it wasn't a good idea for her to be in this room alone."

I looked up to my mother-in-law standing in the doorway to the bathroom, shaking her head in condemnation.

"Mom, we have it," Charles said as he made sure I was situated okay in the wheelchair. "Babe, you gotta let me take care of you. You could have been seriously hurt." He eased my wheelchair back out of the room.

"I just want to lie down," I said, fighting back the river of tears that was threatening to crest.

"Come on," he said.

I expected him to wheel me back over to the bed, but instead he took a right and headed out of the bedroom door.

"Charles, what are you doing?" I asked.

He ignored me as he continued pushing my chair.

"Charles, stop," I said.

He still didn't say a word as he wheeled me down the hall and to the foot of the stair. Then he swooped me up out of the wheelchair and carried me up the stairs to our bedroom.

"This isn't open for debate," he said, opening the double doors to our bedroom. "You could have been seriously injured. You're coming back into our bed."

"Charles . . ." I said.

He was carrying me like I was a rag doll. He gently laid me onto our bed. I cried silent tears as he tucked me in. Then he disappeared. He came back with the little container that I brush my teeth with and my electric toothbrush with the toothpaste on it. He handed it to me.

"And this is what you've been trying to do? You see how easy it is to just let me do it? Why is it so difficult for you to let someone else take care of you for a change?"

I took the toothbrush and brushed my teeth. Then he handed me a small cup of water. I gargled and spat into the plastic basin as he handed me a towel to wipe my mouth.

"Now I'm going to get your breakfast, call for them to send a nurse to check you out, and you're going to sit here," he moved the remote next to me, "and relax until the nurse gets here." He turned and left the room like there was nothing else left for discussion.

Anika stood staring at me. "Mom, what is going on with you and Dad?" she asked.

"What are you talking about, sweetheart?"

"I don't know. It just seems different. And then Grandma is really mad at you."

"Your grandmother is always mad at me," I said, exasperated. This whole situation had just worn me out.

"No, this is unlike anything I've ever seen. I heard her on the phone with Aunt Jean," she said, referring to Judy's sister.

"You know your grandmother is always gossiping."

She sat down on the edge of the bed. "Mom, I know you think I'm still a child, but I'm an adult now."

"Does that mean I can turn the cell phone bill over to you?" I chuckled, trying to ease the tension.

"I'm not kidding."

"Me either," I said with a smile.

Anika blew an exasperated breath. "Mom, will you be serious? What's going on?"

Her expression tugged at my heart. I took a deep breath. Charles would be devastated if I had this conversation with Anika without talking to him first, especially now that I honestly didn't know what was going to happen to us. If I didn't get better, I would need to stay here for Charles to take care of me.

The thought made my stomach scrunch up into knots.

"Your dad and I are going through some things, that's all," I said.

She nodded like I was just confirming what she already knew. "Are you two getting a divorce?"

"Look, let's not talk about this, okay?"

"Mom . . ."

I squeezed my daughter's hand. "Your dad's right. I'm just going to lie here and get some rest."

"Mom, I don't know what's going on, but you see how much Daddy loves you. So, whatever it is, I hope that you guys will fix it."

I couldn't reply to my daughter because I didn't know what to say. I loved her daddy, but despite my current situation, I couldn't say that I wanted to fix anything.

Chapter 24

I was sick of watching *Family Feud*, talk shows, and CNN. I was sick of being in this room and was now teetering between being depressed and being distraught. What happened to the story I was rewriting? The new chapter of my life? Instead I was stuck in this stupid wheelchair in a home with my mother-in-law giving me the evil eye. Yeah, all that concern Judy had had in the hospital was long gone. She acted like she resented Charles taking care of me.

And my husband was taking care of me. He'd set aside all of the hurt that I had delivered to him on a silver platter before my accident and he tried to nurture and love me past my pain—the physical and the mental.

Every day since I'd been home, I was reminded of how much Charles loved me.

But despite my accident, despite his caregiving, that love no longer felt like enough.

All the joy I'd felt prior to my accident had been stripped away, and now each day was just another day trying to heal.

My husband walked into the living room and handed me a cup of tea. "Here you go," he said.

I took the cup as he adjusted the afghan across my lap. He moved the remote on the tray table closer to me and said, "Are you comfortable? You need anything else?" Then he flashed a grin.

A horrible thought crossed my mind. What if Charles didn't want me getting better? Maybe he liked seeing me as an invalid, confined to this chair and dependent on him. When I was in the rehab facility, I'd asked him to call the lady from the quilting shop and explain what happened and pay up for several months. I didn't want to lose out on the building. He'd agreed—but only after trying to convince me that I didn't need to be thinking about that.

I shook away that thought. My husband wanted his wife, but I'm sure he didn't want me like this. "Thank you," I said, taking a sip of the tea.

Charles stared at me for a few minutes. "How are you feeling?" he asked.

I shrugged but didn't reply.

"I know that this is all difficult for you." He kneeled so that we were face-to-face. "But you will get through this. I see drastic changes already. And you know that I'm here for you." He took my hand and kissed it. "I'll always be here for you."

My hand rose and caressed his face. I sighed. I would forever love this man.

"Charles . . ." I began.

"I know. I know everything we have been through," he said, cutting me off. "But just know that I understand that you were going through some things, a serious midlife crisis. But God has a way of working things out on His own. He brought us back together."

That comment caught me a little off guard and I pulled my hand back. "So, God almost killed me so we could be together?"

"Come on, babe. You know I didn't mean it like that."

I sighed and then took a sip of my tea. I didn't want to get into it with Charles. And as if I needed anything more to be irritated about, Judy appeared in the doorway. I was starting to wonder if she just lurked around, looking for the best moment to come in and aggravate me.

"Is everything okay?" she asked. "You all need anything?"

I didn't even look at her. Charles nodded. "Yes, Mother. Everything is fine."

She walked in the room and kept her gaze on me. "Do you need anything, Aja?"

I couldn't tell if the smile on her face was genuine, and at this point I didn't even care. "I'm fine," I said.

"Isn't it wonderful," she ran her hand over her son's head as he remained kneeling in front of me, "how Charles is so doting and taking such good care of you? I'm so proud of my son."

He looked up at her and smiled.

"A lesser man would've left you out in the cold since you had left him."

"Mom!" he said, losing his smile.

She raised her hands in defense. "I'm just saying." She smiled again. "Well, I'm going to go get dinner started. I'm making zuppa toscana soup."

She smiled at me before turning and exiting the room. She knew I hated zuppa toscana soup but I didn't have the energy to argue.

I glanced over at my portfolio. It had been untouched since the DR trip. Maybe painting would improve my mood. Maybe I'd even paint a woman running a marathon to give me some inspiration. That thought gave me my first ray of light. Yes, that's what I needed—to connect with my canvas.

"You know what?" I said. "My mind is just in a bad place."

"That's because you've been through so much, some serious trauma, babe. Why don't you lie down and take a nap?"

I pointed toward the portfolio.

"No, I think I want to try and paint some. Clear my head. Do you mind getting my supplies?"

"Sweetheart, I think you should lie down. Those art supplies aren't going anywhere," Charles replied.

Before I could react, he stood and moved behind my chair and started wheeling me toward the bed. "The doctor said rest is vital to your healing. I'm tired, too. Let's just take a little nap."

Inside, I screamed, "Did you not just hear me?"

Outside, I said nothing.

Defeat blanketed me as I let Charles ease me into the bed.

"You know, after you get better we're going to recommit to each other." He tucked the covers around me. "I was talking to Reverend Caldwell at the church and he said we could come see him, or one of the marriage ministers there would be happy to talk to us. Or if you prefer, we can go see a professional therapist just so we can deal with the root of our issues and fix things." He climbed in the bed next to me, pulled me close to him, and wrapped his arms around me. "Fix us. Yeah, nothing would make me happier." He snuggled closer to me, and as he spooned me, I felt the love radiate from his body. I hated that as much as I loved him, right now, in this moment, I couldn't return his love. In fact, lying in my husband's arms was the last place I wanted to be. But the reality was, I was an invalid. And who knew how long I'd be one. Maybe Charles was right. Maybe this—being a wife—was my destiny. And the sooner I faced that, the better off I would be.

Chapter 25

I swear, I wanted to scream. Trying to navigate this stupid wheel-chair through the front door was the most aggravating thing ever.

I didn't know why suddenly everything Charles did was irritating me so. Maybe it was just because I was grumpy about not having control of my own life. I'd finally gotten up the courage to seize my life by the reins, and one bad decision had snatched it all away.

All the warnings, all the lectures I'd given Eric and Anika about texting and driving flashed through my mind. I'd taken steps to make sure my kids were safe on the roadways. I hadn't heeded my own warnings and now I was paying the price.

"At least it's not the ultimate price—death," Roxie had said the first time she'd come to see me in the hospital. She was so devastatingly hurt by my actions, but I could tell she was trying to temper her chastisement.

"Sweetie, how many times . . ." She'd let the unspoken part of her sentence dangle in the air.

"I know," I'd replied. "I just . . ." The rest of my sentence hung midair as well. I thought I'd mastered texting and driving. I couldn't even utter those ridiculous words now. My "mastery" had left me crippled.

My husband grunted, pulling me out of my blame game, which was good because Lord knows I had played it enough these last six weeks.

"Ugh," Charles said again as he pulled the back of the chair over the step in the front room.

"I really don't understand why you won't let me build a wheelchair ramp," Charles said. My husband had broached the idea while I was still in the inpatient facility. It's bad enough that he had to rearrange the furniture. I wasn't about to let him permanently rearrange our lives.

"Because I'm not going to be in this thing that long and it would be a complete waste," I said just as Charles once again banged my leg up against the wall.

"Ouch!" I exclaimed.

"I'm sorry. I'm so sorry, babe," he said.

"Be gentle, please," I moaned, massaging my knee.

"Sweetie, I'm trying."

He sounded so exasperated, but I didn't have room to be sympathetic to him right now.

"This has been an adjustment for us all," he added.

"How about we trade places, then?" I snapped.

His expression turned serious. "If I could, I would."

I took a deep breath. I didn't need to be snapping at Charles when all he was trying to do was help.

"Sorry," I mumbled. He closed the front door as he pushed me into the living room. We were returning from another doctor's visit. I swear, I felt like I had a never-ending litany of doctor's visits.

I shook off my sour mood and hoped that being in a foul space wasn't a side effect of my condition.

"So, I'll get you settled in our bedroom so you can be comfortable," he said.

"Charles, would you mind if I went back to the guest room?" I said. I'd been thinking about this since last week when he snuggled with me. That's how he'd gone to sleep every night since then. Some nights I welcomed his touch. Most nights I didn't.

"What?"

"Like you said, this is a big adjustment for all of us, and you know I'm having to deal with this both physically and mentally," I told him.

"But you need me," he protested.

"Please?" I said. I wasn't in the mood to argue. "It's just more comfortable. That way, you don't have to fool with trying to get me up the stairs."

Every time Charles carried me up those stairs made me sadder and sadder. He'd tried to joke about it "being our honeymoon every day," but it was just a reminder that he was carrying me because I couldn't walk.

"Then we'll both move into the guest bedroom," he announced.

"Charles, I need to be alone," I said, my voice raising an octave. "Just until I can get used to this . . . this new reality."

"It's okay, baby," he said, touching my arms to soothe me. "I'll move you."

"That's not a good idea," Judy replied, appearing at the bottom of the stairs. My sour mood intensified with just the sight of her.

"Judy—"

Charles cut me off. "Mom, I don't need you to fight me on this. This is hard enough on all of us. I just need your help with Aja. I'm going to get her comfortable here on the sofa while I go set up the guest room."

She shook her head like she couldn't believe her son was being so stupid. Then she walked over to the wicker trunk that sat in the corner of the living room. She took out an afghan as Charles struggled to help me stand. My legs felt extra wobbly today, and it brought tears to my eyes.

"You need a real physical therapist to help around here, Charles," Judy said as he struggled against my weak legs. "None of us are cut out for this, especially since she's put on all that extra weight."

If I'd had any energy, I would've told my mother-in-law that she was one Pillsbury biscuit away from being overweight herself, so she needed to be quiet.

Charles sounded exasperated. "I have to work on that, too. The physical therapist was supposed to start last week and something happened and she can't start. Now the agency has to find someone else." He finally got me seated and took a deep breath like it had sapped him of all his energy. "I have this project at work. I don't have time to be interviewing other therapists."

I fought back tears. I was already becoming an inconvenience.

Judy sighed as she covered me with the afghan. "Look, I'll find the therapist. This is a lot on you, sweetheart. Go get the guest room together and then take some time to yourself this evening."

I wanted to scream that Charles wasn't the damn victim. Charles looked at me with pity.

"Honey, I would never generally leave you, but it's just that LeBron is talking about coming to the Rockets and I have the exclusive interview . . ."

"It's fine," I said. It really was. I welcomed the opportunity to be left alone. I just didn't want to be left alone with Judy.

"Okay, babe. I will get you settled and then I'll be back."

I shrugged my left shoulder. At this point, I didn't really care.

Judy put the television on *Gunsmoke*, a show I hated, then set the remote on the coffee table just out of my reach.

"Let me get to work," Judy said. "I'll make you some lunch and then I'll make some calls."

I wanted to tell her to hand me the remote, but I didn't want to give her the satisfaction. So as the sounds of gunshots filled the room from the black-and-white TV show, I just pulled the afghan over my head and cried myself to sleep.

I don't know how long I had been asleep, but the sound of Judy's voice snapped me out of my slumber. It didn't take long; when Judy set her mind to something, she dove right in, so it was no surprise when she said, "So, I have a list of PTs. Charles actually wants someone in this week, so I pushed the agency. I have a folder of some people that can actually start ASAP. Do you want to review them?" Judy asked.

I inhaled, then exhaled and glanced at the TV. *Gunsmoke* was off and *In the Heat of the Night* was on. I liked that show and decided giving my attention to it was much better than talking to my mother-in-law.

"I'm watching TV," I said.

She tsked her frustration. "So, you're just going to sit here and feel sorry for yourself?"

I didn't say a word, just kept staring at the TV.

"Fine," Judy replied. "I'll choose the therapist myself." She turned and walked out of the room.

———※———

It took less than forty-eight hours and Judy had a new therapist on tap. I had rolled into the living room just in time to hear the conversation between her and Charles.

"Mom, you have no idea how grateful I am to you," Charles said. "The LeBron interview was great and now he wants me to come up to Philly to cover his new school, but I really don't want to leave Aja."

"Son, you have already done more than most men would've done by taking her back and taking care of her after what she did to you." She patted his cheek. "So you do not need to put your life on hold trying to nurse her."

I ignored her words, even though they stung, and rolled closer. Both of them turned to me. Charles looked embarrassed. Judy looked like she could not have cared less that I overheard her.

"Your mother's right, Charles. Go. I'll be fine. Plus, the therapist will be here, so you'd just be in the way."

"Babe, are you sure?"

"I'm positive."

He leaned down and hugged me, then stood to embrace his mother. "Thank you so much, Mom. I don't know how we'd do all of this if it wasn't for you."

"It is my pleasure, baby. Anything I can do to make life better for you since I know this is very difficult on you."

I rolled my eyes. I was the one in the frigging wheelchair, but it was difficult on him? Okay.

The doorbell rang and I couldn't help but say, "I would get it, but I can't walk."

Charles took a deep sigh and headed over to the door and opened it, "Hello," he said.

I heard a perky female voice say, "Good morning. You must be Mr. Clayton, right?" she said.

"Yes, that would be me. You must be the physical therapist. You can call me Charles."

"Well, Charles," she giggled, "I'm Sunnie Ray. The new physical therapist."

Great, a sunny physical therapist named Sunnie. *Just what I need,* I thought.

"Well, hello. Come in," he said, stepping aside so she could enter.

Judy walked over and shook her hand. "Sunnie, I am so happy to see you and I am forever indebted that you were able, under such short notice, to fit us into your calendar."

"It worked out, really. My other client got another therapist and I was available."

"Well, their loss is our gain," Judy said.

My eyes scanned up and down the perky girl that looked like she was a mixture of black and Asian, and with her butt-length hair, she was better suited for a music video than physical therapy. "Are you even old enough to be a licensed physical therapist?" I asked.

She released that annoying giggle again. "I get that a lot. I'm actually twenty-seven."

"And you wear your twenty-seven so well," Judy said, beaming like Sunnie was her daughter-in-law and not me.

I took in her too-tight scrubs and shook my head at the way the material was hugging her thick hips and 34DDs. Yeah, real professional. Even still, her appearance made me instinctively brush my unkempt hair down. I'd been wearing it in a ponytail since the accident and pretty much lacked any motivation to do anything to it.

"Well, you must be Aja," she said, not at all fazed by my attitude.

"Yes. Did the wheelchair give it away?" I asked.

Charles stepped on the side of me. "You'll have to excuse my wife. She isn't usually this rude."

She kept her smile as she approached me. "Something about being confined to a wheelchair can bring out the worst in a person. Rudeness is a natural part of the healing process for trauma victims." She knelt in front of me and motioned toward my legs. "May I?"

I reluctantly nodded and she began gently massaging my legs.

"Well, Aja, I've been told I have some magic hands," she said as she kneaded my thighs for a few minutes. Then she stood. "So, we're going to get right to work. And before you know it, I'm gonna have you up and walking and dumping that chair."

That actually made me perk up. "I would love nothing better," I said.

"I've reviewed your medical files, and you're one of the better cases I've had. So we'll get you up and going in no time."

That brought a smile to my face, and suddenly I saw perky Sunnie Ray as my new best friend.

Chapter 26

It's funny how quickly your friend can become your enemy. Okay, Sunnie wasn't my enemy, but there were some days when I wanted to inflict immeasurable pain on her. Even though I knew all of her demands were designed for one thing—to get me out of the chair.

"How bad do you want to walk?" Sunnie had asked me the first full day of therapy.

"More than anything else," I'd replied. I'd worked so hard today that there was a thin layer of sweat covering my brow.

"Then you're going to have to let me lead," she replied. "You're human, so you're entitled to cry, to cuss, to want to give up. But no matter what, we will not quit. Deal?" she asked.

I'd agreed, and it had been nonstop work ever since. Sunnie wasn't playing. For the past three weeks, she'd been a drill sergeant.

And this morning, she was in full metal jacket mode. We were standing in front of some metal bars she'd erected in the den. The entire area had been transformed into a state-of-the-art rehab facility. Charles had spared no expense, getting the best equipment money could buy, including a ZeroG Gait and Balance Training System, a robotic body-weight support system that I'm sure had to have cost as much as a car.

"Come on, Aja, you said you wanted to be walking in six months. You're not going to do that with this half-ass effort," she barked.

"It hurts," I moaned. She had me doing some type of squatting exercise, and my whole body felt on fire.

"I need you to work through the pain," Sunnie continued. "Mind over matter. As long as the pain isn't unbearable, we're going to keep pushing." She stood in front of me, her arms outstretched to catch me in case I fell.

Sunnie had insisted that I set a goal. So I'd written down "Walk again in six months." And I placed that on the wall in the den right in front of the parallel bars.

"It's a matter of motivation if you have feeling below your waist," Sunnie had said, when telling me how achievable my goal really was.

But today was one of those days when I just wanted to sit on the sofa and watch TV. I'd even take some episodes of *Gunsmoke* over this torture.

"I told you, you have to focus," Sunnie said. "Apple."

I managed a laugh as I inhaled. She had insisted that I think of my body as an apple and keep my focus on my core because "a strong core leads to steadier sitting, standing, and walking."

"Come on, Aja, you can do this," Sunnie said, her voice raising an octave like a cheerleader. "Resist the temptation to hunch over. Stand tall like a tree."

"Do you want me to be an apple or a tree?" I snapped.

Sunnie remained unfazed by barrage of verbal attacks.

"Evenly distribute your weight on your legs . . . You're not breathing. Exhale."

How could she always tell that I wasn't breathing?

"What if I fall?" I asked.

"Then you get back up." She adjusted my leg. "Dig in with your toes. Use your toes for all they're worth. If you're falling forward, press your toes into the ground and fight to remain upright.

But falling is part of learning how to walk again, so accept it and don't be scared of it."

Back when I was in middle school and taking gymnastics classes at the Y, we learned how to fall. We lined up on the mat and our teacher would push us. Our job was to draw our arms in and roll around on the floor like a ball. We were to try not to put our arm out if we fell because it might break or get otherwise hurt. I had mastered the art of falling back then. But now, for some reason, I couldn't muster up the confidence that I had back then.

"Stop worrying about falling. Mr. Clayton didn't buy these plush mats for nothing. They'll protect you. And if anything does happen, I'm right here." She moved closer so that I could feel her presence. "When you start moving around, you have a wall radar," she said. "You know where the walls are and if you fall, you will break the fall against a wall."

Sunnie's optimism and confidence was often enough to squash my fears. Most of the time, anyway.

Unfortunately, today wasn't one of those times.

"Come on, Aja," she said. I could tell I was frustrating her. "There is no magic in attaining these skills—it's purely repetition. If you want to walk again, you have to repeat your physical training and activities day in and day out, and be willing to push yourself in a situation where there is so much pressure. After all, pressure builds diamonds."

"I'm tired," was the only response I could muster.

"Soft tissues heal faster through movement, so we can't stop."

"I'm tired," I repeated as I plopped down in my chair.

She stepped back. "Okay, fine. Guess you're more tired of trying than you are of being in that chair."

I rolled my eyes at her, and huffed, then pulled myself back up on the bars. Dang, she was good.

Chapter 27

There would be no extra working out today. Sunnie had worked me until my body begged for mercy. I couldn't be mad—well, I was, but I got over it, because yesterday, I'd taken two steps without help. Sunnie had pushed and pushed me today, and while I pushed myself just as hard, I couldn't go any farther than the two steps.

"Well, it's been a great session," she said, gathering her things. "I am sooo impressed with your progress." She turned toward the kitchen and called for Charles, "Mr. Clayton, did you still need to go to the store? I was going to leave, but I can wait for you to get back."

Charles stepped from the kitchen, wiping his hands on a dish towel. "No, it's fine. I'm cooking dinner now. I'll go in a bit, but Aja will be fine. I won't be gone long."

"Okay, great. See you tomorrow," she said, bouncing out the door.

She hadn't been gone five minutes when I heard the doorbell ring, and even if I wanted to get up to get it, my body wouldn't cooperate.

Usually, when Sunnie left, no matter how exhausted as I was, I would continue my standing and moving exercises. But today I could barely move. The doctor had given me a good prognosis, so I was confident that it wouldn't be long before I was up and moving again.

"I got it," Charles said, heading past me from the kitchen. As soon as he opened the door, I heard Simone squeal.

"Hey. Hey. Hey," she said.

"Hello, ladies," Charles said. "So nice to see you. Aja is in the den. Come on in."

I know my girls had been trying to get by here to see me, but I'd been giving them excuse after excuse. The only one I had really let come by was Roxie. But I guess they were no longer waiting on an invitation since they were now standing over me in my den.

"You look a hot mess," Nichelle said.

"Hello to you, too," I replied.

"Just because you almost died doesn't mean you need to look like you almost died," Simone added.

I couldn't help but smile. I hadn't wanted them to come, but now that they were here, I was glad to see them.

"I've been in my intense PT," I said. "But you guys just can't listen, huh? I said I wasn't up to visitors."

Simone shrugged and came over to hug me. "And I said we don't really care what you said. We haven't seen you since you left the hospital and that is totally unacceptable."

Roxie and Nichelle also hugged me and then got comfortable on each side of me as Simone sat across from me.

"So, what's up? How's life?" Simone asked.

I glared at her, then glanced down at my legs, then over at my wheelchair. "How do you think it is?"

"Roxie told us the good news that you were up and moving," Simone continued, not feeding into my negativity.

I took a deep breath and sighed. "Yeah. I'm actually feeling a lot better, at least physically. My PT is a beast."

Roxie glanced back over her shoulder toward the kitchen where Charles had gone back in. "How's everything here?" she whispered.

I shrugged. "Charles is Charles. His usual loving self."

The look on Nichelle's face softened. "Maybe. Maybe everything happened for a reason."

"Let's just hold off a little bit," I whispered. "Charles mentioned that he was about to head to the store." They nodded. No more words needed to be said and we began chatting about something else.

Five minutes later, Charles came through and said, "Okay. I'm heading out. I'm going to pick up some wine now that your girls are here because I'm assuming you all will be joining us for dinner."

"Are you cooking?" Simone said.

"My Cajun shrimp and pasta specialty," Charles replied.

"Oh, yeah. You might need to get me some fresh sheets for the guest bedroom," Nichelle added.

They all laughed.

"I'll bring back wine," Charles said.

"Stella Rosa," Simone called after him.

"Hennessy!" Nichelle added.

We all watched as Charles walked outside. They gave him a few minutes until they heard the car backing out of the driveway and then Simone said, "So, spill."

"Spill what?" I replied.

"How is it? I mean, you had left the man," she said.

I sighed. "It's like I never did. It just makes me feel even more guilty. He's not missing a beat taking care of me."

All three of them looked at each other knowingly.

"Well, that's because he's that type of guy," Simone said.

"I know," I said, sighing. "Maybe this is a way that I was supposed to look at my husband in a new light. Maybe this is a sign that I'm supposed to be right where I am."

Roxie hadn't said a word since Charles left. She studied me throughout our whole conversation. "What do you have to say?" I finally asked her.

She looked sad as she bit down on her bottom lip like she was weighing her words. Finally she said, "The woman I saw dancing around my apartment to Barbra Streisand as she worked on a painting, where is she?"

Tears filled my eyes as I shrugged. "She died in the car wreck, I guess."

"That makes me sad," Roxie said.

"You?" I threw my hands up in defeat. "But it is what it is. I have been thinking about this, though. Charles rearranged our lives." I motioned around the den. "I mean, look at this place. He bought all of this PT equipment. He waits on me hand and foot. I hurt him so bad and he's still stepped up—without hesitation—to take care of me. His mother is right. I'd be a fool not to see how much he loved me."

I waited on my friends to say something. No one did. So I added, "I mean, it's not like I don't love him."

"But what happened to all that self-discovery?" Roxie asked.

"It went out the window with one text," I said, somberly.

"Don't look at it like that," Simone said. "Charles is indeed one of a kind and maybe you just needed something to make you appreciate that."

"Maybe," I replied.

"You know what?" Nichelle said. "I have a suggestion. Until he gets back with the drinks, let's have fun. You know, like we had in the DR."

"Have fun how? I can't even walk," I said.

"Well, I could tell you guys about my latest date," Simone said.

"That online dating is something else. This guy had a gorgeous picture on his profile. I go to meet him and he was forty years older and looking like my great-granddaddy. Had the nerve to tell me that was his grandson's picture."

"Ha, you got catfished," Roxie laughed.

"Right? That's what I'm telling Aja. It's nothing out here. She'd better hang on to her good man."

Roxie shook her head. "This journey Aja is on has nothing to do with a man. And that's a good thing."

"Well, maybe it would make sense if it did. I can see tossing aside one man for another. I can't understand wanting to leave in the pursuit of happiness. Don't you know happiness is fleeting?"

"Don't listen to negative Nancy," Simone said. "We just want you to find your joy . . . whatever that may be."

Nichelle had just waved her comment off as the doorbell rang.

"You expecting someone?" Simone asked.

"No, maybe it's my mother-in-law and she forgot her key."

Nichelle walked over and opened the door. "May, I help you?" I heard her say.

"Hi, um, I'm Sunnie Ray, is Aja here?"

"That's my therapist," I called out.

Sunnie bounced into the room and each one of my friends grew silent as their eyes roamed from Sunnie's head down to her tiny Nike tennis shoes.

"Hey, y'all, this is Sunnie, my physical therapist. Sunnie, these are my very best friends."

"Hi!" she exclaimed.

None of them spoke, they just kept staring at her.

Roxie was sitting next to me, so I elbowed her.

"Oh, ah, hi, I'm Roxie. That's Nichelle and Simone," she said pointing across the room.

"Nice to meet you, ladies," Sunnie said. "Aja, sorry, I forgot my phone." She motioned toward the fireplace mantel, then stepped over and picked it up. "You know we can't function without this these days." She giggled as she held the phone up. "Well, nice to meet you ladies. I just adore Aja and she's making tremendous progress."

"Yeah, Sunnie is working her magic," I said.

"I bet she is," Nichelle said, not cracking a smile.

I frowned, but Sunnie didn't seem to notice the tension in the room.

"Well, I have to get going. Enjoy your girl time!" she said before disappearing out the door.

As soon as the door slammed, Nichelle turned on me. "Have you lost your ever-loving mind?" she said.

"What?" I asked. "And why were you guys so rude?"

"I know doggone well you're not having that Pamela Anderson–Kimora Lee bombshell bouncing all up and through this house," Nichelle said.

"Yeah," Simone added. "You might as well just put her in a bowl of gravy and hand Charles a biscuit."

"What?" I said. "You guys are tripping. Sunnie is a professional. She's here helping me."

"And she's going to help herself to your husband," Simone warned.

I shook my head. "Why, because she's a pretty girl, I should hold that against her and not have her in my house?"

"Hell yeah," Simone and Nichelle said at the same time.

"It was just a little surprising," Roxie said. "I'm sure, you know, with your condition, you and Charles aren't intimate so having Miss Thang parade around your house might be a little too tempting for my taste."

"Exactly," Nichelle said. "And the last thing you need is to be have that Nicki Minaj ass bouncing around your house."

"And I'm sure she'd be happy to snag her a man like Charles," Simone said. "You'd better keep one eye on that chick at all times."

I couldn't help but laugh. My girls were doing the most. Sunnie was here to help me, just like she'd been doing. I couldn't let them fill my head with doubt and get me off my mission. But I did take a moment and think. Of course Charles would move on if I ever left. I waited to see if I'd feel any kind of jealousy at that thought. My heart hurt when I realized that I didn't.

Chapter 28

I remember when Anika and Eric took their first steps. We were so excited and Charles used his video camera to document every step. Anika, especially, was particularly proud when she was able to balance herself and move. She kept falling but she kept getting up until she was able to walk from my arms to her dad's.

My fifteen-month-old child was the visual inspiration I was using right now. I needed her determination and fearlessness in order to follow Sunnie's commands.

"Come on, Aja. You got this."

Sunnie was standing about fifteen feet away, urging me to walk. She was in full cheerleader mode. For the past three weeks, I'd been on an intense regimen, and my improvement had shocked everyone. My mobility had improved drastically and I was able to walk with assistance. But today was the first time Sunnie wanted me to walk on my own.

"Come on, they said you wouldn't stand up and you did," she encouraged when I wouldn't move. "They said you wouldn't get out of the wheelchair and you did. You can do this!"

"Did you used to be a cheerleader in another life?" I asked her.

"I'm a cheerleader right now," she said, clapping her hands. "Come on."

"Okay," I said. I took a huge breath, then a smile spread across my face because I felt it in my bones. Whatever circuits went from my brain to my legs were ready to do their thing. I slowly moved my right foot, maintained my balance, and moved my left foot.

"Yes," Sunnie said.

Right. Left. Right. Left.

"Yes, yes, yes!"

My heart was racing, but I stayed focused and moved and moved until I was on the other side of the room. When I reached Sunnie, I squealed with joy and threw my arms around her neck.

I turned around to Charles, who was standing in back of me, recording just like he'd recorded Eric's and Anika's first steps. A mist filled his eyes.

"Did you see that, babe?" I asked.

"Yes. You walked." He stopped filming and took a step toward me.

I held up my hand to stop him. "No. I'm going to walk to you."

He stopped as I repeated the walking process, each step getting a little easier. I imagined this was where Anika's joy must've come from the day she learned to walk. She wanted to walk everywhere. A trip to the mall would take twice as long because she insisted on walking. I now understood what my toddler was feeling.

Charles took me into his arms and smothered me with kisses. "Oh my God, sweetheart. I'm so happy."

I pulled away and looked at my physical therapist. "Sunnie did this."

She blushed and waved my comment off. "It wasn't me. It was your wife's determination," she said.

Charles was all grins and walked over and hugged her. "We are so grateful to you." He pulled her tight.

I was thrilled about my achievement, but my girls' words were in my head.

"You'd better watch her." So, instinctively, I began to watch.

I noticed the way her hands curved into the small of his back.

The way her body seemed to relax in his embrace. She was about three inches shorter than me, so her head stopped in the middle of his chest.

Watching them made my smile slowly fade. But then, Charles pulled away from her and turned back to me. "This is just wonderful. I can't wait to share the news."

I kept my gaze on Sunnie. Was that a flash of guilt? I shook it off. I was letting my girls' words get to me. Sunnie had saved my life. The last thing I was going to do was look at her side-eye like she was trying to steal my husband.

Chapter 29

My happiness at being able to walk was tempered by my husband's constant doting. As usual, he had taken control, telling me when I'd had enough exertion, dictating how much was too much, and even monitoring the food that I ate.

Charles was getting on my nerves. I knew he meant well, but right about now, I was wishing that he had some friends, some fraternity brothers, something outside of work to occupy his time. Before, it just felt like life in general was suffocating me. Now Charles had the suffocation covered all by himself.

"We're here, babe," he said as we pulled into the parking lot of St. Luke's Hospital.

"I'm not blind," I said. The sarcasm came out before I could rein it in. I'd wanted to go to the art store to get some more art supplies so I could resume painting, but Charles had been late getting home to take me to the doctor and told me that he had to rush to a meeting afterward.

Charles ignored my sarcasm as he jumped out of the car, raced around, grabbed a wheelchair that was sitting by the front door, and returned to the car. After he opened my door, I glanced down at the wheelchair, then back up at him.

"You know I can walk, right?"

"I know you can walk, sweetheart. But I just want to make sure the doctor gives you a clean bill of health. I want Dr. Hubbard to sign off on everything before we let you loose to run your marathon," he joked.

"I don't want to run a marathon. I just want to walk into the damn doctor's office." My tone was short and I didn't care.

Charles stood in front of me on the passenger's side, unfazed by my attitude.

I sighed, knowing it would be useless to argue with him. He patted the back of the wheelchair and said, "So, have a seat."

I got out of the car, then sat down and struggled to suppress my frustration at being ordered around.

Charles shut the car door, locked it, and began talking about something that happened at the Rockets game and I didn't even bother trying to appear interested in what he was saying as he wheeled me into the doctor's building.

"So, babe. I was thinking maybe I can get Mom a place and we can downsize. Something a little more intimate," he said as he navigated my chair through the door of the first-floor doctor's office. Navigating my wheelchair had become a skill he had mastered.

I rolled my eyes. "Your mother would never want to leave you," I said. Judy had long ago recovered from her surgery, but she had her own mother-in-law suite, complete with a kitchenette. And she didn't have to pay a single bill. So why would she want to leave?

"Well, I think it's time," he continued. "We need to just focus on us. I was serious when I said that."

"Hi, may I help you?" the nurse said as we approached the receptionist's desk.

I was just about to speak up when Charles said, "Yes, my wife has an appointment at two. Aja Clayton."

A flash of recognition then a gigantic smile filled her face. "Oh yes, Mr. Clayton. How are you today?"

I rolled my eyes and slumped back in my chair. Now not only

was Charles speaking for me but the receptionist wanted to know how he was doing—not me, the patient. On top of everything else, I was invisible next to my celebrity husband.

The receptionist tapped her keyboard, peered at the screen, then said, "You're all set. I have you all signed in. Please have a seat until the nurse calls you."

Charles thanked her, then pushed my chair over to the other side of the room.

He took my hand as we sat in the waiting room and after a few minutes, he said, "Aja, I know you're angry at the situation you're currently in, but I'm a firm believer that everything happens for a reason. I know we have been through a lot these past few months, but God works in mysterious ways and He brought us back together so we can focus on us. He took us through a storm so we can appreciate the sun," he said, squeezing my hand. "I'm not going to lie. I didn't know we were broken. But now that I do, I want to do everything in my power to fix it."

My husband's words made some of my irritation dissipate. Charles was a rare breed. I'd left him, mistreated him, disrupted his life . . . and yet, he was still here.

"Mrs. Clayton, Dr. Hubbard will see you now," the nurse called out.

Though I said no words, I squeezed his hand back, then slowly stood.

"Are you sure you don't want to wheelchair into the doctor's office?" Charles said.

"No, that man said I wouldn't walk again. I want him to see me walk again. I want him to see me walk into his office," I replied. I was going to fight Charles on this one. I had something to prove to my "you'll never walk again" doctor.

Luckily, Charles just extended his hand and motioned for me to lead the way.

Once again, the nurses were eyeballing my husband. But I wasn't the jealous type. I never had been because Charles had always made me feel secure. Besides, I had more important things to focus on—like showing Dr. Hubbard that I was the exception.

Sunnie had been right about one thing. Setting a goal for myself made achieving it that much more rewarding. I really do think if I hadn't said, "I'm going to get out of this chair," I might still be in the chair. But I had given myself a date to walk again, and not only had I made that date, I'd beaten it by two weeks.

It took me a little longer to make it back to the examination room. I just didn't move as fast as I used to. But the fact remained—I was moving. I'd just rounded the reception area when I saw Dr. Hubbard. He was standing at the edge of the counter talking to a nurse about another patient. He looked up and his eyes met mine. His mouth dropped open in wonder as he looked down at my legs.

"Oh my God, Mrs. Clayton," he said, scurrying over to me. He ran a mental scan over my body.

"In the flesh." I beamed.

"Do you need some help?" he asked, coming and trying to slip his hands under my arm.

I gently tapped his hand to push him away. "No. No. I got it."

He stood back and watched me take a couple steps. "That you do," he said. "Extremely impressive." He turned to his nurse. "Which room?"

"C," she said pointing to the third room down the hall.

"Mr. Clayton, good to see you, too. The two of you can go right in here," Dr. Hubbard said. "I'll be just a minute."

Charles walked behind me, carrying my purse. I guess he was making sure I didn't fall. We got in the room and I got settled on the doctor's table. A few minutes later Dr. Hubbard tapped on the door.

"Knock knock knock," he said, pushing the door open, then stepping inside. "Thank you for your patience. I wanted to make sure I closed out my other patients so that I could come in here," he folded his arms and looked me up and down, "and just marvel at you." A smile lit up his face.

"You said I wouldn't walk again." I held out my arms as I stood, took two steps, and turned around.

He held up a finger. "I said you *may* not walk, but honestly, I was leaning more toward the 'not.' But I always love it when my patients prove me wrong. Let me take a look at you." He patted the table and I sat back down. He pulled out a stethoscope and put it up to my chest, listening to my back, taking my vitals, and then he took some type of hammer-looking thing and hit my knee. "How does that feel?"

"Ouch," I said.

"I love that sound." He hit the other knee before I could say anything else. I winced at that as well.

"Really? That hurts," I said.

"I am sorry about that," he said, "but I just wanted to make sure that you're in tip-top shape."

He ran his fingers along my legs, pushing and prodding. He nodded his approval with every knead, then tapped on a laptop to study my records. "Well, Mrs. Clayton, this is amazing. Considering where you came from and where you are at this point, I'd call you nothing short of a miracle."

"While we know God helped her get here, my wife was determined," Charles interjected, his voice dripping with pride. "My wife said she was going to walk again, and when she sets her mind to something, she gets it done."

I couldn't help but feel a twinge in my stomach because I'd set my mind to move on, start a new life, and yet here I was. Charles couldn't have been more wrong.

Dr. Hubbard nodded. "Well, I don't know what your motivation was, but I'm sure glad you had it because your recovery is remarkable."

"Thank you, Doc."

He examined me some more, but I could tell from the expression on his face that he was pleased with everything that he found.

"Of course I want to continue to monitor you and make sure you don't have any setbacks, but," he closed his laptop, "Aja Clayton, I'm giving you a clean bill of health."

"That's awesome," I said.

"I don't know what your previous schedule was, but as long as you're not exerting too much energy, I think life as you know it can return to normal. If at any time you start feeling any pain, don't be ashamed to grab a cane to help you around. You do have one, right?"

Charles nodded. "Yes, and I'll make sure she has everything that she needs to continue her recovery."

"Wonderful. In addition to continuing your recovery, any big plans coming up?" Dr. Hubbard asked.

I was just about to open my mouth and tell him all the big plans I had with my gallery when Charles said, "We're going to take it slow and I'll be right by her side as she recovers." He squeezed my shoulder.

"Well, that's just perfect," Dr. Hubbard said. "Every woman should be so lucky."

I was lucky to have a man like Charles by my side. Everybody told me so.

I inhaled, then expelled the little voice that kept trying to whisper "but" in my head. In that moment, I decided to stop fighting the side of me that was begging to break free.

"Yes, every woman should be so lucky," I said, with no sarcasm in my voice because I truly meant it. And my words brought a gigantic smile to my husband's face.

Chapter 30

Silencing that inner voice was becoming a constant source of mental anguish. It seemed the more I tried to convince myself to accept that how things were was how they'd continue to be, the more my mind was fighting me. But every day Charles proved to me why I was a fool to even think about leaving him. Judy was right about one thing: Not many men would take their woman back, then nurse her back to health after she'd broken his heart. But Charles had done that and more.

Since we'd left the doctor's office and I got my clean bill of health last week, I'd tried my best to not think of the things I wanted in life and simply appreciate the things I had. Every morning, I reminded myself that I needed to do what I had done the last twenty years for the next twenty years. Love the life I lived. And even if I couldn't get to the point of loving it, I needed to find a way to like it.

That's why I'd spent the last week trying my best to ward off thoughts of the life I'd begun creating before my accident.

"There's no reason you can't have your gallery and your husband," Roxie had told me just yesterday. I'd tried to talk to Charles about the gallery a couple of times during my rehabilitation, but he always managed to change the subject by telling me to focus on total healing.

I didn't know when or why I'd developed an either/or attitude, but my best friend had a point. And that thought had consumed me all night—to the point that I'd awakened with a new resolve: I would stay with my husband *and* open my gallery to showcase my work. Even if it was a scaled-down version of what I initially wanted, having a slice of the happiness pie was better than nothing at all.

I was grateful that I had paid my deposit and Charles had called to pay up the monthly rent so I wouldn't lose my building.

We were all gathered now to celebrate Charles's forty-eighth birthday, Eric and Anika had come in for the weekend. Judy was there, along with Eula, one of her friends. And of course, my girls. The lopsided balance of friends reminded me of how antisocial my husband was.

Clink. Clink. Clink.

Charles tapped on his glass with his fork as he stood. "I just want to say thank you to each of you for coming out and helping me celebrate my birthday. A few months ago, I didn't think I'd have a cause for celebration. But if ever you doubted the power of God," he put his hand on my shoulder, "we are a living testimony. And all of you know what Aja and I have been through."

I glanced up at him out the corner of my eye. Surely he was not going to put me on blast in front of everybody, especially my children, who didn't know that I had actually left their father. Anika had noticed us settle back into our normal routine, so that must've satisfied her because she didn't ask any more questions.

I was glad when Charles skipped all the details and continued his speech. "Nursing my wife back to health has been heartbreaking because there have been times I wanted to chop my legs off and give them to her."

A chorus of "awws" resonated throughout the room.

Charles continued, "Aja is my rib, my source of completion. She is everything that I've ever wanted in a woman."

I inhaled, then glanced over at Judy, whose lips were tight as she kept her eyes focused on her son. A few times over the last few weeks, Charles had put her in her place when it came to dealing with me.

"So, on my birthday, I want to thank God for the greatest gift of all—my wife." He leaned down and kissed me on the lips as everyone clapped.

Simone was clapping the hardest. Nichelle looked happy that I had come to my senses. My eyes met with Roxie's and her faux clap summed up how I felt inside.

The clapping subsided and Charles held up his hand. "Hold on, there's more," he said, turning to my friends. "I know you ladies went to the DR for Aja's birthday and probably don't need another vacation," he winked as they chuckled, "but I'm hoping you'll be ready to go again in three months as I'm requesting, and this is a surprise to Aja, that you all join us for our twenty-first wedding anniversary and vow renewal in Turks and Caicos—on me."

Everyone started clapping again as I stared at my husband in shock. He hadn't discussed any of this with me. I wouldn't be able to go to Turks and Caicos in three months. I would just be getting my gallery off the ground.

"I can't wait to renew my vows," Charles told me. "I can't wait until you stand on the beach and we pledge our love to one another again. I want to spend my lifetime making you happy."

More "awws" as Charles took me into his arms and hugged me like I was a soldier about to go into combat.

I was speechless. And not in a good way. Even though I'd resolved to make this marriage work, I hadn't told Charles, so this announcement meant that he just assumed I wasn't going anywhere. It meant that he had just discounted my feelings. Again. Everyone but my friends seemed oblivious to my change in demeanor. Both Nichelle and Simone had stopped clapping and were studying me like I was chemistry homework. Finally, after about ten minutes of chatter in the room, Roxie stood and said,

"Charles, do you mind if I borrow your wife to escort me to the restroom?"

Charles laughed and turned to Eric. "Son, in case you don't already know, women have to travel in pairs to the restroom."

"Make that quadruplets," Nichelle said, standing and flashing a smile as she pulled Simone up and followed me and Roxie.

Inside the restroom, Nichelle pulled a scene out of a movie and checked the stalls. When she noticed everything was clear, she turned to me.

"Could you be any less interested in your husband's enthusiastic announcement?" she asked.

"Who said I was disinterested?" I replied.

"Your body!" Simone exclaimed.

"Look," Roxie said, stepping next to me and taking my hand, "I know you've been to hell and back. And I know you're grateful to Charles, but if this isn't what you want . . ."

I pulled my hand away and walked off. "I don't know what I want. I mean, I do. I appreciate everything that Charles has done. But that scene out there—that's what I've been living for twenty years. Doing what he wants. Doing what the kids want. What about what I want?" Fresh tears sprang to my eyes as Roxie hugged me.

"Calm down, sweetie."

I sniffed, wiped my tears, then added, "I want to do what I was doing before my accident. Start my new life. I don't want to show my gratitude for Charles taking care of me by giving my life back to him."

This seesaw of indecisiveness was too much. I would never be happy if I stayed. That was the brutal truth. That was the reality I needed to face. Oh, I might convert back to my complacent life—but my heart grimaced at that idea.

"I want more," I added, my voice low.

"Then go get it," Simone said, turning me around to face her. "The worst thing I ever did was guilt Ben into staying with me when he told me he was ready to go," she said, referring to her ex. "I cried and acted such a fool that he stayed, but his heart didn't. For the last four years, his heart wasn't there, and that made our marriage miserable."

"Guys, I understand we want to support her," Nichelle said, "but marriage is about ups and downs. Hard work. Forgiveness. We all get bored. But maybe you need to find a way to put a spark back into your marriage."

I looked out at three sets of eyes. One telling me to go. One telling me to stay, and the third . . . I couldn't make out the expression on Roxie's face.

"What do you think, Roxie?" I asked her.

She folded her arms. "I think this is something you have to come to terms with yourself. I think you have lived for others all your life and it's time for you to live for you. Whether that's with Charles or without is a call only you can make. But I will tell you this, Charles is a good guy and you can't begrudge him for trying to make it work, whether it's the vacation, the vow renewal, or his persistence. But you shouldn't stay with him out of guilt. Whatever you decide to do, just talk to him about it."

"Just not today," Nichelle added. "It is his birthday."

I nodded as I grabbed a paper towel to wipe my tears. I knew she was right. They all were. There was no more indecisiveness. It was time to go.

"Thank you, ladies. I love you so much." I extended my arms until we were all in a group hug.

"Know what else I think?" Nichelle said, pulling back. "I think we need to get back out there before Ms. Eula drinks up all the Dom Pérignon."

"Nichelle!" I said.

"Girl, what?" she replied. "Y'all know Ms. Eula is a lush."

"Takes one to know one," Simone said.

We laughed as we headed back to our table.

Chapter 31

I took my time walking across the room. One end of the room to the other, over and over. I marveled at the ease with which one foot went in front of the other. I had been doing that for about twenty minutes when I felt some eyes on me. I turned to see Charles standing in the doorway, a smile across his face.

"That is a beautiful sight," he said.

"It is." I let out a long sigh. "I'm so grateful that I was able to get up and move."

"It's just absolutely wonderful," he said.

I'd listened to my girls and decided not to berate Charles for that stunt at his birthday dinner yesterday. After all, what did it look like getting upset because my husband wanted to plan a vacation for our anniversary? I had to talk to him. I had to tell him that I was leaving. However, I decided that I'd tell him about moving forward with the gallery first, as if my good news would soften the blow of the bad.

"So, I was thinking," I said, taking a seat on the edge of our bed. He rushed over to help me ease down. I raised up my hand to stop him. If I was going to be independent, I needed to be independent all the way around. "So, what I was thinking," I repeated once I was seated, "I'm ready to move forward with my gallery. I was thinking I could make it like a wine and cheese bar,

where you can view original artwork. Maybe even do some painting classes to help offset the bills. We told the owner three
months and I don't want her thinking the building will just sit
there empty. I want to call the owner and see when I could pick
the keys up."

Charles lost the smile on his face. "I . . . I just assumed you
wouldn't want to do that anymore," he said.

I stared at him. "Do what anymore?"

"You know. Open a business. You're in no condition to run a
business."

"I'm walking," I told him, confused because we had talked
about this. He knew this was my dream. I'd shared my dream
while I was still in rehab. He acted like he supported me.

"Yeah, but your full recovery is still a while away. You don't
need to be running a business," Charles said. "I know you want to
paint, but maybe you can just paint here after you get off from
work. I know you told Karen you quit but she'll give you the job
back."

I took his hands. "Honey, I know you're worried," I said. "But,
it's fine. That's my dream. I don't want it to die." I left out how
being a wife and mother for twenty years had left my dreams dor-
mant.

"But I thought this all was a phase you were going through."

"A phase?" I said, cutting him off and pulling my hands from his.

"No, I . . . I mean," he stammered, "a business just takes a lot
of work. I know you love painting. You can just paint more here."
He motioned around the house.

My hands went to my hips. "I don't want to paint here, Charles.
I want to open my own gallery like we discussed." I stood and
walked toward the closet, not about to indulge in this debate.
"Where did you put the box with all my paperwork from the car
when you went to total it out?"

"Uh, well. I went through everything."

I stepped out of the closet and flashed him an "and?" look.

"Please tell me that you didn't throw my stuff away," I said when he didn't answer.

"No. No. Of course not," he replied.

"Oh good," I said, going back into the closet. I searched on the top shelf until I saw the box I'd seen when he'd put in the closet. I pulled out the stuff from my mangled car. I sifted through the box and pulled out an envelope, and shattered glass fell to the floor. I shook off memories of the car accident, refusing to get sidetracked by my memories from the day I almost died.

"Here it is," I said, pulling out the lease agreement. I walked back into the room with a huge smile on my face. "It's a good thing we paid that deposit and rent."

"Um." Charles's eyes darted from side to side.

"What's wrong, Charles?" I asked.

He paused, then blew a long breath and said, "Well, she actually refunded your money."

"Refunded? What do you mean?" I asked, confused.

It was his turn to pace. "Well, you had me call her, and since the doctor said you probably wouldn't walk again, I thought—"

I interrupted him. "Charles, we talked about this. You said you called her."

"I did, but I just . . . I didn't think you wanted to still do that."

I blinked. Paused, pushed down the bile in my throat and blinked again. "So you lied."

"No. I mean, I did call her back, but . . ."

"You know what? It doesn't even matter. I want to still do it."

"Well, I told her you were no longer interested in the property because of the accident. And she put it back on the market, and in fact she said she had someone else that wanted it, so she wasn't even that upset and that's why she refunded your deposit."

"Are you kidding me?" I said. I had to sit down. I was so stunned. "Are you freaking kidding me?"

"Aja, just calm down."

"You lied to me." I stared at him in disbelief.

"I was looking out for you."

"You sabotaged my dream." My voice was calm, like it was coming from someone on the brink of exploding.

"Sweetheart, I was just thinking about your well-being. You need to be taking it easy. I get it that you want to paint. That's cool. Everyone needs a hobby."

"It's not a damn hobby!" I screamed. "It's my passion! It's a dream I've had since I was a little girl and you destroyed it!"

My outburst must have caught him by surprise because he took a step back. "Look, I told you you can paint here or I could even lease out a small space for you, that way you can get out of the house for a little bit. I understand if you don't want to go back to social services. I can more than afford to take care of both of us and we can just enjoy each other."

"I don't want to paint here or in some small space you rent for me," I said, wanting to add that I didn't want to enjoy him either. My fury was building. "You're always making decisions for me," I snapped.

He paused, even more taken aback. "Well, somebody had to make decisions. You weren't able to. You were incapacitated and mentally . . ." He let his words trail off.

"Mentally what?" I snapped.

He took a deep breath. "You haven't exactly been in the right state of mind. Even before the accident. And after the accident, you've been too busy around here snapping at everyone, treating us like your servants."

"I never asked any of you to do a damn thing for me."

"You didn't have to ask," he said. "That's what families do."

I closed my eyes and willed my anger to subside. I wasn't about to fight with him. "Well, I am making a decision now. And I want my gallery. I want to proceed with my original plan."

"You know you sound like a spoiled child right now."

"I. Want. My. Gallery!"

He took a step toward me, his eyes bucking in surprise. "Okay.

Calm down, baby. Let me give you time to sleep on this and then we can figure out an alternative."

"Unless that alternative includes telling that owner you messed up and want to get my building back, I don't want to hear it."

He sighed, his expression resolute. "Look, I'm going to have to put my foot down on this one. I don't believe now is the time for you to open a business. Maybe this is something that we can re-visit later," Charles said. "You're fragile, and that's not a smart business move right now."

I stared at my husband. "You must think I'm Eric or Anika. I'm not your child and you don't get to command me."

He shook his head like I was being unreasonable. "Nobody is commanding you. I'm just making a decision that is in your best interest. And right now I need you to go to bed and get you some rest."

Suddenly I lost it and just started crying, "I can't do this," I told him. "I just can't."

"Okay," he said, trying to hug me. "Calm down. Good grief. I will find you another facility. If that's what it will take to make you happy, I will find you one if it's that big a deal."

"You're missing the whole point," I screamed, wiggling from his embrace. "It is a big deal. I told you it was a big deal, and not only do you not listen to me, you just straight lied to me! Nobody told you to take this from me in the first place." I lowered my voice and began emphatically nodding as the break-free voice grew louder. "You don't respect my dreams, that's why you did this."

"Okay. See, now you're being ridiculous," he said.

"I can't do it," I cried, now muttering to myself as I paced back and forth across the room. I felt delirious, like I was having an out-of-body experience. "I need to go. This place is suffocating me. There's more to life, there just has to be more to life," I looked around the room, "than this. Than you." I didn't mean for those last words to come out, but it was too late, and I could tell they cut Charles to his core. I closed my eyes and wished I could snatch those words out of the air and ram them back down my throat.

"So," he cocked his head as he studied me, "after everything?" He took a deep breath. "In *spite of* everything, you still want to leave?"

I nodded, the tears streaming down my face. "I *need* to leave. I'm better now, I just have to go," I said.

"You're better thanks to me," he growled.

His tone made me step back. But I composed myself and said, "Yes, and I appreciate you because of that."

Before I could respond, he picked up the lamp that sat on the nightstand and threw it across the room. "But you want out because I'm such a terrible husband!"

I jumped but kept my voice calm as I said, "This isn't about you."

Judy came running in our bedroom, Sunnie right behind her. I'd lost track of the time and forgot Sunnie was coming for a PT session. Though my therapy wasn't as intense, Sunnie still came once a week.

"Is everything okay?" Judy asked. "I heard a crash." Her eyes went to the shattered lamp, then back to us. "What is going on?"

"No," Charles said, slipping his shoes on. "Everything isn't okay."

Sunnie stared at me and then at him. "Mr. Clayton, is everything all right?"

"Y'all need to help Aja pack. She hates it here. She hates being married to me. She wants to leave. So help her get the hell out of my house," he snapped.

Sunnie looked stunned, like she never envisioned walking into the middle of a marital dispute. Judy looked pissed.

"She's leaving after everything that you've done?" Judy said in disbelief.

I looked at Charles, thinking he would say, "Mom, I have this," or something to somehow put a leash on his mother. But instead, he glared at me, grabbed his keys, and headed toward the bed-room door.

"Where are you going?" I said, following him down the hall. I wobbled trying to keep up with him.

"Out."

"Out?"

"None of your damn business," he said. "I'm through begging you to be my wife. You want to leave? Go. I'm done." He threw his hands up as he stomped down the stairs.

"As well you should be, son," Judy called out from the top of the stairs. "You don't have to beg anybody to be with you. I have a Rolodex full of women I can fix you up with tomorrow."

Charles didn't say anything as he went out the front door, slam-ming it so hard that the picture on the wall fell off.

"Sunnie, go with him, please. He doesn't need to drive like that," Judy instructed.

My physical therapist took off after him. Then Judy turned her wrath on me.

Chapter 32

My mother-in-law and I were in a face-off. Every ounce of her that disliked me but she'd kept bottled up was being unleashed from the fury in her eyes.

I'd seen that look before—though it was a tamer version. That look said one thing—she wished her son loved anyone other than me.

Mrs. Clayton sat on the sofa, her back straight, poised like she was about to take a family portrait.

"Why do you have a problem with me?" I asked.

She ran her eyes up and down my body, a stoic expression plastered on her face. She hesitated before speaking. "Charles is all I have."

Her voice had lost its usual confidence. She sounded surprisingly defeated.

"My husband, God rest his soul, always told me that I babied him. But that is my baby. He has a big heart and I don't want him hurt."

"I won't hurt him."

"You already have."

I flinched.

If I ever doubted whether Charles had told his mother about my breaking up with him, this confirmed it.

"I was the one Charles came to when you left him," Mrs. Clayton continued. "I watched the sadness and pain in his eyes. Pain that was multiplied because he didn't even know why you left him—at least that's what he told me."

I didn't know what to say. I had left Charles right after he professed his love for me because all my time was devoted to my brother, and when Charles's ex had shown up, claiming that the two of them were having an affair, I believed her, and instantly broke things off with Charles without ever telling him why. Later, when Charles had found the real reason, he'd demanded that his ex come clean and reveal that she had lied.

"I was relieved when he first told me you broke up with him," Mrs. Clayton continued. "I was hoping that he'd get over you quickly and move on. So imagine my surprise when he told me you two were back together."

I struggled to keep my composure. "I'm sorry I hurt Charles. I was just confused. I come from a background where you don't put a lot of faith in relationships," I responded.

"Well, we come from a background where you do. My Charles is a good man. Are you a good woman?"

I lowered my eyes. Was I a good woman? I had enough drama to fill a lifetime of soap operas. I reflected on Mrs. Clayton's words. Then finally, I said, "Yes, I am a good woman. And I will make Charles happy." I paused, letting that sink in. "I don't ever want to disrespect you, Mrs. Clayton," I continued, "but I love Charles and we're together now. I hope that you will learn to accept that."

Mrs. Clayton sighed heavily. "I guess I can learn to accept it. That doesn't mean I have to like it."

I blinked away that memory. On second thought, that was disdain back then. This was full-on fury now, but I wasn't going to let Judy get to me today.

"Judy, I'm not in the mood," I said, stopping her rant and pushing past her.

"You think I give a damn what kind of mood you're in?" she snapped.

"Call your Rolodex, Judy," I said, heading toward the staircase.

"Don't worry. I will," she sneered as she followed behind me. "And I'm going to make sure that you don't try and take my son for all he's worth."

"*We're worth*," I corrected. "We've been married twenty years."

"And you're a damn social worker," she snapped.

I took a deep breath as I massaged my temples. "Judy, I don't want to fight with you." I didn't want to, but a fight with Judy was like that *Waiting to Exhale* book I'd checked out from the library when it was a new release—long overdue.

"Oh, we're not fighting," she said, stepping in my face. "I'm telling it like it is. Everyone around here walks on tiptoes, trying to make sure Aja is taken care of. Trying to make sure Aja's needs are met, and meanwhile, Aja doesn't care about anybody but herself."

I didn't care about anyone but myself? The whole reason I was losing my mind was because all of my life I'd cared about everyone but myself.

I turned to face her. Not that it mattered, but I hoped that Judy could see my sincerity. I suppose if someone had hurt Eric like Charles was hurting, I'd be mad, too. "You've got to know that I never wanted to hurt my husband."

"And yet you did. Again," she said. "I'm just trying to make sense of it because he surely can't. We didn't the first time and we sure don't now."

"Judy, it's just . . . I don't expect anyone to understand. But I'm at a point in my life where I have to live for me."

"That's a bunch of bull," she snapped. "You created this life and now you just want to walk away from it."

I knew she was right, but I couldn't help but feel like my life was like those emergency situations on the plane when they advise the parents to put on their mask first.

"Be careful what you wish for," Judy warned. Her words sounded ominous. "You reap what you sow," she continued, "and the hurt you do unto others will come back to you tenfold."

"You never thought I was worthy anyway," I said.

I expected her to protest, try to tell me that I was overreacting. But instead she said, "Because I saw you for who you were." I couldn't be sure, but it seemed like she was misty-eyed. The anger had somewhat subsided and her voice filled with painful regret. "My mother used to always tell me, never marry somebody who you love more than they love you. My son loved you more and now he's paying the price. That's why I've had issues with you when it comes to him. His love is genuine. Yours seemed to be a part of this perfect story you were trying to create. I know about your past. Your abusive father. Charles is everything that your father was not. My son gave you the family that you wished you'd had. And when you'd had your fill of him, you repaid him by walking out."

Her words brought tears to my eyes. Was she telling the truth? Did I want this life because it fit some type of narrative? *No*, I told myself. My love for Charles was real.

"I loved Charles. I *love* Charles," I protested.

She stared at me, her anger now gone, replaced with sadness. "If this is your definition of love, I'd hate to see what you did to people you hate." Her tone turned icy. "You're right. You're not worthy of my son."

Her words were shaking me to my core. "Judy, I am not doing this with you. I really am sick and tired of you," I said.

"Then the feeling is mutual." She stepped to me like we were two girls about to go at it on the playground.

"What you need to do," I continued, vowing that she wasn't going to reduce me to a sniffling basket case, "is get you some business and stay out of mine. Here's a thought. Go get a man of your own. And release the hold on your son."

She wasn't moved. "Trash like you can come and go. Mothers are forever."

"You know, it's a good thing that I'm leaving because I would hate to have to put your ass out on the street," I told her.

"My son would never allow that to happen," she protested.

I managed a laugh. "Then you don't know your son as well as you think," I said. "The only reason you've been here is because I allowed you to be. And we were already talking about ways to get rid of you. But it's a moot point now. You've made your feelings known. I didn't want to hurt my husband. And I pray every day that he forgives me."

"And I pray every day that he doesn't."

"Well, it doesn't matter because I've forgiven myself."

"I don't see how."

My laugh this time was real. I was done. "Whatever. You can take your sanctified hate and go somewhere because I'm done."

She literally followed me up the stairs. "My son cared for you when you were on your deathbed."

I turned around at the top of the staircase, sorrow filling my face. "And I will be forever grateful for that, Judy." I took a deep breath, then released it. "I will be grateful to you. To everyone who helped me, but it doesn't change the situation that was at hand before my accident."

"I can't believe you're doing this to your family. God forgive me, but I wish you had died in that accident."

I just stared at her before shrugging. "But I didn't. Not only did I not die, coming close made me want to live. And that's what I'm going to do. Charles may not understand it. You may not understand it. My kids may not understand it, but I'm saving me."

I walked into the bedroom to pack my things, slamming my bedroom door on my mother-in-law. Twenty minutes later, I had my suitcase and a duffel bag slung over my shoulder as I stood at my front door. I paused and looked back over my shoulder, knowing this time, my departure was for good. At some point I'd have to come back, get the rest of my things and clear up all my loose ends. But something told me it would be a while before that happened. Charles had to heal and I had to get to happy.

Chapter 33

I sat across from the Quiet Quilt as tears streamed down my face. How had my dream been so completely derailed?

The Quiet Quilt was no more. The awning had been painted. The sign had been removed and a Coming Soon sign placed in the window. I peered over my steering wheel but I couldn't make out what the name of the business was.

Curiosity got the best of me so I eased open my car door and stepped out.

As the sign came into focus, my heart dropped to my stomach. "Coming Soon: We Work It." I leaned in closer to read the tagline—"a work space designed to help creatives reach their dreams."

Not only had I lost my building but the new tenants were opening a business to help people live their dreams. What kind of cruel joke was God playing on me?

"Excuse me, may I help you?"

I turned toward the voice and saw a pretty doe-eyed woman with long blond hair.

I pulled myself together. "Umm, I . . . I'm sorry, I was just reading your sign."

She smiled. "Yes, We Work It. We open next week. You ever heard of us?"

I shook my head.

"We have offices all over the country. Basically, we provide shared workspaces for entrepreneurs, freelancers, artists, start-ups, small businesses, stuff like that," she said. She sounded like she was reciting a pitch straight off a postcard. She extended her hand. "I'm Ruth, by the way."

"Hi, Ruth." I contemplated telling her I had planned to use this space, but if I said much more, I would probably break out into tears. "I came here when this was a quilting shop and just wanted to see what was here now."

"Yes, I actually bought it from the owner of that shop. She wanted to move to be near her grandkids. My husband and I had been looking at this area for a while. We bought the franchise and thought this was a perfect spot." She laughed. "When we first inquired about it, the owner had just leased it out then something happened and voilà! it opened up for us. Isn't God good?"

I swallowed the lump in my throat. Thankfully, she didn't wait for me to reply.

"When we first found out the place had been leased, I told George, that's my husband, what God has for us is for us."

I managed a smile. "I guess this was for you, then."

She stood back and admired the building. "It sure is. Well, I would ask you to come in, but the place is a mess. I'm trying to get it ready for our grand opening next week. If you know any creative types, let them know we're here."

"I will," I replied. I pushed down the queasiness in my stomach. "Well, I'll let you go. Goodbye."

I turned and scurried back to my car. I'd expected to get inside my car and burst into tears. But when I set foot in my car, no tears would come.

"This was a detour, not a derailment."

The words of that old lady from the DR continued to follow me. But this time, I knew exactly what she meant. My mother once told me that my name meant "fighter." My brother, Eric, had laughed and said that Mama made that up to make me sound important. But I'd fought my way back to mobility. I could fight my way back from this.

Yes, this was a detour, not a derailment. Now I just needed to figure out how to get my dreams back on track.

Epilogue

Nine months later

My dream had come to fruition.

I glanced around the room and a smile not only filled my face, it filled my heart. This was the culmination of months of hard work, of nonstop painting, and what Roxie called "sweat equity."

But looking around the room, I knew that it was all worth it.

"So, is this all the drinks you're going to have at this shindig? Wine?" Nichelle approached me as I stood in the back of the room, overlooking the small crowd that had started to gather for my grand opening. "You got us all the way out here in the boonies and we can't even get the good stuff?" She held up the bottle of wine. "And you're buying stuff we can't even pronounce?"

"Yes. First of all, Katy isn't the boonies. I moved out here because the area doesn't have a place like this. Secondly, that is eiswein. It's from Germany." I snatched the bottle back. "It's an art and wine gallery, not art and chug-a-lug, Chug-A-Lug Queen. If you want real liquor, go down the street."

"Or to my purse," she said with a wink.

"Nichelle Shavonne Humphrey, if you pull some liquor out of your purse at my grand opening—" I warned.

Simone stepped up and draped her arm through Nichelle's. "Don't worry. We're going to make her behave."

The two of them giggled as Eric approached us. He'd come home for my event. Anika had been unable to make it. Or rather, she decided against making it.

"Yo, Mom. This is really nice and all, but can I bounce? Jason an 'nem are getting together."

I smiled at my son and patted his cheek. He'd been here longer than I ever thought he would be able to take it. "Yes, son, thank you for coming out to support. Make sure you tell Jason an 'nem hello."

I was just happy that Eric had shown up. When Charles and I sat Anika and Eric down and told them we were divorcing, it had been harder than I imagined. Anika had taken it the hardest, re-fusing to speak to me for weeks. I knew she was upset that her fa-ther had nursed me back to health and I was still leaving him. I echoed Jewel's words and told her it would have been unfair to stay. She didn't get it. But I knew at some point my daughter would come around. Eric took the news better, but I could tell he was hurt. Ultimately, he told me that he just wanted me to be happy.

I was grateful that Charles had taken the high road, not once bashing me to our children. And in fact, he was helping Anika work through her anger with me, which I knew was difficult since he still harbored some anger and resentment.

I didn't expect Judy to be here because in the four months since my divorce had been finalized, she was the one person I had never spoken to. Charles made it a point to have her out of the house when I officially moved all my stuff out. And when Anika and Eric came to visit me, they came to my loft overlooking downtown Houston. I hadn't gotten a Roxie-level apartment, but my place was good enough for me.

"Your first VIP guest is here," Roxie said, motioning toward the front door as the leggy woman who looked more like a fashion model than an art critic walked in. "Is that the reporter from the newspaper?"

"Art critic, not reporter." I nodded. "She goes to my church. I didn't know if she was going to show."

"Well, do your thing," Roxie said as I inhaled, brushed down my silk African skirt that I'd had made just for this event, and went to greet my guest.

"Hi, Joy," I said. "Welcome. I'm so glad you could make it." I extended my hand.

She shook it. "Thanks for the invitations. All six of them." She winked.

I smiled. "Just wanted to make sure you got it."

"Oh, I wouldn't miss this, especially with your huge 'get.'" She glanced around, taking in the artwork. I'd prided myself on taking my time to make sure the gallery was set up just right. I'd decided to feature art primarily from Nigeria and West Africa, along with original paintings from U.S. painters of African descent, including my work, of course. I was so proud of my paintings, which covered an entire wall.

I'd finally taken them out of the closet.

I'd lined another wall with wine from various parts of the country.

"This is really nice," Joy said, looking around. "I will admit, I didn't know what to expect."

"Well, I hope you'll be pleased. Not only with my work," I pointed to a large painting that hung over the bar, "but all of the artists featured here."

I could tell she was impressed because she nodded her approval. "Well, you must tell me how you snagged a LaTerus original. That's all of the buzz of the art conference at the convention center. How this small upstart Katy gallery snagged one of the hottest artists in the industry."

That made me smile. "A wise woman once told me that when you walk in your purpose, you'd be amazed at all the doors that would open up," I said.

"Is it true that you reached out to him on Twitter and told him that you were a small gallery owner starting over in life and requested to showcase his newest piece?"

I nodded. "I knew the art convention was coming to town, so I figured, what did I have to lose. I sent him a direct message, told him about our shared passion, and was shocked when he replied and said he was looking to do something different for his newest work and he believed in giving back, so here we are." That had been an unexpected blessing. I never in a million years dreamed an internationally known painter would agree to my request, but I chanced it and asked anyway.

"Talk about amazing." Joy shook her head in awe. "The little gallery that could."

I smiled my appreciation. My new life had given me a new outlook. I wasn't afraid to take chances. I didn't hesitate to step outside the box. And the only opinion that mattered to me now was mine.

It was an exhilarating feeling.

"If you don't mind, before I leave, I'd really like to talk to you about stepping out on faith and following your dreams," Joy said. "My photographer will be here later and we'd love to get some pictures of you in your element."

I beamed. "Of course."

"I love that you are following your passion." She leaned in. "Between you and me, I've been thinking of writing a book of all the things I've collected that bring me joy this past year."

"A year of Joy," I said. "I love that."

"And that sounds like a perfect title," she replied. "You're inspiring me to do just that." She glanced around. "Well, I'm going to take a look around and I'll talk to you a little later."

I smiled just as the door chimed and some more VIP guests came in.

"King, Tiffany, Osayer." I beamed. These were three of the top art reviewers in the country and they were here in my gallery. I figured Tiffany would come since we went to school together at Texas Southern University and had taken some art history classes together. When I found out they'd be in town for the art convention, I'd personally invited them as well. Tiffany had agreed to drop by if she could squeeze it in. Of course, King and Osayer had blown me off—until they found out about the LaTerus piece.

"Aja," Tiffany hugged me. "You look marvelous. Girl, how do you go from being a social worker to this?"

"You just do it," I replied. "Your desire to follow your passion has to become greater than your resistance," I said, echoing my seat mate from the airplane. "I'm so glad you all could make it."

"Well, we just had to see the little shop that snagged a LaTerus original," Osayer said, looking around. "I take it that's it?" she said, pointing to the covered piece by the front entrance.

"It is," I said with a proud smile.

King added, "You know you've generated quite the buzz at the conference. The Houston Art Gallery had been trying to get this piece for a year but he turned them down."

"I guess I'm just blessed," I said. "Please come on in, enjoy our wine, look around. LaTerus will be here in about thirty minutes."

I eased to the back of the room and marveled at the magnificence of seeing my dream come to fruition. After soaking it all in, I walked around and mingled with more guests.

"Um," Roxie eased up behind me, "don't act surprised, but Charles just walked in."

I looked up, and for a moment, I had a nostalgic flutter. My ex-husband was, and always would be, fine.

"Hi," he said, stepping toward me. He'd cut his hair and now wore a close-cropped fade. The haircut, along with his paisley shirt, dark blue blazer, and khaki pants gave him a youthful appearance.

"Hi."

He paused, like he wanted to make sure it was okay, then he hugged me. "This is really nice, Aja."

"Thank you," I said.

"I would say I can't believe you did it, but I can." He paused, then added, "I'm just really sorry that I didn't help you achieve this dream."

Charles had sat through our divorce proceedings in a daze. At one point, he'd told me that he was stunned because he thought that we had a good life.

"Where did I go wrong?" he'd asked through tears as we sat with the mediators.

Though I'd told him about my biggest issues, I could tell he still didn't get it. I didn't know if he got it yet. I could no longer be focused on that.

I snapped out of the past. I wanted to leave all those thoughts in the past and focus solely on my future.

"I would never belittle all that you did. I am grateful for everything we had and everything we built," I told him.

He looked around the room and we stood in an awkward silence for a moment.

Finally, I said, "Where's Sunnie?"

His eyes bucked and I couldn't help but chuckle.

"You might want to get an Instagram account so you can monitor how much your girlfriend is posting your business," I told him.

"I-I . . ." He stammered like he didn't know what to say.

The first time I'd seen the picture of Sunnie and my ex-husband, I have to admit, I felt a pain in my stomach. My immediate reaction was to get mad, wonder if that had been Judy's goal all along. If that had been Sunnie's goal. But then I decided it didn't matter. Sunnie had helped me heal, and for that I would be eternally grateful. Maybe she was brought into my life to heal my body and heal Charles's heart, because he definitely looked happy in the pictures she posted last weekend.

"I promise I'm not stalking you. I just happened to see them because one of your fans shared it."

"I, uh—"

I cut him off. "It's okay. I do want you to be happy. Though between me and you, Anika will never call someone less than ten years older than her, mom."

"It's not that serious. I wouldn't . . ."

"I'm kidding, Charles. I really do want you to be happy." I meant that. I knew that some couples divorced and had contentious relationships, but I hoped we could be mature enough to want nothing but the best for one another.

"I want the same for you," he said and I could tell he meant it, too.

We hugged, then broke away for the last time—and went our separate ways.

"LaTerus is pulling up," the party planner I'd hired to help with the event whispered just as I stepped away.

I took a deep breath and prepared to corral the crowd to welcome my favorite painter.

I grabbed a glass of wine off the bar and turned to my guests. "Hello, everyone! May I have your attention." The chatter subsided and all eyes were on me at the front of the room. "While we wait on LaTerus, I wanted to thank you all for coming out this evening and to welcome you to Utopia Art and Wine . . . I am grateful to each of you for being here this evening and sharing in what is truly a dream come true. I am proof of what can happen when you find your passion . . ."

A Note from the Author

They say writing is therapeutic. Because I love the craft of storytelling, I never understood how true that statement was—until I began writing this book. When I sat down to write this story, life as I knew it had been turned upside down. Many people don't know it, but I was in the midst of a storm while writing this book. No, bump that, I was in the middle of a full-fledged hurricane.

My perfectly constructed life had come toppling down.

I probably should've called this book *The Devil Sure Is Busy*. That didn't really have anything to do with this storyline, but that's the life I was living. From the outside, it looked like I had a dream life. And publicly, I kept a smile, even as I cried inside. Behind closed doors, I was dying. I call it my on-the-sofa time because I literally and figuratively was on the sofa. Life had knocked me down and I just didn't want to get up. I found myself facing a divorce after twenty-plus years, a stalker tried to ruin my life, my children—my heartbeats—were suffering, falling apart, and I felt helpless. I was also dealing with some medical issues, helping my sister take care of our disabled mother, and then, my career—one ripe with forty-plus books and two movies—had become stagnant and eventually, hit rock bottom. My bank account was drained dry and I lost virtually everything—including a book deal I'd had for nearly twenty years.

I was broken, and when my ride-or-die friends didn't want to come to my pity party, I found some different folks who didn't mind wallowing in negativity with me. But that's the good thing about the right circle, they won't come to your pity party and they won't let you stay long at it either.

Still, picking myself up was hard. And then, one day, I realized my children were watching. And how I pulled myself up could make all the difference in the world when it came to shaping who they would become. So as one year morphed into another, I made myself a vow. There was more to life than what I was living—or in this case, not living. And though I took a different twist on this book, ultimately, it's about finding that which brings you joy— and doing it. And realizing that sometimes, God has to knock us on our behinds so that we can get up and fly!

I cried and cried about all that I had lost. What I didn't know then was that God was preparing me for something greater. I'm still working toward that greatness every day but I'm so happy to say I'm moving. Maybe I lost my book deal because I'd gotten comfortable and God knew my destiny was greater than that. I was blessed to land with another publisher (hence the reason you're reading this book ☺) . . . and back with my original editor who helped put "ReShonda the author" on the map in the first place. Maybe God moved me so that we could go to the next level (I'm ready, Selena James).

I don't know the reasons for everything I went through, but I do know that which didn't break me made me stronger. I changed my attitude, and it changed my life. The happiness I thought I'd never know again greets me daily with an intoxicating hug. And yeah, I may have my down moments, but they're just that—moments. Now I dance every day like no one's watching.

That's what this book is all about—finding your joy, finding the strength to start over, releasing your fear, pursuing your passion, and stepping out on faith to follow your dreams! I'm ready to soar!

Now that I've let y'all all up in my personal business—it's cool because hopefully my testimony will inspire someone else to walk in their purpose—I need to get down to the hard part: thanking all of those who made this possible. I know with fifty books, it's like do you really need to thank all these people again? Yep. Because each book is made possible by some amazing people and I will continue to recognize them again and again.

First and foremost, my babies—the reason I do what I do—Mya, Morgan, and Myles. You three are the strongest, most amazing children any mother could ask for. Though I may have fallen short at times, know that the most fulfilling job I have is being your mother and I will work tirelessly to make you proud.

My sister . . . words can't even express my love for Tanisha Tate. She has been my biggest cheerleader since the day she entered this world. Our mother did her best to raise two amazing daughters, and watching the way my sister steps up to the plate—as a single mother, as a daughter, as a sister, as a soror, as a friend—fills my heart with joy. To my mother, a stroke and brain tumor sidelined you, but the love you have for us is still evident and I am forever grateful God decided to make me yours.

To Victoria Christopher Murray (the friend that almost wasn't) . . . you have become more than my business/writing partner, you are my sister for life. I truly would not have gotten up off the sofa if it were not for you. Thank you so much for not bailing on our business or our books when I was that monster that made your life miserable. This book—like all the others—is better because of you. My life is better because of your friendship.

To my forever friends who literally kept me sane, dried my tears, and slapped me around and told me to snap out of it: Jaimi Canady, Raquelle Lewis, Kim Wright, and Clemelia Humphrey Richardson. Love you for life!

To Pat Tucker, thank you for the hours and hours and hours . . . of just being my friend. Of helping me find laughter when all I wanted to do was cry.

To Jeffrey . . . thank you for helping me find balance, for listening, for laughing, for encouraging and making me remember to always "Choose kindness."

To my BGB family . . . thank you so much for all that you do.
To our amazing partners . . . Thank you for your patience and
understanding.

I've already mentioned my editor Selena James, but I want to
thank her again for believing in me, and I want to give a shout-out
to the whole Kensington family. I'm getting my hustle on to make
you proud. As always, thank you also to my agent, Sara Camilli.

To some very special friends who help my muse be her best on
this book: my sisters in Da Baddest Authoresses (Tiffany Warren
and Renee Flagler) . . . you ladies have no idea how our interac-
tion (along with VCM) help me get through the day. Thank you
Raine Bradley. Special shout out to Eric Jamal, Nakecia Bowers,
Yolanda Gore (thank you for helping me get this done), Shay
Smith, Sonny Messiah Jiles, Norma Warren, Sedaris Preston,
Eddie Brown, Lisa Paige Jones, Marilyn Marshall, and Jay T. Car-
raway.

Much love to my Texas Southern University family: Melinda
Spaulding (an amazing boss and even better friend), Isoke, Karen,
Dominique, Shenetra, Crystal, Bosede, Jeff, Joneen, Connie, Louis,
Tan, Ernest, and Donna. Thank you for all that you do.

A thousand thanks to my literary colleagues: Nina Foxx, Terri
Ann Johnson, Landis Lain, Eric Jerome Dickey, Victor Mc-
Glothin, and Curtis Bunn. Special shout-outs to: Davion Ander-
son, Jason Frost, Monique S. Hall, Sharon Lucas, Naturopath
Cecie Reed, Sophie Sealy, Isiah Carey, Tres Dunmore, April
Moore Gipson, Bridget Crawford, King Brooks, Tiffany Tyler,
Orsayor Simmons, Radiah Hubbert, Jessica Hill, Monica Green,
Pam Gaskin, Ivy Levingston, Shajra Austin, Jean Cormier, Addie
Heyliger, Erika Gentry, Lisa Meade, and Monique Bruner.

I could list book clubs for days. But I want to give a special ac-
knowledgment to Black Orchid Bookclub, A Novel Idea, Brownstone Book Club, Bettye Jean, Sistahs in Conversation and Sistahs
in Harmony, Black Butterfly, Cover 2 Cover, Savvy, Nubian Page-

turners, Cush City, Black Pearls Keepin it Real, Mahogany, Women of Substance, My Sisters & Me, Pages Between Sistahs, Shared Thoughts, Brag about Books, Mocha Readers, Characters, Christian Fiction Café, Sisters Who Like to Read, Readers of Delight, Tabahani Book Circle, FB Page Turners, African-American Women's Book Club, Women of Color, Zion M.B.C. Women's Book Club, Jus'Us, Go On Girl Texas 1, Book Club Etc., Pearls of Wisdom, Alpha Kappa Omega Book Club, Lady Lotus, Soulful Readers of Detroit, Brownstone, and First Baptist Church— Agape Book Ministry (please know that if you're not here, it doesn't diminish my gratitude).

Thank you to all the wonderful libraries that have also supported my books, introduced me to readers, and fought to get my books on the shelves.

People often ask why I take time to thank my Facebook friends. But I've gotten so much love, encouragement, and support for my social media family, I would be remiss if I didn't acknowledge them. While I'm sure I'm missing someone, thank you to: Bernice, Allison, J'son, Natalie, Davina, Michelle, Karla, Tracey, Karyn, Crystal, Nina, Eddgra, Tonia, Kimberlee, Cindy, Annette, Nicole, Chenoa, Brenda, JE, Tanisha, Beverly, Dwon, Noelle, LaChelle, Kim, Princis, Joe, Charlenette, Karla, Yasmin, Terri, Tres, April, Cheryl, Kelley, Katharyn, Tashmir, Bridget, Juda, Alicia, Arnesha, Tamou, Antoinette, Cynthia, Jackie, Ernest, Wanda, Ralph, Patrick, Lissha, Tameka, Laura, Marsha, Wanda, Kym, Allison, Jacole, Stephanie, Dawn, Paula, Nakia, Jodi, Cecily, Leslie, Gary, Cryssy, KP, Tomaiya, Gwen, Nik, Martha, Joyce, Yolanda, Lasheera. (Y'all know I could go on and on . . .)

Lots of love and gratitude to my sorors of Alpha Kappa Alpha Sorority, Inc. (including my own chapter, Mu Kappa Omega), my sisters in Greekdom, Delta Sigma Theta Sorority Inc., who *constantly* show me love . . . and my fellow mothers in Jack and Jill of America, Inc, especially the Missouri City—Sugar Land Chapter.

And finally, thanks to YOU . . . my beloved reader. If it's your first time picking up one of my books, I truly hope you enjoy. If you're coming back, words cannot even begin to express how eternally grateful I am for your support. From the bottom of my heart, I thank you!

It's my fiftieth book, y'all. Here's to fifty more.

Livin' my best life . . . Much Love,
ReShonda

MORE TO LIFE

ReShonda Tate Billingsley

ABOUT THIS GUIDE

The suggested questions are included to enhance your
group's reading of ReShonda Tate Billingsley's
More to Life!

DISCUSSION QUESTIONS

1. From the beginning, it's evident that Aja loves her family; however, she seems exasperated with Charles, Anika, Eric, and even her mother-in-law, Judy. Are her feelings justified? What was the most challenging aspect of each character? And what role did she play in "creating those monsters," as Roxie said?

2. Aja constantly feels like there's a void that needs to be filled. What was the catalyst that made Aja truly feel like there had to be "more to life"? Did she set out about achieving her new chapters the right way?

3. Aja often talked of feeling suffocated. In what ways was this manifested throughout the story?

4. Aja set her dreams on the shelf to take care of her family and they continued to belittle her dream. Since it's obvious they loved her, why do you think they repeatedly stepped on her dream? Who was to blame for their actions?

5. How could Aja have avoided losing herself in the marriage? Is this something that women do quite often? How can they keep this from happening?

6. Judy never felt that Aja was worthy of her son. Why do you think she felt that way? What role did Judy play, if any, in making things difficult between Aja and Charles? How should Aja and Charles have handled Judy from the very beginning?

7. Everyone dismissed Aja's painting as a hobby. Is this something she should've addressed early on? How could she have better gotten her loved ones to understand her passion?

8. In the Dominican Republic, Aja interacts with both Jewel and Don Juan. What role does each of them play in helping Aja rediscover herself? What role does the stranger on the plane play?

9. On the surface, Charles appeared to have it all. What were some of his biggest drawbacks? Could you overlook some of his negative attributes because of all his positive ones?

10. Would you consider Aja's friends supportive? Why do you think they initially didn't want her to quit her job? Should they have talked her out of leaving her marriage?

11. Charles took Aja back and nursed her back to health without hesitation. Were his actions understandable? Did you agree with them? Why or why not?

12. Should Aja have found a way to make her marriage work after the accident since Charles took her back?

13. Do you believe that Sunnie Ray had intentions on developing a relationship with Charles from the beginning? Was that Judy's goal? Would you allow a therapist like Sunnie into your home?

14. Aja talked about how she had gone from taking care of her brother and sister to taking care of Charles to taking care of her children. Did that play a role in her feeling unfulfilled? Do you think at some point, most women burn out?

15. Was Aja's desire to open a gallery realistic? Should a mother be prepared to let some of her dreams go when it comes to raising her family?

Connect with Us

Visit us online at
KensingtonBooks.com
to read more from your favorite authors, see books
by series, view reading group guides, and more.

Join us on social media

for sneak peeks, chances to win books and prize packs,
and to share your thoughts with other readers.

facebook.com/kensingtonpublishing
twitter.com/kensingtonbooks

Tell us what you think!

To share your thoughts, submit a review,
or sign up for our eNewsletters, please visit:
KensingtonBooks.com/TellUs.